SHEISTY
CHICKS

SHEISTY CHICKS

KIM K.

www.melodramapublishing.com

Library of Congress Control Number: 2011927246
ISBN-13: 978-1934157473
ISBN-10: 1934157473
First Edition: December 2011
10 9 8 7 6 5 4 3 2 1

Interior Design: Candace K. Cottrell
Cover Design: Marion Designs
Models: Janeen, Farrahn, and Gabriella

CHAPTER 1

"Watch, when I get put on and I sign my deal, I know I'll sell more records than Nicki Minaj, Rihanna, and Beyoncé all put together!" Ashanti boasted, while watching the three superstars perform on a rerun of the BET Awards.

"Ashanti, you ain't gon' do shit! You ain't shit now, and you never will be shit, and that's why your ass is in here. So sit the fuck down and shut up with all that dreaming-big bullshit."

Big Momma, the obese, dark-skinned, forty-year-old supervising manager of The Waverly Girls Group Home, located in the Bedford-Stuyvesant section of Brooklyn, New York, was trying her best to intimidate Ashanti, one of the new girls in the group home, but the sixteen-year-old half black-half Puerto Rican from the South Bronx wasn't easily intimidated, and she definitely wasn't one to hold her tongue.

"I might not be shit, but at least I'm not four hundred fuckin' pounds! You fat bitch! You're fat, you'll always be fat, and you won't ever look as good as me! And that's why your fat ass needs to stop hating on me and just lose some fuckin' weight!"

Ashanti's words drew snickers and laughter from some of the other girls lounging in the living room of the group home watching the awards.

"The only one hatin' on you is your own mother. She ain't want your ass, and your daddy ain't want your ass. And you know why they ain't want you? They ain't want you because you ain't shit, Ashanti!"

The truth of the matter was, Ashanti's Puerto Rican father wasn't in her life, and her mother couldn't control her, and that's why she was in the group home. Big Momma knew all of the girls were battling with low self-esteem and that they all wanted to feel worthy and have a sense of belonging, so her words were purposely designed to hurt Ashanti's feelings.

Big Momma's words stung Ashanti. She'd always wondered how her mother could actually say that she loved her but yet just leave her in the care of the group home, like she was some unwanted mutt taken to the dog pound after the owner had had enough.

"Whatever!" Ashanti said under her breath. "You and I both know that my mother only put me here on a temporary basis, so *ska-beat it* with all that hate. You too old to be hatin' on chicks more than half your age anyway."

Big Momma felt like she had won that verbal confrontation, so she pushed herself away from the desk she was sitting at and prepared to walk to the kitchen for some Twinkies.

Ashanti said to the girls within earshot, "That bitch just sexually frustrated because don't nobody wanna fuck her fat ass. Dudes probably couldn't even find her pussy underneath all them jelly rolls of fat."

All of the girls burst out into laughter.

Big Momma didn't clearly hear the crack. She turned and asked, "What did you say?"

Ashanti stood to her feet and projected her voice above the sound of the TV. "I said, 'Nobody wants to fuck you and that dudes probably can't even find your pussy underneath all them jelly rolls of fat and that you're fat and sexually frustrated!'"

Everybody in the large living room heard Ashanti that time, and they all burst out into laughter.

"When your birthday comes around, I'll make sure I buy you a two-foot dildo so you won't be so damn miserable!" Ashanti knew she was dinging Big Momma really good.

Big Momma put up her middle finger to Ashanti. She never backed down from a verbal confrontation, but she was distracted by Jazzy, Cha Cha, and Maya strolling through the front door of the group home, carrying large Duane Reade shopping bags.

Jazzy, Cha Cha, and Maya said what's up to everybody, but they didn't hang around the living room to socialize. Instead they went straight up to their room.

Since none of the girls had gotten their bi-weekly stipend from the state and none of them had a job, Big Momma knew the bags were full of stolen merchandise, and was focused on getting some free products, like she'd always done in the past whenever the girls went out boosting.

"You see this shit? It's thirty minutes past curfew, and Big Momma don't say shit to them three bitches. They come and go as they please. Now let me or you walk up in here thirty seconds past curfew and she'll be all up in our ass," Ashanti said to one of the girls that she was sitting next to. "I'm so tired of them three chicks walking around here like they better than everybody. It is so fuckin' annoying!"

The other girls, drooling over Chris Brown and Trey Songz as they watched them perform during the awards show, could have cared less about whether or not Jazzy, Cha Cha, and Maya were coming or going.

Big Momma hated walking up the one flight of stairs to get to the sleeping quarters of The Waverly, but she had to make the hike if she wanted to get her cut of the loot.

Without knocking, she used her master key and let herself into the bedroom that Jazzy, Cha Cha, and Maya shared.

"Lord knows I can't wait until the city solves this budget crisis so they can install that damn elevator. Those stairs is liable to give a sister a heart attack." Big Momma was breathing heavily and sounding as if she was having an asthma attack, even though she didn't have asthma.

Jazzy shook her head as she looked at Cha Cha and Maya. Of the three girls, Jazzy was the most resentful when it came to including Big Momma in on their hustle, when it was them who was taking all of the risks. Yet, Big Momma was sharing equally in the rewards.

Big Momma caught her breath and began talking again.

"Now I done told y'all that if it's after eleven o'clock to just call me and I'll unlock the back door because I don't want everybody seeing y'all walking up in here late and them thinking that they can all just do the same."

Jazzy, originally from Bedford-Stuyvesant and, without question, the ringleader of the three girls, rolled her eyes at Big Momma and handed her one of the four shopping bags. Jazzy, to most, was a pretty girl who had the worst attitude. She had light skin, shoulder length dark brown hair and catlike eyes. She was top heavy, sporting double Ds and a flat ass—compliments of her mother's genes.

Big Momma looked through her bag and saw bars of deodorant, lotion, lipsticks, two clock radios, perfume, potato chips, soda, devil dogs, Nathan's Hot Dogs, Häagen Dazs ice cream, and maxi pads.

"Here," Big Momma said as she handed the two pints of ice cream to Cha Cha. "How many times I have to tell y'all that I'm allergic to anything with peanuts in it and I don't like no kinds of nuts in my food? And what do y'all bring back? Peanut butter fuckin' ice cream and butter muthafuckin' pecan ice cream? And I love Häagen Dazs too. Shit."

"Well, it ain't like we got time to be all choosy. We have to get in and get out as quick as possible. We don't have time to be looking at labels and shit," Jazzy said with an attitude.

Big Momma then took it upon herself to look in the girls' bags and helped herself to whatever she wanted and left them with whatever she didn't. When she was done helping herself to the best of the spoils, she opened up a pack of Chewy Chips Ahoy! and started eating them.

"So, Maya, what you gonna do? The state is on my back. They just sent me your sixty-day notice. They ain't playing. Whoever turns eighteen, they want them up outta here sixty days after their eighteenth birthday." Big Momma stuffed her face with cookies.

"I know, I know," Maya replied. "I'm working on something."

"Working on something?" Big Momma asked, her mouth full. "Listen to me. This ain't a game. You only got one option—You either get pregnant, or they bouncing that ass up outta here in sixty days. They ain't playing, I'm telling you, the state ain't tryna support you forever. But if you get pregnant, then you can stay here until six weeks after the baby is born. So that would give you almost a whole year. You feel me?"

"Well, what you want her to do? Just go out in the street and fuck any Tom, Dick, and Harry just to get pregnant?" Jazzy asked as she put away the Duane Reade merchandise she'd kept for herself.

"Well, I guess I'm outta here because I'm not trying to have no baby. Don't nobody want stretch marks and swollen ankles and all of that."

Big Momma continued to eat the chocolate chip cookies, and then she spoke up after a brief silence. "Listen, you get me two stacks and I can get you a pregnant girl who can go to the clinic and pose as you and get a letter from the doctor saying how many weeks pregnant she is. Then I can get that to the state, and all of your problems can go away. See, Big Momma takes care of my babies. And all of y'all are like my babies."

"Two stacks? Big Momma, come on? Why you can't just look out for her on GP?" Jazzy asked.

"GP? GP don't pay the bills! I'm not putting my job on the line for no got-damn GP. And, besides, it ain't like the money is all going in my pocket. I gotta give one stack to the pregnant chick for her to do this, and I'll keep the other stack for myself. Shit ain't free. You gots to pay like you weigh!"

Maya looked at Jazzy.

"What the fuck you looking to her for? She's gonna be alright. You the one who'll be tossed up outta here. And, believe me, that one thousand dollars that you'll pay me is the minimum amount you're going to have to pay to rent a one-bedroom apartment anywhere in this expensive ass city. So I don't see what there is to even think about."

Maya looked at Big Momma and nodded her head.

"Just let me know what you wanna do. But don't be waiting to the last minute," Big Momma gathered up her bag of goodies and made her way out of the girls' room.

"Yo, I am so tired of that fat fuck using us!" Jazzy said.

"Me too, but at the same time, it's not like I really have any options."

"Fuck that. You got options. We all got options. We'll get the two grand for that fat bitch, but after that, the three of us is getting the fuck up out of here and we getting our own apartment," Jazzy said. "Big Momma will get this pregnancy exception from the state for you, but then what we gotta do is think past that and think about what happens in a year from now. Because, Maya, you eighteen now, but in a year from now, me and Cha Cha will be aging out of the system too, and then what? Big Momma is gonna want two grand apiece from us to get us an extension. Fuck all that. We gotta get focused now. Start stashing our paper and let it stack and let's get the fuck up outta here."

"I'm with whatever," Maya said.

"You know I wanna get the fuck up outta here like *yesterday*— fuck tomorrow!" Cha Cha said.

The three girls were determined to do what they had to do to get out of The Waverly Girls Group Home and to get from underneath the control of Big Momma. And they had the heart and the desire to make it out. The only question was, would they have the toughness to make it through all of the obstacles that would stand in their way?

CHAPTER 2

School had ended a little less than a week ago, and the curfew for the summertime had been extended one hour, until midnight.

It was currently fifteen minutes past midnight, and Jazzy and Maya were still sitting outside on the front steps drinking vodka and cranberry juice. Cha-Cha was inside their room with her shorty that she had snuck inside more than an hour earlier, and Jazzy and Maya were trying to give her as much time as she needed, since it was her night to have *company*.

Ashanti walked out from inside the group home. "Whatch'all doing out here?"

"Ashanti, go back inside and don't worry about what we doing," Jazzy replied with an attitude. "We ain't in the mood for no bullshit."

Ashanti reached inside her pocket, pulled out ten dollars, and handed it to Jazzy.

"What's that for?" Jazzy asked.

"Pour me some."

Jazzy was reluctant, but she wasn't a dummy. She wasn't going to turn down any money, if Ashanti was offering. She took the money and poured Ashanti a drink.

"Absolut? That's that shit that'll give you a headache. Don't nobody drink Absolut no more. What's up with the Ciroc?"

"You want it or not? That's all we got," Jazzy said.

Maya remained silent. She'd already had three drinks, so she was feeling nice.

"You got your drink. Now bounce," Jazzy immediately said after handing Ashanti a drink.

Ashanti sat down next to the two girls and finished her first drink in a few gulps and then held out her white Styrofoam cup for more.

"Ten dollars only gets you one drink," Jazzy barked at her.

"What the fuck! This is more expensive than Club Amnesia. At least y'all could have the large red plastic cups." Ashanti then reached inside her pocket and pulled out a twenty-dollar bill. She asked Jazzy to give her ten dollars in change and to pour her another drink.

"I can count," Jazzy poured her another drink.

"Where you getting all this dough from?" Maya asked Ashanti.

Ashanti's first drink had her feeling nice, so she drank the second one a lot slower. But it wasn't like she needed any alcohol at all to get her mouth talking.

"I keep telling everybody that my mother has paper, but don't nobody wanna believe what the hell I be saying," she responded.

"Oh that's right. I forgot you said your mother be trickin'!" Jazzy laughed.

Ashanti looked at her and rolled her eyes.

"Seriously Ashanti, you said your moms is a paralegal for the police department. Cops don't make shit so how much could she really be making?"

"I swear, if I didn't know any better, I would think I was talking to Big Momma. Why is it so hard to believe that my mother is rich? You see the clothes I be rockin' every day. I been in here for more than a month, and can't nobody say they seen me wear the same outfit more than once. And I put that on everything!"

"So? That don't make you rich. That might make you hood rich, but that don't mean you Donald Trump, wake-up-and-do-whatever-the-fuck-you-wanna-do-when-you-wanna-do-it rich," Jazzy replied.

Ashanti stood up and finished her second drink. At that point she was really feeling nice from the liquor.

"See, once again, that's where you wrong, because I can wake up every day and do what the fuck I wanna do when I wanna do it. If I wanted to go shopping tomorrow I could."

"Ashanti, just knock it off please," Maya said.

"She's annoying, right?"

"Yes!"

Ashanti then went in her pocket and pulled out a wad of money. She handed Jazzy another ten dollars and asked for another drink.

"It ain't that I'm annoying. It's just that you and you are just like everybody else. Y'all hate on what y'all can't have. But it's all good in the hood. I understand." Ashanti took her third drink from Jazzy.

Jazzy was way too proud to admit it, but Ashanti had her attention and she was intrigued. She wanted to know just how much money Ashanti had and if in fact her mother was actually rich.

"Damn! Whoever that nigga is that's up in that room with Cha Cha, he must be serving her up some good-ass dick," Ashanti said.

Jazzy and Maya looked at each other, but they didn't say anything, not knowing if Ashanti was planning on ratting Cha Cha out in the morning to one of the social workers.

"Y'all know she up there fuckin'?" Ashanti added.

"So how does your mother get her paper?" Jazzy asked.

"She get it how she get it."

Maya took a stab at Ashanti. "Oh, so in other words she be selling pussy just like a trick," Jazzy said.

"Yup, she be selling pussy," Ashanti said with sarcasm. "But I know one thing—She don't be hustling backwards like y'all be doing with all them petty two-dollar items that y'all be boosting."

"Yo, I swear, I ain't never seen nobody talk as much shit as you talk. You really think you know everything about everything." Jazzy stood up.

Ashanti drank some more vodka and cranberry. "All I know is what I know." Then from out of nowhere, she said, "Heyyyyy, cutie. Why you running from us?" Ashanti was talking to Cha Cha's shorty, who was silently making his way out of the yard of the Group Home, and to his car parked down the block.

Troy, a twenty-two-year-old hustler from Queens, was wearing a Yankees snap back baseball cap, a pair of brand-new Nike Airs, and his jeans was sagging off of his ass. Cha Cha was working for him, selling weed, but she was regularly crossing the line and letting Troy fuck her. It was a mistake on Cha Cha's part because fucking Troy wasn't benefiting her in anyway, and he was just using her.

Troy looked backed in the direction of the steps that the girls were sitting on and smiled.

"You better keep it moving. Don't get fucked up out here tonight," Jazzy shouted to him.

Troy nodded his head and kept walking toward his car with a devilish grin.

"And don't you fuck around like that again 'cause your ass will get slapped behind that disrespectful shit," Jazzy said to Ashanti.

"Don't nobody want Cha Cha's sloppy seconds. I'm just drunk and talking shit." Ashanti stood up and prepared to go back inside and up to her room.

"That's all you do is talk shit," Jazzy said to Ashanti as she walked off.

"But I can back up what I say."

Jazzy tapped Maya and told her that she would be right back, and then she ran off to catch up to Ashanti, which she did just as she was approaching the kitchen. The house was quiet, with everyone either 'sleep or in their rooms' preparing to go to sleep, and the only noise that could be heard was the sound of Big Momma snoring.

Jazzy whispered loudly to Ashanti, "So you be boosting or what?"

"Maybe. Why?"

"You was talking like we don't know what we doing—"

"Y'all don't!" Ashanti quickly responded, cutting Jazzy off in the process. "Especially not if y'all be hitting drug stores."

"So then what's up with Friday? Let's head out to some high-end spots, and you can show us what's what, since you talk so much shit," Jazzy said to her.

Ashanti took the rest of the remaining vodka that Jazzy had in her bottle and told her that Friday wasn't a problem.

Jazzy wasn't actually trying to be all buddy-buddy with Ashanti. In fact she hated the ground that Ashanti walked on, but she wanted to know if Ashanti actually could teach them some things that they didn't already know about boosting.

CHAPTER 3

"Cha Cha, please tell me you were not fuckin' on my bed again!" Maya screamed at Cha Cha as soon as her and Jazzy returned to the room.

Cha Cha had just come from taking a shower and was still feeling good after her two rounds of good sex with Troy. She smiled a devilish smile as she applied lotion to her body, and she apologized to Maya.

"See, this is another reason we got to get up outta here and get our own spot," Maya added as she removed the sheets from her bed.

Maya was referring to the fact that she and Cha Cha shared a bunk bed, and Cha Cha slept on the top bunk. Cha Cha was always adamant that she wasn't fuckin' anybody on a top bunk, so it was always some kind of drama when it came her turn to sneak boys inside.

"Why you stay fuckin' that cheap-ass nigga anyway?" Maya asked Cha Cha. "There's a whole lot of other dudes out there that can fuck, eat pussy, and trick off on you all at the same time."

Cha Cha just looked at Maya and smiled. As far as she was concerned, she was in love with Troy, and there wasn't anything that anybody could say or do to change that.

Jazzy and Maya always got on Cha Cha because Troy would drop off bundles of weed for Cha Cha to sell, and he was only letting her keep ten dollars off of every hundred dollars that she sold. The girls had told her a million times that Troy was just pimping her, but their words were going in one ear and coming right out the other.

Jazzy and Maya both knew to never really press Cha Cha too hard because out of the three of them she was by far the most ruthless. Cha Cha had the prettiest face of the three chicks and looked the most innocent, but her looks were definitely deceiving.

Cha Cha was from a single-parent home in New Orleans, and she had stabbed her mom to death over a Po'Boy sandwich. Fortunately for her she had been acquitted of the charges, but after the trial, she ended up bouncing around from home to home of different relatives, until she ultimately found herself in New York and at The Waverly. Cha Cha, like most girls at The Waverly was rough around the edges. She was a nice looking girl—no beauty queen. But what she didn't have in looks she made up in body. Cha Cha was thick in all the right places and never had a problem getting a man. Her dark chocolate skin was highlighted by her extremely white teeth. She always sported a weave, preferably curly, and wore tons of makeup to brighten up her skin tone.

Jazzy changed the subject, purposely trying to get Cha Cha heated.

"Yo, I had to check that bitch Ashanti. She was all hollering at Troy, talking about, '*Heyyyyy, cutie.*'"

"My Troy?" Cha Cha asked.

Jazzy nodded her head and tried to shield the smile coming to her face. She wanted Cha Cha to believe that she was really angered by what Ashanti had done.

"Yo, I swear to God, I will fuck that bitch up! When was this?" Cha Cha asked.

Maya's hand accidentally hit a wet spot on the bed sheets. "Oh my God! Cha Cha, I know this ain't cum on these sheets? Fuck on Jazzy's bed next time, or fuck on the damn floor."

Cha Cha totally ignored Maya. "When did she say this? Tonight when he left?"

Jazzy looked at her and nodded her head yes.

Cha Cha slipped on her pair of flip-flops, and was ready to go confront Ashanti at that very moment.

"I'm going to fuck that bitch up right now! She gets on my fuckin' nerves! Always lying about shit and walking around here thinking she all that." Cha Cha reached in her drawer and grabbed a roll of quarters, which she held inside of her fist to make her punches more powerful. "I'm getting ready to light that bitch up."

Jazzy started to laugh. She ran up to Cha Cha. "Oh my God! Yo, Cha Cha, I swear on everything, you are my muthafuckin' girl! You be ready to fight at the drop of a hat. You got your pajamas and flip-flops on, and you ready to two piece that bitch at one o'clock in the morning," Jazzy said through laughter while trying to calm her down. "I already told you I checked her ass. And, besides, she was drinking, so that was just the liquor talking for her."

"Fuck that 'liquor talking for her.' She knew exactly what she was doing." Cha Cha tried to move past Jazzy.

"No, Cha Cha, chill. I got a better plan for her ass. Since she be talking all them lies, we can make her our Vic when we go out boosting. You been saying all along that we need to hit the high end stores, and now we can do that. But why should we take all the risk of getting arrested? Let's put that shit on Ashanti and her lying ass."

Cha Cha was listening to what Jazzy was saying, but she was still heated from the disrespect. "You feel me?" Jazzy asked Cha Cha.

Cha Cha slowly nodded her head. She walked over to the dresser that the girls shared and placed the roll of quarters on top of it.

Although Jazzy was the youngest of the three girls, it was almost as if she was their big sister. Cha Cha and Maya trusted her as if she was a blood relative and usually went along with whatever she said.

Jazzy, who was from the streets of Brooklyn, was by far the most street-smart of the three chicks. Her father had died of a drug overdose when she was eleven years old, and her mother died the following year from AIDS complications when Jazzy turned twelve. Right after her mother's death, Jazzy was forced to grow up quick, bouncing around from foster home to foster home, until she eventually landed at The Waverly.

Since the age of twelve Jazzy always had to think like an adult just to survive. But it was being forced to grow up so quickly that gave her the natural ability to lead, and have others gravitating to her as their leader.

"Alright, sis, I'm hearing you, but if that bitch so much as looks at me the wrong way, I am bussing her light-skinned ass!" Cha Cha said to Jazzy.

Maya was definitely the biggest follower of the three. Never really paying attention to what was going on or caring too much about details, she always seemed to be just going along for the ride.

Much of her personality had been shaped when she was sexually abused by a family member and neighbor as a young girl. The neighborhood pedophile, who went by the name of Tiny Tim, started molesting her when she was six. Tiny Tim was a grown-ass man, but being barely five feet tall, kids took to him as a playmate because of his short stature. Unfortunately for Maya, Tiny Tim loved to play doctor with her, which usually included an examination of her genitals.

Starting with Tiny Tim, Maya learned to disassociate herself and her feelings from the sexual abuse she was subjected to. Whenever Tiny Tim touched or kissed her vagina, she always would imagine that she was a princess living in a castle. Or she would imagine that she was an Olympic figure skater performing a gold-medal-winning routine. She would use her imagination to take her anywhere and everywhere for as long as she needed to, to endure the abuse she was going through.

Maya also had the misfortune of having the fully developed body of a woman at the tender age of thirteen. And her voluptuousness seemed to bring out the worst in her uncle, her mother's boyfriends, and even strangers, all of whom took sexual advantage of the girl with the body of a woman.

Maya had gotten to the point where she no longer had to disassociate her feelings from the experiences simply because by the age of fourteen she had pretty much become Newark, New Jersey's neighborhood whore and was giving her fruits away to just about anybody who wanted to take them. All this abuse on her body and tremendous stress at such a young age had seemed to age Maya. She was eighteen but looked almost thirty. Her naturally thin lips were down-turned into a scowl, which she couldn't control. Her chocolate colored skin framed her oddly black colored eyes, which gave her a menacing stare. Her hair was thick and coarse and hair relaxers barely worked so she usually kept it pulled back into a tight ponytail.

But like most of the girls at The Waverly, Maya had also come from some serious dysfunction, aside from the sexual abuse. Her biological father was an alcoholic with anger issues that he routinely took out on the women in his life. And her mother was a three-time felon who was just sent back to state prison for aiding and abetting a convicted murderer.

So with Maya, the eighteen-year-old who looked like a thirty-year-old fitness instructor, it was easy to see why she so desperately wanted to cling to The Waverly and why she cherished the sisterly relationships she had with Jazzy and Cha Cha.

"Maya! Maya!" Jazzy yelled to snap her out of la-la land and to get her opinion on Ashanti.

Maya apologized for not paying attention to what they had been talking about, and then she chimed in. "Well, personally, I don't think we should fuck with somebody we can't trust. All that's going to do is get us in trouble. The three of us got a good thing going. We got our plan to stash our money and get our own crib, so what do we even need to put her down for?"

"See, I feel you, and I was thinking the same way, but at the same time we can't cut off our nose to spite our face. And Maya, you saw how much money she was holding. She had to have a knot with at least five hundred dollars."

"Say word?" Cha Cha added.

"Word up. Me and Maya were sitting on the steps drinking, and Ashanti comes out asking for a drink. So just to blow her annoying ass off, I told her that it was ten dollars a drink, and the chick went in her pocket and was just peeling off paper like it was nothing. She bought three drinks from me. It was like she was at the bar in a club or some shit." Jazzy laughed and pulled out the money to show Cha Cha.

Cha Cha looked at the money and thought silently to herself for a moment. She slowly nodded her head. "That's how that bitch always be rockin' new designer shit."

"Exactly!" Jazzy said. "And now we need to use that bitch to find out what the fuck she knows, so we can come up off of her and get this money quicker than we been getting it. And if her ass is a bullshitter, then it won't matter, because she'll get locked the fuck up. What the hell do we care?"

At that moment the three girls heard a knock on their door. They knew it wasn't Big Momma because Big Momma never was so polite as to knock before entering their room.

Maya walked over to the door, unlocked it, and Ashanti walked in wearing a gold all-silk pajama short set and matching Gucci slippers. Ashanti's naturally long, jet-black hair was flowing with loose curls against her pale, light skin. Her slender, yet curvy body was on display in her short set. Her ample breasts, tiny waist, and athletic thighs made all three girls envious.

"I ain't staying long. I just came to say that I hope ain't none of y'all snitches. Because if you are, please tell me now," Ashanti said with neck-twisting attitude. She was really there just to show off her slippers and her pajamas.

"If you know what the hell you're doing, you don't have to worry about getting caught," Jazzy said.

"I'm just saying."

"Good night, Ashanti," Jazzy said to her.

Ashanti looked around the room, scoping it out to see what she could comment on. She made her way to the door. "Friday?" she asked.

Jazzy nodded her head.

Cha Cha had tried her best to hold her tongue, but she just couldn't. "Ashanti, I heard about your slick-ass mouth. Watch that shit!"

"Oh, please. Girl, stop it with the insecurities. Don't nobody want your little man," Ashanti said and quickly exited the room. She had heard about Cha Cha's hand skills and definitely didn't want to test her.

Jazzy got up and went over to the door and called out, "Ain't none of us in here snitches," she said. "Just be ready on Friday at eleven." She closed the door behind Ashanti.

CHAPTER 4

When Friday came, Ashanti was true to her word, and Jazzy, Maya, and Cha Cha all found themselves on the subway, headed to Manhattan. Jazzy wanted to go to Macy's, but Ashanti insisted that they only go to Saks Fifth Avenue.

"Why do y'all keep wanting to fuck with small shit? If we doing this, then let's do it. If y'all scared, then tell me now, so I can turn back around," Ashanti said.

"That store is massive," Cha Cha said. "And expensive."

"Yup, and that's exactly why we're going there. We ain't walking in together, and all of y'all have a half hour to scope out your floor. And by twelve o'clock, Maya you text me and tell me where you're at, and I'll come make a pickup from you. Then at twelve fifteen, Cha Cha, you text me and tell me where you're at, and I'll come pick up from you, and at twelve thirty, Jazzy, you text me, and I'll come pick up from you. And after I pick up your shit, I want y'all to leave the store, and I'll meet you back at The Waverly at two thirty." Ashanti spoke like a seasoned pro, and she definitely had the attention of all of the girls.

"So you got this by yourself?" Jazzy asked. "We ain't leaving with nothing ourselves?"

"Yeah, I got this. Trust me, this is how you pull shit off if you don't wanna get bagged. If we stay separate, then we stay off security's radar. If I roam the store too long by myself, then I'll pop up on the radar. But if we separately roam the store for a little while, with me making the pickups and y'all bouncing at separate times, then we won't have nothing to worry about," Ashanti explained. "And I won't have to worry about anybody snitching because won't nobody get caught to snitch."

Jazzy, Cha Cha, and Maya all felt like Ashanti's plan sounded too good to be true. It all sounded way too easy. Cha Cha knew that where there was little risk there was also little reward, but she didn't challenge Ashanti. Maya was pretty much down for whatever and kept her mouth closed.

But Jazzy, although she loved the sound of the plan, there was no way she was going to tell Ashanti her true feelings. She had to challenge Ashanti simply because she wanted to know just exactly what it was that Ashanti knew that made her feel so fuckin' confident.

"Your plan is bullshit!" Jazzy said as they rode on the A train.

"Why is it bullshit?"

"Because I already know how this is going to go. We're going to head back to Brooklyn and wait around for you to show up, and you're going to show up empty handed with some bullshit-ass excuse about too much security in the store or some bullshit like that."

"No, I'm not," Ashanti replied.

"Well, I think at least one of us need to stay behind and make sure your ass don't back out. Otherwise, we're just wasting our time, when we could be boosting on our own," Jazzy said, just to argue.

"Listen, if you and Cha Cha and Maya wanna go and boost tampons and toothpaste, then y'all can do that after you leave Saks.

I don't give a fuck. All I know is what I know, and I ain't wasting my time on no petty-ass shit. But, by all means, knock yourselves out. I guarantee you, when we meet back up tonight, I'll have my high-end shit, while the three of y'all sift through your scraps."

Everybody was quiet for a moment.

Meanwhile, the other passengers on the train were shocked at how brazen the girls were in discussing their robbery plans.

"So how are you going to get the shit out the store?" Jazzy asked Ashanti, fishing for Ashanti's MO.

"I'll get the shit out the store the same way I would if all four of us were leaving together. I'm gonna walk that shit right out the front door."

"What about the alarms?" Jazzy asked. "Are you sure you good with that?"

"I got that covered."

"So you know how to remove the security devices?" Maya who was finally paying attention asked. "You weren't just talkin' shit?"

"Why the fuck are y'all asking me all these damn questions? I got this. If everybody just plays their position, we'll be good."

Forty-five minutes later the girls found themselves at the ten-story high-end department store. They all entered the store at different times and did exactly as Ashanti had said, going separate ways.

Jazzy was certain that Ashanti had a device to remove the security tags from the clothes, and that was the secret to her being super confident. But at the same time she wanted to follow Ashanti throughout the store, just so she would know for sure just how Ashanti was going to go about getting the clothes out of the store.

Ashanti was no dummy. She knew that Jazzy and the other two chicks didn't have her best interest at heart. What was driving Ashanti was, she wanted to be able to brag and show off later at The Waverly, once everybody in the group home was around. She desperately wanted the three leaders of the group home, Jazzy, Cha Cha, and Maya, to have her back and vouch for her credibility.

Ashanti's biggest need was to feel validated, something she had never gotten from her mom or any of her relatives. She knew if she was successful in boosting with Jazzy, Cha Cha, and Maya, they were going to provide her with all of the validation she needed. Maybe then everyone would finally stop labeling her a pathological liar.

Ashanti headed straight to the men's section of the store, thinking that security was less likely to take notice of her there. The first thing she did was purchase three men's dress shirts and three neckties. She had to shell out close to three hundred dollars for those items, but she wasn't worried about it because she knew she could always return them.

Ashanti loved the men's department because the men who worked in the store were always so much friendlier than the women, and usually men worked the cash register in the men's department.

"Do you think my dad will like these shirts and ties?" Ashanti smiled and asked the white male cashier, who looked like he was flaming gay.

"Oh, I definitely think so," the cashier responded. "That's a very popular brand of ties that you chose, as well as the shirts."

"OK, that's good. It's so hard shopping for a man. I was thinking about getting some of the shirts and ties from Donald Trump's line, but I wasn't sure how the cut would be and I was going for a more fitted look for my dad," Ashanti said, running the cashier some bullshit.

The gay guy nodded his head and told Ashanti that she had definitely made the right choice. "Trump is nice, but it's a more straight-laced, stuffy, corporate businessman look. What you chose are much more trendy," he explained as he finished bagging everything. "Cash or credit?"

"Oh, I'll be paying in cash." Ashanti handed the cashier three crisp hundred-dollar bills.

The cashier smiled and thanked Ashanti as he handed her change and the bag of clothes.

Just as Ashanti was about to walk off, she stopped in her tracks as if she had forgotten something. "I'm sorry to bother you, but can I please have two Saks shopping bags, if you don't mind?"

The cashier didn't hesitate and reached down underneath his register and handed Ashanti the shopping bags without any questions. Ashanti and the cashier smiled at each other, and she walked off, headed straight for the ladies' room.

When Ashanti reached the ladies' room, she went inside one of the stalls and quickly went to work. She reached inside her Gucci bag and pulled out a brand-new roll of aluminum foil. She then opened up both of the shopping bags the cashier had just given her and lined the insides of both with two layers of aluminum foil. Then she reached inside her Gucci bag, took out masking tape, and taped the aluminum foil in place so it wouldn't shift. She put two shirts and one tie inside one shopping bag, and inside the other shopping bag, she put the other shirt and the other two ties. Ashanti then left the stall and exited the bathroom.

Two older white ladies inside the bathroom looked at each other horrified that Ashanti had just bolted from the bathroom without as much as sprinkling a droplet of water on her hands.

Ashanti, a seasoned high-end booster, knew the aluminum foil would prevent the alarms from detecting the security tags on the clothes once she walked through the detectors. That was the secret to her magic, and she most definitely wasn't going to share it with Jazzy, Cha Cha, or Maya.

After exiting the bathroom, she headed straight to Café SFA, located on the eighth floor, where she ordered an apple Danish and a small orange juice, and then patiently waited ten minutes for Maya to text her location to her.

When Maya's text came through, it said that she was on the fifth floor, near the Juicy Couture section. Ashanti almost lost it. She couldn't believe Maya was wasting time on bullshit such as Juicy.

Ashanti headed to the fifth floor and quickly found Maya. They acted as if they hadn't seen each other in years. After fake small talk, Maya began to show Ashanti the five pairs of jeans she had. Maya had done well. She had a $190 pair of 7 For All Mankind jeans, a $350 pair of Burberry five-pocket boot-cut jeans, a pair of $560 Chloe wide-leg denim pants, a $235 pair of Vince skinny stretch jeans, and a $178 pair of True Religion shorts.

Maya had some other items in her hand, but what she handed Ashanti was what she wanted to boost. Ashanti took hold of everything, and then they talked briefly before giving each other a hug and kiss on the cheek.

Ashanti reminded Maya to totally bounce from the store, and then she continued to roam the store. As she walked around, she slipped the items into her shopping bags in an inconspicuous manner.

Right at twelve fifteen, Ashanti got a text from Cha Cha, whom she met on the seventh floor, and they made a similar exchange.

At twelve thirty, she got a text from Jazzy. They met up on the third floor, where they made their exchange. After talking for a few minutes, Ashanti didn't want to give Jazzy a hug and a kiss because she didn't want to start looking too obvious.

"Bounce, and I'll meet everybody back at Waverly by two thirty," Ashanti said to Jazzy.

Jazzy nodded her head and did as she was told.

At that point Ashanti went back upstairs to the café and ordered a peppermint tea. She sat down and took her time drinking the tea, and also looked at her bags to make sure everything was all good.

After about fifteen minutes, when she felt confident that everything was in order, she stood up, grabbed hold of both of the heavy shopping bags, and made her way to the nearest escalator.

The eight flights down the escalator to the ground floor was a nerve-wracking trip for Ashanti. Her heart pounding, she felt like every eye in the store was fixed on her, and she was certain that security was in a back room watching her every move and talking into their walkie-talkies, just waiting to give the order to an undercover to rush in and apprehend her.

Ashanti's heart continued to pound out of her chest as she walked past the cosmetics section. And the exit seemed to move farther and farther away.

"Hey, excuse me, miss."

Ashanti was too spooked to turn and look to see who the person was talking to, so she kept walking as briskly as she could.

"Miss," the same person said.

This time Ashanti felt a hand grab her shoulder. Her heart in her feet, she turned and saw a security guard.

The security guard looked at Ashanti, and then he looked down and pointed at her shoe. "I was just trying to tell you that you have a napkin stuck to the bottom of your shoe," he said.

"Oh, OK." Ashanti smiled. Inside she was letting out the biggest sigh of relief. "I'm sorry. I was in another world, and I didn't hear you." She dragged her right foot on the floor to remove the stuck napkin.

The security guard nodded his head, and then Ashanti walked straight out the door and passed the detectors without a hitch.

It was a bright and sunny day with a cloudless sky and no humidity. Ashanti smiled her ass off as she headed for the train station thinking that the July weather was perfect, just like the crime she had managed to pull off. She knew she was the shit, and she was damn sure going to make sure that all of the girls in The Waverly knew it too.

CHAPTER 5

When Jazzy, Maya, and Cha Cha hadn't heard anything from Ashanti by four thirty, they were certain that she had gotten locked up. Jazzy wanted to call her and check up on her, but she didn't want the cops to have Ashanti's phone and for them to see her number on the caller ID.

Seeing that it was mid-afternoon, The Waverly was buzzing with activity, with a full staff on duty, visitors, and of course the majority of the girls from the group home present. Jazzy had checked with everybody that Ashanti was cool with, and no one had heard a word from her.

"I'm calling her ass," Cha Cha said.

It was close to five o'clock and Ashanti's phone just rang out to voice mail, but Cha Cha didn't leave a message.

"Voicemail," Cha Cha said to Jazzy.

"I knew it, that bitch wasted our time," Jazzy replied.

"I'm calling her ass back because I know she ain't get locked up and I want my shit!"

Cha Cha called Ashanti three times in a row, and it wasn't until the third time that she called her when Ashanti picked up, giggling into the phone and sounding distracted.

"Ashanti?" Cha Cha asked, unsure if it was her who had picked up.

"Yeah, what's up, girl?" Ashanti replied as if she didn't have a care in the world.

"*What's up?* Where the fuck are you?" Cha Cha screamed into the phone. "We was supposed to meet back at The Waverly at two thirty."

"Well, something came up!"

"Something like what?" Cha Cha yelled. "We were worried!"

"Something like me getting some dick!" Ashanti yelled back. "Last I checked, you don't run my show."

"Yo, take this phone and talk to this chick because, I swear, she about to send me to jail." Cha Cha handed Jazzy the phone.

"What's good, Ashanti?" Jazzy asked.

"You tell me."

"Where's the shit? We been waiting on you all day."

"First of all, I don't answer to nobody. Second of all, I am allowed to fuck when I want to without asking you or Cha Cha for permission," Ashanti said, stroking the leg of her thirty-year-old fireman boyfriend in his all-black X6 BMW truck. "And last I checked, we ain't never speak about how we divvying up these clothes."

"Ashanti, where are you?"

"I'm on my way with my dude. I'm about ten minutes away. I just left Queens ten minutes ago," Ashanti replied. "Can I live?"

Jazzy was silent, and she had a serious attitude. She was certain that Ashanti had already dipped into the goods and probably had sold some off already.

"So when we sell everything off, we'll split everything four ways. But just get here, and we'll talk about all that," Jazzy explained.

"I'm not into all that hustling shit off. I already got money. All I want is two outfits, and y'all can split the rest amongst the three of y'all," Ashanti explained.

Jazzy was somewhat surprised to hear Ashanti say that. She also wondered exactly what was Ashanti's true hustle...

Fifteen minutes later a black BMW truck with dark-tinted windows pulled up in front of The Waverly, and Ashanti slowly exited the car wearing some really nice designer shades and now carrying two Conway shopping bags full of the stolen loot. She walked as if she was a supermodel, smiling extra hard and making sure everyone saw her waving good-bye to her married fireman cradle-robber.

"I have to make sure I introduce y'all to Marquis the next time he drops me off. He was rushing because he's late to the firehouse." Ashanti handed Jazzy the Conway plastic bags filled with clothes.

"Firehouse?" Maya asked. "You fuckin' with a fireman? How did you manage that?"

Ashanti smiled and she didn't answer Maya directly, but she did chuckle to herself. "Marquis definitely knows how to work his fire hose and put out my fire. Ten long thick inches of pipe," she said, and then she shook her body as if she was having a convulsion.

"Ashanti, these clothes still got the security tags on them," Jazzy barked after inspecting the bags.

"Yeah and?"

"And these clothes are worthless with the tags on them."

Ashanti shook her head. "All you need is two pairs of pliers. You squeeze down on each end, and the tags will come off," she explained.

Big Momma emerged from the group home and came over to inspect the bags.

"I know there better be some plus size clothes up in them bags. Big Momma needs a new outfit."

"Ehh, no!" Ashanti replied, quickly dismissing Big Momma's words. She reached inside both bags and took the two outfits she wanted for herself, and she walked off to her room.

At that point Jazzy was more intrigued than ever. She desperately wanted to know how Ashanti had gotten the clothes out of the store with the security tags still intact. And she also wanted to know how Ashanti learned to remove the security tags.

"We got you, Momma, don't worry." Jazzy had to calm Big Momma down, telling her they were going to raise the two stacks she wanted for the pregnancy hookup by selling the clothes.

Big Momma smiled and waddled her fat ass back inside but not before telling Jazzy to make sure that they got her two cartons of Pringles potato chips the next time they hit up Duane Reade.

"Yeah, get me the plain ones and the bar-be-cue," she said.

Jazzy nodded her head and smiled a fake smile at Big Momma, but inside she was seething.

An hour later, Ashanti was in Jazzy's room with the pliers showing the girls how to remove the security tags.

"That's it?" Cha Cha asked.

"That's it."

Jazzy looked on in envy at the attention Cha Cha and Maya were giving to Ashanti. Ashanti was wearing a pair of the jeans that they had just stolen, and Maya was complimenting her on how good she looked in them.

Jazzy couldn't wait for Ashanti to go with them on their next boosting trip. She was determined that Ashanti either show her how she was getting the items out of the store, or for her to get locked up.

Just to make sure, Jazzy asked, "And you don't want none of the cash?"

Ashanti frowned up her face as if hustling off stolen products was beneath her.

"Money is money," Cha Cha said.

"I know that's right," Maya replied.

"Yeah, but time is money," Ashanti told them. "And ain't nobody got time to be hawking no products on the street. I ain't one of those African's who be peddling products on 125th Street."

"Why the fuck do you think you are so much better than everybody?" Jazzy said.

"I'm just explaining how I do me. Don't hate, Jazzy."

"Hate? Bitch is you stupid?" Jazzy shook her head and directed her words at Ashanti. "We got three thousand dollars worth of product. It don't matter how we sell it, just as long as we get the money. I'll sell this shit right alongside those Africans if I have to, it don't make me no difference."

"Yeah well that's the difference between me and you. You stay focused on that worker shit and I stay focused on that boss shit! But if you can sell it don't talk about it be about it. And regardless, it's gonna take you a minute to get rid of it," Ashanti said.

"I'll have the three grand within three days. Believe that! You may be a *boss* but I'm a hustler!"

"Three grand in three days?" Ashanti asked.

"No doubt."

Ashanti smiled at Jazzy. She knew Jazzy wasn't going to be able to pull that off, but she played along with it anyway. "OK, so then that's when we'll make our next run," Ashanti said to the girls just before leaving the room.

Jazzy's plan was to sell off all the goods on eBay. She had never actually sold anything on the site, but she had heard chicks in her school talking about how they'd shopped on eBay and found real good deals, so she was certain the products would sell. And she wasn't going to tell Maya or Cha Cha just how she was planning on selling the merchandise. She needed to make sure that they continued to look up to her and not Ashanti.

CHAPTER 6

A week after the girls had successfully boosted the items from Saks, Jazzy had managed to sell all of the items on eBay, where they moved like hot cakes. Within two days all of the items sold, and in total the girls brought in $3,800.

They decided to give Big Momma her two grand just so they could get the whole pregnancy test thing out of the way. That left them with $1,800 that they could split three ways. But instead of splitting it, they decided to just stash it and continue to save toward their goal of having enough money to move out of The Waverly and get their own apartment.

The Waverly was hosting their annual summer basketball tournament at Boys & Girls High School. The first day of the tournament was on a Saturday, and teams from all across the city came to Brooklyn to take part in the tournament. At the tournament Jazzy walked up to Big Momma, who was working the scoreboard, and sat down next to her.

"We got that paper for you." Jazzy slid the cash to Big Momma underneath the table.

Big Momma didn't want the other supervisors from The Waverly standing nearby to see what was going on, so she quickly took the money and stuffed it between her two huge breasts. As fat as Big Momma was, she had the nerve to be wearing a tube top and some spandex pants. And her open-toe sandals made her pudgy feet look like pigs in a blanket. She was showing off every roll of fat, and couldn't no one tell her that she didn't look good.

"Big Momma, you so crazy," Jazzy said.

"I don't have no handbag on me and no pockets, so what the fuck am I supposed to do?" Big Momma sipped on the soda she was drinking.

"Well, the money is all there. Don't lose it."

"I won't, and I'll get with my friend and set everything up for Maya. Don't worry."

The second game wasn't scheduled to start for another fifteen minutes, so everybody was walking around and mingling with each other. Jazzy was looking for Cha Cha and Maya. She bumped into Ashanti, who was walking with some chick that was new to the group home.

"You looking for your two sidekicks?" Ashanti asked.

"Why you always in our business?" Jazzy remarked. "If I was lookin' for them I know how to find them. Nobody *needs* you, Ashanti." Jazzy meant that last remark literally. She couldn't stand Ashanti.

"I got the most haters," Ashanti quipped. "You hatin' when all I was trying to do was show you love and give you the 4-1-1."

Jazzy's interest was piqued. "What 4-1-1?"

"Oh, now you wanna politick?"

Jazzy placed her hand on her hip. She knew Ashanti wanted her to beg. She must have bumped her head. "Fuck it…no better yet, fuck you!"

Jazzy was just about to storm off when Ashanti replied, "All I was gonna say was you better go outside and check on your girl. Her man look like he was about to get in her ass."

Jazzy frowned up her face and then she quickly left the school building and headed outside to Fulton Street. She looked around for Cha Cha but couldn't find her. She called Cha Cha on her cell phone, but Cha Cha didn't pick up. Then she called Maya, who picked up. She heard Maya yelling for Troy to get his hands off Cha Cha.

"Maya! Maya, what's going on?" Jazzy screamed into the phone.

"This muthafucka is crazy! He putting his hands on Cha Cha. We about to fuck this nigga up!"

Maya told Jazzy where they were, and Jazzy quickly ran down the block and across the street, where she spotted Maya standing in the middle of the street, flailing her hands in the air.

"You a fuckin' pussy, Troy!" Maya yelled as she yanked on the driver's side door of Troy's Yukon. "Open up this fuckin' door!"

As soon as Jazzy arrived, she could see Troy reaching across the front seat of his truck and punching on Cha Cha, who was doing her best to fight back, but she was no match for him.

By this time people had started to notice what was going on, but none of the guys nearby did anything to help Cha Cha. At this point, Troy had a handful of Cha Cha's hair weave and was smashing his fist into her face.

"What they fighting for?" Jazzy asked Maya.

"He saying Cha Cha came up short on his money. But that's bullshit he's just trying to jerk her ass."

Jazzy quickly trotted across the street and got a metal city garbage can from the corner and turned it over, emptying all of the garbage onto the street. Then she dragged the garbage can right next to Troy's car.

"Help me lift this shit up," she said to Maya.

Without hesitation, Maya and Jazzy lifted up the garbage can and smashed Troy's window on the driver's side. The shattering glass caught Troy off guard, and he instantly released the chokehold he had on Cha Cha.

Jazzy jumped up on the running board of the truck, reached inside, and started punching Troy. "Don't you be putting your fuckin' hands on her!" she yelled, throwing blows.

If somebody didn't know, they definitely would have thought it was two dudes going at it.

"Cha Cha, get out the car!" Jazzy yelled to her.

Cha Cha didn't listen, and she also started to throw punches at Troy.

Meanwhile, Maya used all of her strength to lift up the garbage can and smashed out the rear window of Troy's truck. And then she rammed the garbage can into the side of the truck and put a big dent in it.

Troy pushed Jazzy off the running board, and as soon as he was about to step out of the car, he started to wince in pain. Some of the shattered glass had got into his eyes, so he wasn't able to see. All he could do was cry out in pain as he repeatedly blinked his eyes.

When Jazzy and Maya both saw that he was covering his eyes in pain, they ran up on him, and together they threw him to the ground and started to stomp on him. Cha Cha exited the truck and joined in, and the three of them stomped out Troy in the middle of the street.

As the crowd of onlookers cheered the three girls on, the sound of a police siren could be heard in the distance. Cha Cha, Jazzy, and Maya all scattered, and they didn't even go back to the basketball game. They ran a couple of blocks to the train station, hopped the turnstile without paying, and boarded the A train, which they took to the next stop.

"That nigga still got my money," Cha Cha vented.

"Cha Cha, I swear to God, you better not fuck with that nigga no more. He ain't no good, hitting on you like that. But I'm telling you now, if I see you hugged up with him, I ain't fuckin' with you!" Jazzy stated as she caught her breath.

"Fuck him!" Cha Cha knew in her heart that it would take just one phone call of apology from Troy and she would be right back up in his face.

Cha Cha equated a beating as her proof of a man's love for her.

"I'm so done with his ass. Y'all been telling me for the longest that he wasn't no good for me, but I couldn't see it."

"The moment his chips get low, he gets on some other shit," Maya added. She laughed at how they had fucked Troy up. "Whatever he took from you, Cha Cha, it's gonna cost him way more to fix his truck, so don't even stress it."

Cha Cha was pissed and she was more bothered by the principle of everything. She really thought that Troy loved her. He would tell her that he loved her every time she let him fuck her. She could have lived with him hitting on her had she done something wrong or had she been out of line, but to accuse her of stealing from him just so he could take all of her money proved to her that he really didn't love her and had just been using her all along.

"Dick is dick," Jazzy said to Cha Cha. "Leave his punk ass alone and find some new dick."

The three girls exited the train station and headed back to The Waverly.

"You don't need that weed hustle no more anyway," Jazzy said. "All we gotta do is stay focused on this boosting, and we'll make enough dough to do what we gotta do."

The girls all agreed that Jazzy was right.

As they walked back to their room, the girls decided that the next day they would take Ashanti with them to Bed Bath & Beyond on 18th Street in Manhattan and boost from there. Only, this time the three of them weren't going to leave the store, because Jazzy was determined to know exactly what Ashanti's technique was.

The Waverly was completely empty, since everybody was at the basketball game, so the girls were free to smoke their weed as they pleased. While they smoked, Jazzy told them that on Monday they would have Cha Cha hot-wire a car for them, so they could head out to the outlets on Long Island and boost from there.

They all agreed that Manhattan would soon become too hot and that their luck was likely to run out if they kept going back to the same stores.

All they wanted to do was to get their stash built up to the point where they had ten to twenty grand, and then they were going to chill and take a break from the boosting, and get away for good from all the leeches in their lives. Leeches like Troy and Big Momma.

CHAPTER 7

Big Momma loved to do two things more than anything else. One was eat, the other was gamble. Every day she was sending one of the girls to the store for her to buy her scratch-off instant lottery tickets and to play numbers for her.

Big Momma always told herself that there was a reason she was so fat, and part of that reason was because her weight was bound to come out in the daily pick three drawing. She weighed four hundred and five pounds, so every day she would play the number 405, hoping to hit it straight. She was so sure that number was going to come out, she had been spending ten dollars a day playing it for a year with no luck. But it didn't matter. She was determined to hit it.

Seeing that Big Momma only made eight hundred dollars a week and lived paycheck to paycheck, her gambling and fast-food addictions were starting to take a toll on her, and she found herself two months behind on her rent. So when Jazzy handed her the two thousand dollars, she saw that as a blessing from God. She'd owed her landlord eighteen hundred dollars and had been promising him that she would get caught up within a week. Big Momma had no idea that Jazzy and the girls would come up with the money so quickly, but it was right on time.

While Big Momma worked the scoreboard at the basketball games, it was hard for her to pay attention to the game because she was so focused on the two grand stuffed in her cleavage.

God don't always come when you want him to, but He's always on time! Big Momma said to herself as soon as the basketball tournament was over. She left the high school gym close to six p.m. and called her best friend Shonnie and told her to meet her downtown Brooklyn at Applebee's.

Shonnie was nowhere near as big as Big Momma, but she loved to eat. And one thing about Big Momma, whether it was male friends or female friends, she was always buying her friendships, always treating them to restaurants and buying them small gifts just so they would like her.

Shonnie lived way out in Staten Island, so it took her some time to get to Brooklyn. By the time she got there, it was close to 7:30, the exact time that the bus going to Atlantic City was scheduled to leave.

"Hey, girl. I just got off the train, and I'm crossing Flatbush Avenue right now," Shonnie said to Big Momma after calling her on her cell phone.

A relieved Big Momma smiled. She had already spent thirty-five dollars buying Shonnie's bus ticket and didn't want it to go to waste. She told Shonnie that she was already on the bus waiting for her and was holding a seat for her.

Five minutes later, Shonnie walked on to the bus. She didn't have to see Big Momma to know where she was sitting. All she had to do was follow the smell of cornbread, barbecue ribs, and French fries.

"I know you not eating without me. And I'm starving too,"

Shonnie said to Big Momma as Big Momma stuffed her face with French fries.

"Girl, you know I got you." Big Momma handed her a bag of food. "The best thing Applebee's ever came up with was that 'Carside To Go.' Don't nobody always wanna be sitting down to eat in them tight-ass booths they got up in there."

Shonnie wanted to laugh at Big Momma, but she did her best not to.

Big Momma had ordered for Shonnie the same thing she had ordered for herself—a full slab of double-glazed baby back ribs, French fries, cole slaw, cornbread, and a large soda.

Just to be politically correct, Shonnie reached into her pocket and she tried to hand Big Momma thirty dollars.

"Girl, you better put that money right back in your pocket and sit down and eat that food. I already told you I hit that 715 last night. I had four dollars on it, and it came out straight as an arrow," Big Momma lied.

"Two grand you hit it for? You should've called me and told me to play it too." Shonnie started to eat her ribs.

"I know, I know. But that's why I got you today. I'll give you five hundred to gamble with, and you ain't got to pay me back. But if you hit, I want half of what you win."

"Oh, no doubt. You know how we do."

Big Momma's self esteem was so low, she did what she had to do to have a social life.

Two hours later Shonnie and Big Momma were in the Showboat Casino. Shonnie only played slot machines because she didn't like the way her money disappeared so quickly on the table games. Big Momma, on the other hand, hated slot machines because it didn't allow her to use her brain, and she also felt that the machines were rigged for gamblers to lose, so she went straight to the blackjack tables.

Shonnie wasn't a dummy. The first thing she did was put away three hundred dollars that she wasn't going to spend in the bottom of her purse. She was going back home with no less than three of the five hundred Big Momma had given her. She had bills to pay and wasn't about to just gamble away free money like that.

Meanwhile, Big Momma pulled out thirteen hundred dollars and laid it on the blackjack table so that the dealer could give her thirteen hundred dollars worth of chips. Already Big Momma only had about seventy-five dollars in cash left from the two grand Jazzy had given her.

As Big Momma sat at the blackjack table and gambled, she didn't have a care in the world. High off the thrill she got from gambling, she didn't care about her past due rent, she didn't care about her nonexistent sex life, and she didn't care about her weight.

Four hours later, Shonnie was done, having lost the two hundred dollars she was playing with. She walked around the casino searching for Big Momma and found her sitting in front of a mountain of chips.

"Don't tell me you lost all that money playing slots?" Big Momma asked Shonnie.

Shonnie put on a sad face and nodded her head yes.

"See, that's why I don't fuck with them damn slot machines.

Especially them dollar slot machines. That shit is a fuckin' scam."

Big Momma then said to the dealer, "Yeah, hit me!"

"Twenty-one!" she yelled in excitement and slapped her hand on the table. "I'm killing they ass. I'm up like five grand!"

Big Momma then handed Shonnie three chips, each one worth one hundred dollars. "Don't play no fuckin' slot machines. Go play roulette or something like that. Get all one-dollar chips and put one chip on all of the even numbers, and watch how much money you start winning."

Shonnie snatched the three hundred dollars in chips, and after thanking Big Momma, she walked off. She cashed in those chips and put the cash in her bag, and then she walked to one of the restaurants and ordered some food. By this time it was close to two in the morning, and Shonnie was tired and ready to go. She knew Big Momma wasn't going to get a room for the night and that the bus wasn't making its return trip for another four hours.

After Shonnie finished eating, she went back over to Big Momma and told her that she had won one hundred dollars playing roulette and that she was going to go play the crap tables.

"See, you listened to me and you made yourself some money. You need to get over here and play blackjack, so you can get some of this money I'm getting. I'm up seventy-five hundred. I'm straight murdering this casino!"

"Wow! You need to get up and cash in your chips and let's go wait for this bus."

Big Momma looked at her watch and she saw that it was only two thirty in the morning. "Please! We got another three hours. I'm sticking them up for twenty grand before I get up from this seat. I'm way too hot."

Big Momma was feeling good. She had enough money to pay her back rent and to pay two months in advance. She also had the money to pay her friend to do the pregnancy thing for Maya, so she knew she was good. No matter what, she was going back home with at least five grand. She had already told herself, if her chips got close to five grand, she was going to stop at that point. Her goal was to get to twenty grand, so she would have enough dough to get her gastric bypass surgery done. Getting that surgery had always been her secret mission and wish ever since she had seen how much weight Star Jones had lost.

"You are focused!" Shonnie laughed.

Big Momma nodded her head, focusing on the action at the blackjack table.

"You want me to get you something to eat?" Shonnie asked.

Big Momma nodded her head and handed Shonnie a hundred-dollar chip. "Get me some Buffalo wings with blue cheese dressing. You can keep the change." She didn't need a drink because she had been getting round after round of free drinks from the casino waitresses, all of whom she'd tipped generously.

Shonnie smiled as she took the hundred-dollar chip, and she walked off in search of Buffalo wings and blue cheese dressing. She was very tired, but she had managed to pocket more than six hundred dollars just by going to Atlantic City with Big Momma, so there was no way she was going to complain. The way she looked at it, she was earning fifty dollars an hour, which was way more money than she made at her job.

Three hours later, well after Big Momma had finished the Buffalo wings, she was calling Shonnie's cell phone to see where she was at.

"Hello," Shonnie answered, sounding groggy. She had dozed off in the waiting area where the buses departed from.

"Girl where you at?"

"I'm in the waiting area for the bus."

"You ready to leave?"

"Yes. It's almost six in the morning. You ain't ready to go?" Shonnie asked.

"No, I ain't ready. I'm a gambler. This is what I do. Let's just chill until twelve thirty, and we'll leave then."

"I can't. I'm sorry, but I gotta work at five this afternoon, and I'm not trying to go straight from AC to my job."

Shonnie was a nurse and worked twelve-hour shifts. She was scheduled to go to work at five p.m. that night, so she wanted to get home and get a good eight hours sleep. Not to mention, she wasn't really looking forward to the ferry ride back to Staten Island after she got off the subway.

Big Momma sucked her teeth and sighed into the phone, contemplating what she should do.

"Girl, just get on this bus with me and come home with that money you won."

"But I ain't at my twenty thousand dollar goal yet."

"Yeah, but you're up, and you're going home with more money than you came here with."

The phone was silent for a few moments, and then Big Momma let out another sigh. "No, I *was* up. I ended up giving all that money right back to their asses," Big Momma said, sounding really dejected.

"No fuckin' way! You practically had ten grand. What happened?"

"Shonnie, I don't feel like talking about it. I'll get it back. You got any more money on you? All I need is a hundred dollars, and I'll get it back."

"You don't even have a hundred dollars? Are you serious? See, I knew I shoulda pulled your ass up from that table when I brought you them wings."

"Yeah, but you didn't, and now I'm broke."

Big Momma was going to stay broke because Shonnie, although she had more than six hundred dollars in her bag, knew not to give her a dime. That would only be throwing money down the drain. So she told Big Momma that she had gone back to the slot machines and lost all of the money she had.

Believing that Shonnie was supposedly also broke, Big Momma didn't feel like a complete loser. But, at the same time, as they boarded the bus to go back home, she knew she had dug herself into an even bigger hole. Now, not only did she owe her landlord, but she also owed Maya a promised favor that she couldn't deliver on.

Big Momma did have enough money left to buy herself a huge bag of Crunchy Cheez Doodles. As she ate those Cheez Doodles, she brainstormed about just what she should and could do to get her ass out of the sling she was in. Big Momma knew that getting her hand on some cash was the only way to solve her issues, and she was willing to do whatever she had to do to get the cash she needed.

But as she sat back and thought about everything, she realized that she was Big Momma and that she didn't have to do shit. All she had to do was figure out just how to exploit the power she had over Jazzy, Cha Cha, and Maya.

CHAPTER 8

Everybody in New York City was familiar with a star high school basketball player named Bobby Patterson. Bobby wasn't as tall as LeBron James, but many of the scouts were saying he could be just as good. It was a given fact that Bobby Patterson, from Queens, was going to go straight to the NBA when he graduated from high school in two years, so it was safe to say that just about every teenage girl in the city wanted to get with him.

While Cha Cha, Jazzy, and Maya were fighting in the street during the basketball tournament, Ashanti was inside the gym, perfectly positioned right near the bench of Bobby Patterson's AAU summer traveling team. The only reason Ashanti went to the tournament was to meet Bobby, and sure enough she got her wish. Bobby took note of her fresh face and spoke to her right after the game ended.

"How you doing, miss?" Bobby asked Ashanti while wiping sweat from his forehead.

Ashanti smiled. "Fine."

"I don't think I ever met you before." Bobby's six-foot four-inch muscular frame walked toward Ashanti.

"No, I don't think we ever met before. I'm sure I would have remembered meeting someone as handsome as you. I'm Ashanti." She extended her hand to Bobby.

"I'm Bobby."

Bobby's coach yelled out to him to hurry up. The game was over, but his team had another game later that day in Manhattan.

"Listen, I have to go. My coach is calling me. But would your man get upset if I gave you my number so you could call me later?"

Ashanti smiled, seductively. "I don't have a man," she paused, making him hang on her every word. "And I would love to call you later."

Bobby loved how assertive she was. Flirty and confident but most importantly she was beautiful. She was just his type. In the few minutes of introduction, Bobby had already peeped her swollen cleavage, bi-racial looking features, and long, soft hair. "Listen, my phone is in the locker room, so text me your number and I'll make sure I store it in my cell."

"You do that."

"What are you doing later?" he asked.

"Not much of anything."

"OK, I'll call you later, and maybe we can get up and hang out or something."

"I'd like that a lot." Ashanti replied, and nodded her head.

"I gotta go. We have another game uptown, but I'll call you later."

"OK," Ashanti said with her soft-sounding voice. "Nice meeting you."

"Nice meeting you too." Bobby smiled and trotted off.

Ashanti was on cloud nine, and later that night when she spoke to Bobby she was even more delighted when he told her that he was going to come by and see her at The Waverly.

Bobby had illegally been given a brand-new Lexus by a sports agent who wanted to represent him when he eventually made it to the NBA. The same agent also gave him a thousand dollars a week just so he would have spending money. And for Bobby the money came in handy. That was the money he was going to use when him and Ashanti would go to Times Square later that night to eat at Red Lobster and to see a movie.

"Oh my God! Girl, look at your neck!" Ashanti said to Cha Cha, who had handprint and black-and-blue marks on her neck from Troy choking her earlier in the day outside the basketball game. "I heard about y'all little brawl, but damn, you look like death on a stick. You need to go to the doctor and get checked out."

The other girls in the group home came up to Cha Cha to see if she was alright.

Jazzy and Maya ignored Ashanti, as did the other girls, and they all tended to Cha Cha's bruises. Jazzy was real animated as she told the other girls in the group home exactly how they fucked up Troy and stomped him in the street and how Maya managed to smash out his car windows.

"Oh, please!" Ashanti said as loud as she could, making sure that everyone in the room heard what she said. "I don't know why y'all insist on fuckin' with all those lame-ass niggas anyway. See, me, I only fucks with real ballers like future multimillionaire NBA star Bobby Patterson." Ashanti had just finished texting Bobby her address, so she knew he was already on his way to see her.

"Ashanti, why are you always fuckin' lying? Shit!" Jazzy shouted.

Ashanti smiled. She didn't say anything because she knew that in a moment she would be able to prove that she wasn't lying.

"And for the record we all know that you're fuckin' one of the bum-ass security guards at Saks Fifth Avenue," Jazzy added.

All of the other girls laughed.

Ashanti didn't laugh, and she didn't feel the need to defend herself. She knew the only reason Jazzy said that was because that was her theory as to how Ashanti was able to freely walk out of the high-end department store with all of the stolen clothes with the Sensormatic devices still attached.

"The hate in here is just so unnecessary. It's sad," Ashanti said to herself, and she smiled.

Five minutes later Bobby was calling Ashanti, and he told her that he was outside. Ashanti asked him if he could park and come inside for a quick minute, and Bobby agreed.

All of the girls were absolutely shocked when Ashanti opened up the front door and Bobby walked in with his crisp brand-new clothes and his gold chain and Jesus medallion hanging from his neck.

"Bobby, this is everybody. Everybody, this is Bobby Patterson," Ashanti said with a smile.

Bobby waved and said hello, and then Ashanti grabbed him by the hand and whisked him upstairs to her room that she shared with two other girls who weren't there at the time. Ashanti knew that Big Momma could literally pop up at any minute, but she still took the chance of bringing Bobby into The Waverly and up to her room.

"I can't wait to get out of this place. My mother is really pissing me off by having me up in here," she said to Bobby.

Bobby didn't say anything in response.

As soon as they reached her room, Ashanti went to her closet and pulled out two nice brand-new outfits along with two brand-new pairs of shoes, trying to impress Bobby, asking him which outfit should she wear.

He smiled and said, "You look good with what you already got on."

Ashanti smiled. "Yeah, I know, but I don't think I should wear shorts. I think it's better to wear some jeans."

Without hesitation, Ashanti took off her shorts and stood there in her bright red lace thong, and then she put on a pair of super tight jeans. She knew she had a very nice body and that Bobby was taking notice of her as she got dressed.

It took Ashanti a couple of minutes to squeeze into the jeans, but when she did, she slipped on some open-toe sandals and asked Bobby if she looked OK.

Bobby didn't tell Ashanti, but his dick was rock-hard, and he wanted to fuck her right there on the spot.

"You look really good." Bobby smiled and walked toward her as she gathered up her clothes to put them away in her closet. "You smell good too," he said to her as he got closer.

"Thank you." She tried to act as if she didn't know he was creeping up closer to her. After she put the clothes away, she turned from the closet, and Bobby was standing right up on her.

"I know we just met," Bobby said. "But I really wanna kiss you right now."

Ashanti looked up at him and didn't say anything. The next thing she knew, her and Bobby were kissing. She stood on her tippy toes as she tongue-kissed him as deeply as she could. And she loved the way he held her body tight as they kissed. And as Bobby pressed his body up against hers, she could feel his hard dick, which turned her on so much and made her kiss him even harder.

After about a minute or so of kissing, Ashanti pulled away from him, smiling as she fanned herself with her hand.

She laughed. "Alrighty then."

"I like the way you kiss," Bobby said to her.

Ashanti looked at him lustfully, ready to fuck, but she didn't want him to think she was that easy. She smiled. "We need to leave," she said, and the two of them left her room and went back downstairs.

Jazzy and Cha Cha were feeling nothing but envy when Bobby and Ashanti walked back downstairs and prepared to leave.

Ashanti didn't have to say anything to anyone because it was clear that she was rocking out with Bobby, and her actions spoke for her.

Maya was the only one who really didn't care one way or the other who Ashanti was with because it meant absolutely nothing to her personal life. The only thing Maya was concerned with was solving the dilemma she was facing due to having turned eighteen years old.

"Ashanti," Jazzy called out just as she was about to walk out the door with Bobby.

Ashanti stopped in her tracks, a little disgusted.

"Let me holler at you for a second." Jazzy said, walking toward Ashanti and Bobby.

Ashanti rolled her eyes. "You can go ahead to your car and I'll be right there."

Ashanti said in a very low but stern voice to Jazzy. "I know you're not cock-blocking right now."

"Bitch, please. I don't care what you do with your vagina!"

"So then what do you want?"

"What time are you coming back?"

"I don't know! Did you change your name to Big Momma or

something?"

"No, but I'm just making sure you'll be back to go with us to the outlets tomorrow," Jazzy said.

"Tomorrow? I thought we were doing that on Monday."

"No, it's tomorrow. Ashanti, you better not front on us."

"Well, I don't know. I don't have time for this boosting shit. As you can see, I got bigger fish to fry. Six foot four inches of future NBA fish, to be exact." Ashanti chuckled.

"Ashanti, I'll fuck you up if you front on us," Jazzy replied.

"Oh, now all of a sudden you *need* me. But I thought I was the big pathological liar. So funny how things change." Ashanti shook her head with an attitude.

"Look, are you coming or not?"

Ashanti thought for a moment. She was on the verge of saying no, but at the same time she wanted to get out of The Waverly. If she got into any trouble at the group home, she knew that her mom would leave her there longer to further punish her.

"I'll go, but this is the last time I'm fuckin' with y'all and this petty-ass boosting shit. And I'm only doing this so you can cover me with Big Momma. Say whatever you gotta say to Big Momma, but I already know I won't be in before curfew. I probably won't get in until after two in the morning. So if you cover me on that and make sure that Big Momma don't make a stink about it, then I got y'all in the morning. But if I catch any flack from Big Momma, it's a wrap, and you and your little posse are on your own with your little boosting expedition."

"It's done," Jazzy said.

Jazzy wanted to slap Ashanti's face, but she needed her, so she kept things cool. Jazzy also knew that a hundred dollars would be all it would take to have Big Momma turn a blind eye to Ashanti missing curfew, even though she had no idea that Big Momma wouldn't be coming back until damn near the next afternoon. She figured that the money they would make from boosting would be more than enough to cover the hundred dollars to Big Momma.

"Hey," Jazzy said to Ashanti as she walked off toward Bobby's Lexus.

Ashanti stopped in her tracks. "Whaaaat?"

"Don't let him fuck you without a condom," Jazzy warned.

Ashanti sucked her teeth and gave Jazzy a smile. "Girl, I'm grown," she said, before heading to Bobby's car.

CHAPTER 9

While Big Momma sat slumped and dejected in her seat on the Peter Pan bus on her way back to New York from Atlantic City, wondering where she was going to get money to hold her over until her next payday, and the girls at The Waverly were literally having a party.

By one in the morning, when the girls at The Waverly realized that Big Momma was nowhere to be found, they got on Facebook and Twitter and started spreading the word that they were having a party. Word started to spread like wildfire because it wasn't just any kind of party.

Almost every girl in The Waverly had some kind of hustle. Cha Cha sold her weed and boosted with Jazzy, who was strictly into boosting, and Maya boosted and got money from dudes whenever she could. Some girls ran credit card scams, others sold pussy. And Trina and Tiny, their hustle was stripping.

Trina and Tiny were the main promoters of the party, and since many of their male friends knew they stripped, it didn't take long for the people to start showing up at The Waverly. By two thirty in the morning, The Waverly was packed with about a hundred guys, all of whom had paid five dollars to get in. Girls also came to the party. They got in for free, but they had to buy a drink for three dollars. There were easily a hundred and thirty people in the party, and the majority of them didn't belong there.

One of the girls managed to hook up her iPod to The Waverly's PA system, which was used to announce fire drills and things of that sort. While the music blasted through the speakers, Trina and Tiny put on their stripper show to the delight of all the dudes in attendance.

Trina did her solo act first. She was super flexible. All it took was for her to get butt naked and put both of her legs behind her head, and the guys were throwing money at her.

Tiny was only four feet, eleven inches tall, but her small frame didn't stop her from inserting an entire Heineken bottle inside her pussy. All of the guys went nuts when she did that, and before long, money was raining down on her.

Jazzy was wondering what had happened to Big Momma. There'd been times when Big Momma dipped out for an hour or so, but she always came right back. This was the first time that she had just completely not shown up without having someone replace her. So Jazzy reasoned that because it was the start of summer and right after the Fourth of July holiday that there must have been some kind of mix-up in the scheduling and that the girls had caught a major break.

Though Jazzy was without question the leader of The Waverly, she wasn't a control freak, and she definitely wasn't the one to knock anybody else's hustle. She wasn't into the whole stripping thing or selling her pussy for money, but she loved to drink and party just as much as the next person, so she, Maya, and Cha Cha mingled and partied in the breaks between Trina's and Tiny's strip shows.

"Yo, that bitch Ashanti better be back before six in the morning," Jazzy said to Cha Cha. She took a sip from her Corona and continued bopping her head to the music.

"She will be," Cha Cha replied. "But we better shut this shit down at five, before she gets here."

Jazzy agreed that five a.m. would be the cut-off time.

Meanwhile, Tiny had disappeared to her "VIP" room to fuck one of the partygoers who had agreed to pay her one hundred and twenty five dollars for sex. And Trina had also disappeared to the same VIP room, where she was dishing out a blowjob for fifty dollars.

Ashanti and Bobby exited Bobby's car and headed into a motel on the corner of Pennsylvania Avenue and Linden Boulevard. Bobby paid fifty dollars for four hours of room time, and him and Ashanti made their way up to room 304.

"So, is this where you take all of your girls?" Ashanti asked with slurred speech and a smile. She was drunk from all of the drinks she had at the restaurant.

"It's not like that, Ma." Bobby unlocked the door to the room, and the two of them went inside. "Don't believe all the hype."

"So then I'm special to you?" Ashanti giggled.

"No doubt."

Ashanti playfully slapped him and told him he was full of shit. "You know you just wanna get in between these thighs."

Ashanti excused herself and went into the bathroom to let out all of that liquor she had been drinking. After she peed, she took a washcloth, wet it with hot water and put soap on it, and washed her pussy in the sink, just to make sure that her shit was clean because she was ready to fuck Bobby. She wanted him to eat her pussy, so she would know she was special.

She exited the bathroom and found Bobby lying on the bed with no clothes on.

"You ready to back up all that shit you was talking at the restaurant?" he asked her.

Ashanti smiled as she walked over to Bobby. She sat down on the bed and started to massage his dick until it got hard. Bobby's six-pack along with his chiseled chest and his hard dick was all turning Ashanti on.

She stood up and took off all her clothes. "You can't be the only one with no clothes on," she said to Bobby.

Then she lay down on the bed, on her back, and spread open her pussy lips, letting Bobby take a good look at what she was getting ready to give him. She smiled at him, and then she inserted a finger into her pussy, which caused her to close her eyes and moan just a little bit. Then she slid her finger out of her pussy and sucked on it.

"Damn, my shit is so fuckin' sweet!" She laughed.

Ashanti was definitely turning Bobby on. Bobby was surprised at how relaxed Ashanti was with him, which made him wonder just how many dudes she was fuckin'.

Ashanti used her index finger to point at Bobby and motioned for him to come her way.

Bobby smiled as he came toward her with his hard dick, ready to stick it inside her and fuck her like crazy.

"Nope, nope. You gotta eat me first, just like you promised." Ashanti then guided Bobby toward her pussy.

Bobby went straight to Ashanti's shaved pussy and started sucking on her clit.

"Mmmm-hhhhmmm," Ashanti moaned and then she smiled and closed her eyes and laid back and enjoyed how Bobby worked his tongue on her clit. Bobby was eating her pussy like a porno star.

He inserted two fingers in her pussy and rubbed her G-spot, while his tongue continued to lick on her clit.

"Oh my fuckin'God! You gonna make me come like that! That shit feels so damn good!"

Her reaction had given Bobby more confidence and incentive to keep doing exactly what he was doing, and in the process Ashanti's pussy got wetter and wetter, and her breathing heavier and heavier.

"You gonna cum for me, baby?" he asked her.

Ashanti was tongue-tied, so the only thing she could do was quickly nod her head up and down. She then grabbed the back of Bobby's head and forced his face right into her pussy, grinding her pussy into Bobby's face, rotating her hips like she was dancing to reggae music.

"Bite my shit, baby."

At first Bobby was caught off guard, but then he softly bit on her clit.

"Don't be scared. Bite that shit!"

Bobby then bit her pussy much harder. It was like biting into a juicy orange and causing all of the juices to squirt out because as soon as he bit Ashanti's clit, it caused a surge to shoot through her body, and she started to have small tremors.

Ashanti screamed when she was coming. She might've as well let the entire hotel know that she was coming; she was so loud.

Making her come that hard and that quickly felt better to Bobby than hitting a game-winning jump shot. And he loved watching Ashanti's reaction. After Ashanti returned back to her normal self, Bobby laughed at her.

"What's so fuckin' funny?" Ashanti hid her face with a pillow.

"Who knew that biting your pussy would make you come like that?" he playfully said.

He turned her over on to her back and, without any thought of using a condom, he slowly slid his dick into Ashanti's pussy and fucked her brains out.

Before they knew it, their four-hour time limit was up, and after literally spending the entire four hours fucking, they were preparing to leave and go back to The Waverly. The last thing Ashanti was thinking about was going boosting with Jazzy, Cha Cha, and Maya. All Ashanti wanted to think about was whether or not she had managed to get pregnant by the future NBA star who had just finished fucking her raw dog for four hours.

It was now seven in the morning, and it seemed as if there was going to be no stopping Trina and Tiny, who were in the middle of a girl-on-girl show, delighting what now seemed like all of the black guys in Bedford-Stuyvesant between the ages of fifteen and twenty-one.

Even though the sun was shining brightly, the party showed no signs of slowing down. The music was still pumping, and the liquor and weed was still flowing and being passed around. And with the way The Waverly was situated on a huge piece of an acre fenced-in property, the party noise and the large number of partygoers weren't exactly a nuisance to the local neighbors, who would have definitely called the cops had the party been at a regular house.

Cha Cha was making so much money selling weed that her

and Jazzy decided to not shut the party down at five a.m. like they'd originally planned. And as time went on, they felt more confident about their decision to keep the party rocking because at this point they figured, if Big Momma showed up and started beefing, they now had something to hang over her head because she was AWOL for so long.

During the last forty-five minutes of the party, Trina and Tiny had done all they could with a double-sided dildo. It was now approaching eight in the morning, and the two were completely exhausted as they picked up all of their cash from off the floor that had been thrown at them while they performed their routine.

Before the two could finish picking up all their money, they almost got trampled on by the partygoers, who all suddenly started running outside to the front entrance of The Waverly to see exactly who was beefing.

A popular Blood from Brooklyn barked on another dude that he had been playing cee-lo against and losing his money to, and a crowd started to gather around to see what was up.

"Give me my muthafuckin' money, or I'll murder your ass!"

"I ain't giving you shit!" the Blood yelled back. Courtney was a Blood from Marcy projects who had just come home from jail only a week ago. Everybody knew he was a hothead, and mostly everyone feared him. Apparently though, the dude he was beefing with either didn't know his reputation, or he didn't give a fuck.

"You just said two hundred that I won't roll a four or better, and I rolled a muthafuckin' five!"

Courtney had purposely picked the seventeen-year-old baby-face light-skinned kid from Queens to gamble against because he looked soft and not too many people in the party knew who he was.

He figured he would take his money fair and square by rolling dice better than the kid, but at the same time, his backup plan was to just front on the kid and hustle him out of his money even if the dice weren't going his way.

Courtney also knew the party was full of Bloods who were all strapped and would have his back, and along with the liquor he had been drinking, that gave him even more heart to talk shit.

"I ain't giving you shit, and if you don't get the fuck out my face, I'll take all your money, you bitch-ass nigga!" Courtney, who was shorter than the light-skinned kid from Queens, stared him down with an ice grill that he had perfected in the yard at Attica Correctional Facility.

"That's that fuckin' liquor talking. I can smell that shit." The light-skinned dude smiled and put both of his hands up to show surrender. "You got it, my nigga. It's all good. Keep the two hundred."

"Yo, Courtney, who is this punk ass?" another Blood asked.

"I don't know, but his pussy ass is getting ready to go in them pockets for me." Courtney pulled out a chrome snub-nosed .38 revolver and pointed it at the light-skinned dude, freezing him in his tracks. "Run your muthafuckin' money, nigga!"

Trina and Tiny had finished gathering up their money, and they both came outside to see what was going on.

"Oh my God! That's my nephew! Tim, you OK?" Tiny ran to his side.

Tim had come from Queens to pay a surprise visit to his aunt Tiny. They were the same age, and their family was as ghetto as they came. When he showed up at The Waverly and saw Tiny putting on a stripper show, it was nothing to him because he'd seen his crack-addicted mother do much worse in his seventeen years on the planet.

"I'm good. Just some cee-lo shit," Tim nervously said to Tiny.

Tiny walked up to Courtney and started screaming on him. "Courtney, you just came home, and you starting shit already. Put that fuckin' gun down. That's my family. Y'all can't be coming at him like that, especially not over a damn dice game!"

Courtney, a smirk plastered on his face, looked at Tiny and nodded his head at her. Then he lowered his gun and put it back into his waistband.

Courtney said to his man, "Pussy must run in the family. This nigga a pussy, and she be selling the pussy." He started laughing, and his man gave him a pound.

The next thing you heard was a loud gunshot. *BLAOW!*

Courtney had just been shot in the head, and his limp body hit the concrete. Immediately, people started yelling and screaming and running crazy.

"What you say, nigga?" Tim screamed, and he came toward Courtney and pumped two more shots into him.

Tiny screamed, "Tim!" and she grabbed him and tried to pull him inside The Waverly.

Courtney's man reached for his gun, but he wasn't quick enough. Tim shot him twice in the stomach and then walked up to him and shot him once in the head.

Screams of panic were coming from every direction as everyone scrambled for cover. Other Bloods pulled out their guns and started firing at Tim, some bullets hitting The Waverly, others hitting innocent bystanders.

Tim ran inside The Waverly for cover, but he quickly ran out a back exit through the kitchen because he had to get out of there.

"Oh my God!" Jazzy screamed, and she and Cha Cha ran for cover by retreating to their room.

Maya was kneeling down low outside, hiding behind a tree. She was the first one to think about calling 9-1-1 on her cell phone. And although it seemed like an eternity to her, it was actually a minute and half before the first set of cops showed up on the scene.

After the first cops arrived and realized exactly what type of chaos they had on their hands, they called for all kinds of backup. Five minutes later, The Waverly was flooded with cops and ambulances.

Twenty minutes later a news van arrived at The Waverly at just about the same time that both Ashanti and Big Momma showed up.

Ashanti couldn't believe her eyes. She immediately called Jazzy to try and find out what had happened, since the police wouldn't let her go around the barricade they had set up with yellow-and-black tape that said "DO NOT CROSS."

Big Momma felt light-headed, like she was about to pass out. She knew her ass was going to be in serious trouble and could possibly get fired, depending on what had happened, but from the outset, it didn't look good.

"Please, officer, please! My girls are in there and I have to get to them to make sure that they're alright," Big Momma pleaded with one of the officers to let her go past the police tape, but her pleas went on deaf ears.

Big Momma started crying and hyperventilating when she saw the city coroner arrive on the scene. "Oh my Lord! Somebody done died up in there! Oh my God!" Soon thereafter she fainted, and her four hundred pound body collapsed to the concrete.

When Big Momma finally did come to, she realized that she had much bigger problems on her hands than just the money she had lost in Atlantic City. She would have to explain just how a party was allowed to take place with the combination of minors, alcohol, and drugs. She would also have to explain how was it that on her watch two people had been killed at The Waverly and four others had been shot and wounded. She also would have to answer to the criminal charges she was smacked with when the police arrested her and hauled her fat ass off to jail for endangering the welfare of minors.

CHAPTER 10

As it turned out, God must have been on Big Momma's side. Big Momma had a cousin who was an attorney, and he came to her defense and got the district attorney to drop all charges against her. Big Momma's argument was that because she had worked at the basketball game doing the scoreboard during the day on that same Saturday of the wild party, she thought that her boss had scheduled one of the other group home supervisors to cover her shift. Big Momma's lawyer successfully argued that the blame needed to lie with Big Momma's boss and also with the supervisor who'd left the group home at the end of her shift without another supervisor there to relieve her.

So because Big Momma ended up not being charged criminally, The Waverly couldn't fire her, but they did suspend her for two weeks without pay, throwing her into more debt than she was already in.

Meanwhile, The Waverly went through a complete overhaul of its procedures. Now everything was being done by the book. Among the many changes, everyone had to follow curfew—no exceptions. Visitors had to show state identification to get on the premises, and they also had to sign in and out. And new security cameras were also installed throughout the facility.

With all the changes that had taken place, Jazzy had decided that it would be best to wait a week or so before going to the outlets on Long Island to boost. She also thought it was best to wait until Big Momma got back from her two-week suspension.

On the day that Big Momma did come back to work, all of the girls, including Jazzy, Cha Cha, and Maya, showed her nothing but love. They were genuinely happy to see her as was Big Momma to see them.

Jazzy didn't waste any time in executing her plan, and an hour after Big Momma had returned to work, she, Cha Cha, Maya, and Ashanti were ready to head out to Long Island in a stolen car that Cha Cha had took from the Bronx the day before.

"Maya," Big Momma yelled out just as the girls had reached the front door. "Come let Big Momma talk to you for a minute. Alone."

Maya told the girls that she would be right back and then quickly made her way over to Big Momma. Big Momma motioned for Maya to follow her into the bathroom located on the first floor, next to the main office. When they both were inside the bathroom, Big Momma locked the door behind them and leaned up against it, breathing heavily. It appeared to Maya that Big Momma hadn't missed one meal during her two-week suspension because she looked about twenty pounds heavier.

"What's up, Big Momma?" Maya wanted to laugh at how hard it was for Big Momma to breathe, but she stayed composed.

"Girl, with all these changes that they got going on, and with all these surprise inspections and all these different people that they been sending here from the state to check up on The Waverly, I don't think we can pull off that pregnancy scam like I thought we could."

"Uggghhh, really?" Maya asked in genuine disappointment.

"Yup. You see they were already trying to send me to jail for that other shit, so they watching everything now. My job would be on the line, and I just can't fuck around and chance it."

Tears were beginning to form in Maya's eyes, but she was fighting with herself to make sure that she didn't let one teardrop roll down her cheek.

"But, Big Momma, all you have to do is put me in touch with your girl, and I'll take it from there. I'll speak to her, and I'll handle everything. Nobody will even know that you're involved, and nothing will come back on you. If something happens and I get caught, then that's on me and I'll take the fall for that. I would never sell you out."

Big Momma shook her head no. "Maya, believe me, if there was a way, I would do this in a heartbeat for you. I mean, I never told you this, but out of all of the girls that ever came to stay at The Waverly, I always like you the most. And I always said that, if I ever had a daughter, I would want her to favor you and be like you."

"Really?" Maya asked, a smile on her face. "Awww, Big Momma, that's so sweet."

Big Momma was purposely trying to distract Maya, just so she could set her up.

They both were quiet for a moment, and Maya's mind was racing, trying to come up with a solution, but no good ideas were coming to her mind.

"So then I guess I'll just get the two thousand back from you and put that toward my apartment. What other choice do I have?"

The last thing Big Momma wanted was for Maya to be talking about having the two grand returned back to her. But Big Momma was just about to rock Maya to sleep.

"You know what? The *only* thing I can say that will probably make this work is if I get in touch with my boy who works up in Albany at the main office for the state. I can talk to him to have him make sure that your pregnancy test results don't get flagged or anything."

"Oh my God! Really? Big Momma, why didn't you just say that before? You got me all paranoid up in here." Maya, feeling a sense of relief, smiled and playfully punched Big Momma.

Big Momma frowned up her face, and then she said, "Hold on now. Don't get your head all gassed up. I said I would talk to my boy. I didn't say that I had spoken to him and that he would definitely be with it. So I'm just saying, I can't promise anything until I speak to him."

Maya nodded her head up and down to show Big Momma that she was clear on where she was coming from.

"But I can tell you one thing, and that's that don't nobody do favors for free. And I already know that he's going to want something out of this, so you better do what you gotta do, but just be prepared to kick out another thousand dollars, just in case I have to hit him off."

"Another thousand dollars? What the fuck? I might as well go and put a down payment on a house or some shit!"

"Well, what do you want me to tell you? If you and Jazzy and Cha Cha had of just held shit down for me that Saturday night that I wasn't here, then we wouldn't even be in this position. It was y'all that decided to have that wild-ass party with muthafuckas getting shot and killed and shit. So now it's coming back to bite everybody in the ass."

Maya sucked her teeth and blew out some air from her lungs.

"Alright. Well, I guess I just have to do what I have to do," Maya said.

"And what the fuck does that mean? Do you want me to contact my boy or not?"

"Yeah, contact him. I was just saying that I'll have to do what I have to do to come up with the money."

Maya's words put a smile on Big Momma's face because in a couple of days a thousand dollars would be greasing her fat palms.

Maya left the bathroom meeting with Big Momma and returned to Jazzy, Cha Cha, and Ashanti and told them she was ready to go. Cha Cha had parked the stolen Toyota Camry about five blocks away from The Waverly, and the girls all walked to the car.

They soon found themselves on the Jackie Robinson Parkway, which led them to the Long Island Expressway.

Jazzy asked Maya from the front passenger seat, "What did that fat bitch want with you?"

"We were talking about that thing. I'll fill you in later." Maya didn't want Ashanti to know what they were planning with the pregnancy scam. The fewer people who knew, the better.

While the girls drove the hour-long ride to Deer Park, Long Island, Ashanti was quiet for most of the journey, until they got to their exit on the expressway.

"This is such bullshit and a waste of time," Ashanti remarked, sourly. "So now it's not even Bed Bath and Beyond. We stole a car and drove all this way just to boost from Bath and Body Works? I swear, this is hustling backwards."

None of the other girls said anything in response.

Ashanti added, "Y'all might as well stay in the car and let me go in by myself. The store is so tiny."

Jazzy and the girls still kept quiet, and when they reached the Tanger Outlet parking lot and parked the car and got out, Ashanti stood by the car, hands on her hips, looking defiant. "So we're really doing this?" she asked.

"No, we just drove all the way out here for our health," Jazzy told her.

"Ashanti, bring your ass on!" Cha Cha said. "These stores are already packed. We'll be in and out. We're going to load the stuff into one shopping cart. After I swipe the shopping bags, I'll get them to you. You and Maya will load the shopping bags with stuff and then put all the bags in the shopping cart that you'll have. Maya will get on line and buy a few things just to make everything look like it's on the up and up. Jazzy is going to walk around the store and browse for a few minutes, and then she'll leave the store as a decoy. Then I'll distract the security guard, and you'll just stroll out the store with all the stuff."

Ashanti shook her head and the girls all walked in tandem into Bath and Body Works.

Bath and Body Works wasn't that big of a store, and on a quiet day, the girls would have stood out like a sore thumb. But on this day it was crowded, and they blended in well. The girls worked their simple plan, and within ten minutes, Ashanti had a shopping cart full of about a thousand dollars worth of products.

Maya had managed to quickly load two shopping bags full of items and she also had a small shopping basket that contained a few lotions and body butter. When she saw that the bags in Ashanti's shopping cart were full, she gave Ashanti the two shopping bags that she had, and then she headed to the cash register, while Jazzy left the store.

Cha Cha walked toward the security guard and started to ask him some questions, trying to make small talk.

Instead of walking out the door, Ashanti froze in her tracks and didn't follow through on the execution like she was supposed to. Standing behind the shopping cart, she gave a signal like she was slitting her own throat. She wanted Maya and Cha Cha to know that she wasn't going through with the plan.

Maya and Cha Cha both saw Ashanti's signal, and they waited a minute or so before approaching her.

"What happened?" Cha Cha asked, thinking Ashanti might have seen something that spooked her.

"Ain't nothing happen. I just ain't doing this shit, that's all."

Cha Cha immediately sent a text to Jazzy and summoned her back to the store and told her that Ashanti was fronting.

Two minutes later Jazzy showed up.

Ashanti told her, "Jazzy, this ain't how I work. Let's pick another store, a high-end store, and I'm good. But I don't do bullshit like this."

"Bitch, just walk the shit out the fuckin' store!" Jazzy said under her breath through clenched teeth.

"You walk it out!" Ashanti shot back.

"Word up, when we get back to the parking lot, I'm fuckin' whipping your ass!" Jazzy took hold of the shopping cart and headed to the exit.

Cha Cha quickly walked ahead of her, trying to distract the security guard again. But by this time security was very suspicious of the four girls, who clearly looked like they weren't from that part of town.

Just as Jazzy was attempting to walk through the front door of the store, Cha Cha said to the security guard, "Excuse me. I forgot to ask you one thing. How would I get to Neiman Marcus from here?"

"Oh, sure. Well, to get to Neiman Marcus, you would have to—

Wait, excuse me for a moment. Hey, miss, may I see your receipt please?" The security guard stepped away from Cha Cha and grabbed a hold of Jazzy's shopping cart so that she couldn't leave the store.

"Yeah, no problem." Jazzy turned and asked Ashanti for the receipt.

Ashanti wasn't smooth at all and didn't know how to play things off. She froze in her tracks and just looked at Jazzy.

"I need the receipt to show the man," Jazzy said forcefully to Ashanti.

At this point Maya knew something was wrong. She put her basket down near the cash register and started to make her way toward the exit.

Out of nowhere a plainclothes security guard walked up to the uniformed security guard and asked him, "Is there a problem?"

As Maya tried to leave the store, the plainclothes guard stopped her in her tracks and wouldn't let her leave the store.

"Excuse me. But can you get your fuckin' hands off of me?" Maya said to the guard. "What the fuck is wrong with you?"

Cha Cha tried to leave the store, but the guard stopped her as well. Then the plainclothes guard reached into his shirt and pulled out a badge that dangled from the silver beaded chain it was attached to.

"Suffolk County P.D.," the guard said to the girls so that they would know he was an off-duty police officer.

Instantly all of the girls got nervous.

"Ashanti, give me the receipt so we can show it to the man. Obviously, this is some racist shit going on out here. I swear, y'all white people always think black people are stealing shit," Jazzy said to the police officer and the security guard.

Ashanti still didn't know what to say, and so she said nothing. The fear on her face was evident. The only thing she could think about was, her mom was going to kick her ass if she got into any legal trouble.

Finally Ashanti started to check her pockets like she was looking for the receipt, but by that point it wasn't hard to tell that she was bullshitting.

"Oh, how the fuck do the white people just get to walk out the store and you don't stop them?" Maya spoke up and said.

"See what I mean?" Jazzy said. "This is some racist shit."

Suddenly, Cha Cha took both of her hands and pushed the security guard in his chest, and he fell backwards. Jazzy was quick on her feet, and she pushed past the police officer. The police officer, who was also caught off guard, stumbled to the side, but he reached out and grabbed Maya by the arm, trying to prevent her from fleeing, but Maya fought him off, wiggled free, and started to run.

The uniformed security guard grabbed Ashanti when she tried to run and quickly applied one side of his handcuffs to her left wrist and the other side of the handcuffs to his right wrist.

"Ahhh, fuck!" Ashanti yelled, trying to break free. "Those cuffs hurt!"

"They hurt because you aren't standing still! Stop trying to run!"

"What the fuck are you handcuffing me for? I didn't do shit!" Ashanti pleaded loudly but to no avail.

Meanwhile Jazzy, Cha Cha, and Maya all ran as fast as they could, trying to make it to their car so they could get back to Brooklyn.

Thankfully for them, the undercover police officer was wearing hard-bottom shoes as part of his attire to make him blend in with the regular shoppers. And fortunately for Jazzy, Cha Cha, and Maya, slippery hard-bottom shoes don't go well with concrete, and as the cop chased the girls, he ended up slipping and losing his footing and fell hard to the ground face first and fractured his wrist, trying to break his fall.

Maya looked back and saw the cop bust his ass, but she wasn't taking any chances. She continued to run as fast as she could, and moments later, she caught up with her partners in crime, Jazzy and Cha Cha.

Cha Cha started up the car and peeled off, and she sped the whole time on the Southern State Parkway before making it back to The Waverly, where she, Jazzy, and Cha Cha waited to see what would become of Ashanti.

CHAPTER 11

Three hours after Ashanti had been busted trying to shoplift with Jazzy, Cha Cha, and Maya, she found herself sitting in a Suffolk County police station, waiting on her mother to arrive. No police officer had to come and inform her when her mom actually arrived, simply because Ashanti heard her mom's loud voice before she actually saw her.

"Where the fuck is that little heifer?" Ashanti heard her mom asking one of the police officers.

Immediately a sick feeling came to Ashanti's stomach. Ever since she was a little girl, all she ever wanted to hear her mom say was that she was beautiful or that she loved her or that she was proud of her. Anything positive. But for some reason her mom always referred to her as a whore, a bitch, or a fucking whore bitch! *Heifer* wasn't all that creative of a term, but it was the first time that Ashanti was hearing her mom use that.

"You can have as much time as you want, Ms. Daniels," the police officer said to Ashanti's mother after he let her into the interrogation room that Ashanti was sitting in.

"OK, thank you," Ashanti's mom replied.

Ashanti wasn't handcuffed as she sat in a wooden chair at a square wooden table with her head hanging low. She looked like a high school student trying to fall asleep.

Ms. Daniels shouted, "Bitch, wake yo' ass up!" She grabbed her by her right arm and forcefully tried to yank her up from the seat.

Ashanti hadn't fallen asleep. In fact, she was fully awake and ready for war. "Donna, get your hands off of me!" she yelled back at her mother and freed herself of her mother's grip.

Ashanti had long since stopped referring to her mother as "Mom." To her, "Mom" was a term of endearment, and since no love ever came her way from her mother, she decided that it only made sense to refer to her by her first name.

Donna stood about five feet eight inches tall. She wasn't heavy, but she was thick in all the right places, and she regularly worked out at the gym to stay in shape. So even in the high-heeled shoes she was wearing, she was more than prepared to beat Ashanti's ass.

WHACK!

Donna slapped Ashanti across her face.

"What the fuck are you hitting me for?"

WHACK!

Donna slapped Ashanti across her face so hard, she caused an instant nosebleed. This time blood splattered across the room, some of it landing on the nearby white painted cinderblock wall.

When Ashanti saw the blood, she became enraged and was ready to charge her mother and engage in an all-out brawl. It took everything inside Ashanti to hold back from attacking her mother.

Donna shouted, "Say something else, and I'll knock your little ass into the middle of next week!" She stood with her right fist clenched, ready to land a right hook if Ashanti said as much as, "Peep."

Tears flowed from Ashanti's eyes. She knew there was no use in trying to say anything to her mother, so she just stood there frustrated and angry, holding her hand to her nose, trying to stop it from bleeding.

"Sit your ass down in that chair right now!"

Ashanti bolted out of the room and went to the desk of the commanding officer stationed nearby.

"Excuse me, officer, but I want to press charges against this person right here who just assaulted me in that room over there. As you can see, my nose is bleeding," Ashanti said, hoping the officer would take some kind of action against her mother.

The officer gave Ms. Daniels a look of confusion.

Ms. Daniels reached inside her shirt and pulled out her gold shield medallion and nodded her head to the officer. The officer immediately assumed she was a cop.

Although Ms. Daniels wasn't actually a cop, she worked for the New York City Police Department and was able to have a gold necklace made for her that had a medallion of a gold police shield that hung from the chain.

"She ain't no fuckin' cop. She's just a police precinct pencil-pushing secretary who fucks rookie police officers! Damn pedophile wannabe cougar bitch!" Ashanti yelled, putting her mother on blast.

The commanding officer shook his head in disbelief at Ashanti's disrespect and handed her a handful of Kleenex tissues and told her to go into the nearby bathroom and clean herself up.

"I'm sorry about that," Ms. Daniels said to the officer as soon as Ashanti entered the bathroom. "That girl, I just don't know what to do with her."

The white police officer was annoyed at the ghetto nonsense he had to deal with, but he was willing to tolerate the annoyance simply because he liked the view of the Serena Williams body Ms. Daniels had. And the skintight leggings she was wearing made her killer body even more appealing.

"Ms. Daniels, I understand that this is a difficult time for you, but you have to *only* talk to your daughter. Please refrain from hitting her. I won't ask you again. This time was a courtesy."

"OK, no problem. And, again, I apologize for that. She just makes me lose it because every minute I turn around it's something new with that girl."

Ashanti emerged from the bathroom and asked, "Why isn't she in handcuffs?" She looked at the officer incredulously. "See, I don't even do anything, and they handcuff me and haul me off to the police station. But this woman right here hauls off and violently assaults me and bloodies my nose, and y'all don't do nothing to her. I swear, boy."

The officer forcefully replied, "Shut your mouth before you make things worse on yourself." He inched toward Ashanti and towered over her. "We're all trying to help you, including your mother to get your life back on track and not end up a delinquent. Now go back into the room and talk with your mother. I'll send one of the detectives in shortly."

Ashanti quietly went back into the room and sat back down at the table. Her mother followed right behind and sat across from her.

Ms. Daniels was quiet for several minutes, as was Ashanti, who sat staring up at the ceiling, her arms folded in defiance.

Ashanti broke the silence and said to her mother, "You just going to automatically assume that I'm in the wrong. You couldn't even give me the benefit of the doubt for one moment and just hear my side of the story, and you running with whatever the cops tell you."

Ms. Daniels knew that her daughter had just spoken the truth. Most good parents would want to hear their child's side of the story before jumping to conclusions.

"Well, I'm waiting," she said to Ashanti.

"Waiting for what?"

"For you to tell me your side of the story."

Ashanti sucked her teeth. "All I know is that Jazzy, Cha Cha, and Maya asked me to go shopping with them. I had never been this far out on Long Island before, so I thought it would be cool to go, and I went. And the next thing I know, I was being arrested for shoplifting, and I didn't even take anything. I don't know what happened or what's going on, and I also don't know why I'm the only one here if I wasn't the only one in the store."

"So you telling me that the four of you just came out here to shop? And, if so, what money were you shopping with?"

"I'm saying that they told me they were coming out here to shop, and they asked me if I wanted to come, and I said yes. I wasn't personally planning on buying anything for myself because I didn't have any money like that to be going shopping, but I still wanted to come."

In her gut Ms. Daniels didn't totally believe Ashanti's words, but she didn't say anything in response.

Moments later a detective walked into the room and introduced himself to both Ashanti and her mom.

"OK, let me just say that I have what I would say is somewhat good news, and I have some bad news. The good news is that the store doesn't want to press charges against Ashanti and she will only be looking at civil fines, as far as the shoplifting goes," the detective explained.

"What does that mean?" Ashanti asked with neck-twisting attitude.

"What it essentially means is that all you'll have to do is reimburse the store five hundred dollars and the larceny charges go away."

"Five hundred dollars? But I didn't steal anything!" Ashanti said in anger.

The cop shook his head and he told Ashanti that the video recording from the store, indicate that she was operating with a shoplifting ring and as long as the attempt to shoplift was made, which it was, then that was enough to have everything stick.

"OK, so what's the bad news?" Ms. Daniels asked.

"The bad news is that we have an off-duty officer who suffered a fractured bone while trying to make an arrest during the crime that Ashanti and her cohorts were committing. And, depending on what the district attorney says, she could be looking at a possible assault charge on a police officer."

"Oh my fuckin' God! You can't be serious right now," Ashanti said to the detective.

"Actually, I am dead serious. And unfortunately, Ms. Daniels, we're going to have to book and process Ashanti, and she will likely have to spend a night or two in jail until she can see a judge."

"Basically, she has to go to Central Booking?" Ms. Daniels asked.

The detective then noticed the gold shield police badge medallion Ms. Daniels was wearing and he asked her was she on the job, which was code for is she a cop.

"I work for NYPD in the administrative area."

The cop nodded his head, and then he thought for a moment.

"Well, I'll see what I can do to try and persuade the district attorney to not be harsh on Ashanti. But I will say that they really frown on people from the city coming out to Long Island to steal, so I don't know what deal, if any, will be worked out."

"I understand," Ms. Daniels replied.

"Ashanti, you can help yourself a great deal if you just give us the names of the other three girls that were with you that got away. I mean, I do think there is a strong possibility that the district attorney will be willing to go very light on you if you're willing to testify against your three friends."

Ms. Daniels spoke up for Ashanti and said, "Oh that will not be a problem at all."

Ashanti just looked totally disgusted with everything that was transpiring.

"From reviewing the videotape, the other assailants were the ones who perpetrated the assault on the officer—not Ashanti. And if she could help the DA in identifying her friends and also testifying, if necessary, in open court then I can guarantee that the assault charges against your daughter will be dismissed as well."

"Well, Ashanti will have no problem helping you out," Ms. Daniels said, looking at her daughter. "Ain't that right, Ashanti?"

"Donna, really?"

"What the fuck do you mean, 'really'? Yes, *really.*"

"Donna, I'm not nobody's snitch. Snitches get stitches."

"Excuse me, but you are Ashanti's mother, aren't you?"

"Yes. Why?"

"Oh, OK. No, it was just that she was referring to you as Donna, and that sort of threw me off."

Ashanti wanted to speak up and tell the detective why she didn't call her mother mom, but she kept quiet. And Ms. Daniels didn't bother with an explanation either.

"Ashanti, you best believe that if you don't tell this man everything that he wants to know, that I will make sure that you are sorry that you were ever born."

"As if I'm not already sorry I was born—born to you at least."

Ms. Daniels closed her eyes and held her hands up toward the sky. *Lord Jesus, please help me.*

The detective did end up holding Ashanti in the cell at the police station until she was escorted down to Riverhead, Long Island, where Ashanti had to spend two nights in jail waiting to see a judge. It was the first time that she had ever been to jail. And after experiencing being around butch and dyke women, and eating stale peanut butter and jelly sandwiches, she quickly realized that she and jail were like oil and water.

Ashanti wanted no parts of anybody's jail, and the way she looked at it, she wasn't even in the county jail as of yet, which she figured, more than likely, would be worse than the Central Booking holding pens she was currently in.

After the first night of sleeping on a cold and dusty cement floor, Ashanti was sure of one thing—She was going to snitch on Jazzy, Cha Cha, and Maya, as long as it meant that her ass wouldn't have to see jail bars again.

Ashanti thought she was way too fly to be in jail. Plus, she had more important things to attend to, such as spending time with a future NBA star. So, quite frankly, to her, the decision to snitch was definitely a sheisty one, but it was an easy one to make.

CHAPTER 12

It took Jazzy, Cha Cha, and Maya forty-five minutes to make it back to The Waverly, and during that time, when they didn't hear from Ashanti, they knew she had gotten caught.

Secretly, Jazzy was hoping that Ashanti had gotten arrested because she wanted her to start going through some adversity, since lately everything seemed to be going her way, which Jazzy was starting to resent.

"She would have called or texted one of us by now," Cha Cha said after they parked the stolen car ten blocks away from The Waverly and got out and started walking home.

"All I know is, that bitch better keep her fuckin' mouth shut," Jazzy added.

Later that night Big Momma confirmed for the girls what they had already figured—Ashanti had been arrested.

Maya was looking in the mirror and fixing her hair with a curling iron. "She's gonna snitch."

"Well, the bottom line is, we don't know shit, and we were here in our room at The Waverly all day. That's our alibi," Cha Cha made clear to the girls. "She could tell the cops anything she wants to about us, but as long as we don't tell on ourselves, then we'll be good."

The next day, which was a Monday, Ashanti was released from jail, and her mother dropped her off at The Waverly.

"Hey, Ashanti," Cha Cha said to her.

Ashanti didn't even look in Cha Cha's direction to acknowledge her. Instead, she and her mom simply walked right past Jazzy, Cha Cha, and Maya, who were sitting outside on the front steps of The Waverly.

"Excuse me, are you Ms. Daniels?" Maya asked Ashanti's mom, trying to be cordial, and to make conversation.

Ms. Daniels just looked at Maya and rolled her eyes, and she kept walking.

Maya said, "Just like stuck up-ass Ashanti. That has to be her mother because both of them bitches are stank. You see how they just walked past us like we wasn't even here? And I was trying to be all nice and shit."

"They ain't say nothing to us because they just salty that we didn't get knocked too," Jazzy said to the girls.

After a few minutes the girls went back inside and saw Ms. Daniels talking to Big Momma inside her office. Ashanti wasn't in the office, so the girls figured she was in her room, and they went up to talk to her.

Without even knocking, all three of them just walked into the room, where they found Ashanti looking for clothes inside her closet.

Jazzy asked her, "Where you going?"

Ashanti looked at her with disgust. She was about to ignore her, but then she said, "Because I'm looking for something to put on, that means I'm going somewhere?" She rolled her eyes. "Newsflash—I haven't been home in two days. I was locked up out in Long Island, so maybe I just want to hop in the shower and change my clothes."

After Ashanti had her change of clothes, she started to walk out of the bedroom, and headed to the bathroom down the hall.

"Wait." Jazzy grabbed a hold of Ashanti's arm. "Tell us what happened."

Ashanti looked down at Jazzy's hand, and then she looked up. "Get your fuckin' hands off of me."

Jazzy removed her hand.

Ashanti kept walking and said under her breath, "Bitches run out on me and leave me hanging, and then they wanna act all concerned and shit."

Behind Ashanti's back, Jazzy held up her middle finger and gestured it at her with emphasis, causing both Maya and Cha Cha to chuckle at her antics.

Moments later, Big Momma and Ms. Daniels arrived at Ashanti's room and saw Jazzy, Cha Cha, and Maya walking out.

"What are y'all doing in here?" Big Momma asked. "Where's Ashanti?"

"We was just leaving. Ashanti went to take a shower," Cha Cha said, and the three girls made their way back to their room and wondered what was going to be Ashanti's fate.

For fifteen minutes, the three girls wondered if Ashanti was going to get kicked out of The Waverly. Was she going to get probation? Was she going to have to pay a fine? Was she going to have to go to court?

They speculated and speculated, but when Big Momma appeared in their room, they got the answers they were looking for, and there was no more need for guesswork.

Big Momma sat down on Maya's bed, shaking her head in disbelief. "What the fuck is wrong with y'all?" she asked.

"What?" Jazzy replied.

"Y'all know what. Don't play me for no fool." Big Momma said after taking a sip of her bottled water. She had decided to start drinking a lot more water and stop drinking sodas in hopes to lose a few pounds.

Cha Cha decided to just cop to the obvious. "She snitched, didn't she?"

"Yes, she snitched," Big Momma said, keeping her voice down.

All of the girls looked at each other.

"Ever since that shooting shit, they been on our ass around here. Y'all already know that. I told y'all to be on the up-and-up with everything. You see they tossed Tiny out of here, and now Ashanti's ass might be next. Why the fuck don't y'all just know how to chill and let shit just blow over? Especially you, Maya. You know you already aged out, so they looking for any reason to say bye-bye to you."

Big Momma was only acting as if she was upset. Since she benefited from the girls' shoplifting, she had somewhat of a vested interest their hustle. But the truth of the matter was, Big Momma could have cared less about Ashanti snitching on Jazzy, Cha Cha, and Maya. Big Momma was just, once again, setting the girls up for further manipulation.

"OK, we promise we'll chill for a minute and lay low on the boosting until everything completely calms down," Jazzy said to Big Momma.

"You a day late and a dollar short with that. I already spoke to someone from Suffolk County P.D., and they'll be out here tomorrow to question y'all."

"What the fuck?" Jazzy replied.

"What you so upset for?" Big Momma said. "You go out there doing this slick shit, you better be prepared for what comes back to you." She then stood up and said to the girls in a more serious tone, "Now listen. Ashanti's mom told me that Ashanti made it clear to her and to the police that, Cha Cha, you stole a car, and that the four of you drove out to Long Island to boost and she—"

"Oh my God!" Cha Cha said, cutting Big Momma off. "I really can't stand that bitch!"

"Would you be quiet and just listen to me?" Big Momma said. "I want us all to make sure that we're clear on this. Now what I did was, I covered for the three of you. I told Ms. Daniels I was certain that the three of you hadn't left The Waverly and that y'all were in your room the whole time. That's the story, and that's what we are sticking to. Is that understood?"

The three girls all smiled with relief and told Big Momma that they understood.

Big Momma told them, "Don't be getting all happy just yet. Because I want to make sure that this is really clear. I covered for y'all with Ms. Daniels, but when the cops come here tomorrow, I'm telling y'all now that if I cover for y'all with the cops, then that's it. I ain't covering for y'all on that pregnancy thing."

"But that's totally separate," Maya said.

"It's separate to you, but not to me. They already looking for the slightest thing to get me outta here, and now when the cops come knocking and I cover for y'all on this, all it takes is one slip-up and they find out that I'm lying, then I'm toast. The three of y'all, no matter what, y'all will be alright. Me, on the other hand, I got a lot at stake, and I can't keep lying for y'all and covering y'all asses."

The girls were all quiet.

"But what about the two grand we gave you?" Maya asked Big Momma.

"What about it?" Big Momma shot back.

"Can we get it back, since we ain't going to go through with the pregnancy scam?"

"Get it back? Maya, are you smoking crack or something? Didn't I just say that I'm covering for y'all on this police shit? This ain't free. Ain't shit *free*. And the way I see it, I'm doing all of y'all a big bargain-type favor by committing perjury for only a measly two stacks. And perjury is no joke. That shit come with jail time. Don't y'all remember Lil' Kim's ass got locked up for a year for perjury? So the two grand that I'm holding, just consider each one of your bill's paid in full with me." Big Momma calmly drank some more of her water and looked at the girls and waited for their reaction.

The girls were all quiet and somewhat shocked and pissed off at the fact that Big Momma was playing them out and had basically pimped and scammed them out of two grand.

"Big Momma, with all respect, but that's some Brooklyn bullshit right there," Jazzy spoke up and said.

"Brooklyn bullshit? OK, I tell you what. How about I suddenly get a better memory and call Ms. Daniels back and tell her that I do remember the four of y'all leaving together Saturday? And then how about I tell the cops the same thing? If I do that, then all three of y'all will be getting tossed outta here, and the free ride on state money will be over. If that's what y'all want me to do, then just let me know, and I'll give y'all back the three grand. Brooklyn bullshit, my black ass! Lying to cops ain't something I just do for the sake of doing it," Big Momma said in a matter-of-fact tone.

"Well, I'm just being straight up," Jazzy said. "And all I'm saying is that you could still look out for Maya and have your friend do the pregnancy thing for her."

"And all I'm saying is, shit is way too hot right now for me to do both. So it's either one or the other. Which one is it going to be?"

All of the girls were quiet.

Big Momma wanted the girls to go with the option of using her as their alibi simply because she had already spent the girls' money, and now this opportunity had provided the perfect out for her.

"Just so y'all know, I told Ms. Daniels that, as far as I knew, it was Bobby who likely took Ashanti to Long Island. So if you know like I know, then that's the story you would stick with and also stick with the three of you were here inside your room."

The girls all nodded in agreement.

"Maya, I know it's summertime and all, but the best I can do is get you an additional six-week extension, but to get that, your ass is going to have to get down with the work-study program and get a fuckin' job. Because if I can at least show them that you're working and just need a bit more time to save up rent and security deposit, then you'll get the extension, one, two, three."

"And how much is that gonna cost me for you to do that?" Maya asked, her tone dripping with sarcasm.

"Maya, come on now. You know Big Momma ain't gonna charge you for that." Big Momma smiled before sipping her bottled water.

"A job? Big Momma, are you serious?" Cha Cha asked. "Uggghhhh!"

"Listen, I'm going downstairs to get on the treadmill, and then I'm going to make me a smoothie. After that, I'm watching *The Real Housewives of Atlanta* marathon, and after that I'm going to sleep. So y'all sort out whatever it is that y'all need to sort out. Just be smart. I said what I had to say. I'm done," Big Momma then tossed her empty water bottle toward the garbage can across the room. She missed the garbage can badly and didn't even bother to go pick up the bottle.

"Jazzy, pick that up for me," Big Momma said, and then she walked her big fat sweaty ass out the room.

"Can you say, '*Getting robbed without a fuckin' gun*'?" Maya said out loud as soon as Big Momma closed the door. "That fat bitch is so sheisty!"

Jazzy, forever the ringleader, tried to lift everyone's spirits. "When you get lemons, all you gotta do is make lemonade. Now, Maya, you can fuck with that work-study shit, and this is why. Cha Cha and me are bouncing up outta here with you when your time is up. So if you get the job, it will look good on paper when we start hunting for apartments. In the meantime, I got a new idea that I'm sure will work and get us some paper. It's the same boosting, but the shit is surefire!" Jazzy said, excitement in her voice.

Maya and Cha Cha listened to Jazzy speak, but they weren't as carefree and fearless as she was. The main thing on their minds as Jazzy spoke was, exactly what would the next few days bring when the Suffolk County cops came knocking on their door?

CHAPTER 13

The next morning when the girls awoke, Maya was dreading having to actually go speak to the work-study people about finding her a job. She opened up the blinds in their bedroom and let the sunlight shine into the room. Jazzy and Cha Cha were thoroughly annoyed because the bright sunlight was disrupting their sleep. All three girls usually liked to stay 'sleep until eleven in the morning, and on some days they stayed in the bed until as late as one in the afternoon.

"Close those fuckin' blinds!" Cha Cha yelled in a groggy voice.

"Nah, if I have to get up for this work-study shit, then both of y'all are getting up with me." Maya then yanked the bed sheets off both Jazzy and Cha Cha.

"It's only seven in the morning. It's too early! The work-study office ain't even open yet." Cha Cha covered her head with her pillow.

Maya then snatched the pillows away from Jazzy and Cha Cha.

"I know the office ain't open yet, but they open at eight thirty. And from what everybody says, if you don't get there early, they will not take you seriously."

"Fuck that job shit!" Jazzy said in her morning voice.

Maya pulled and pleaded until the girls were finally all out of the bed. The three of them made their way down to the dining room for breakfast. Breakfast always ended at eleven in the morning, and the three girls rarely, if ever, made it to breakfast.

"Oh my God!" Nancy said. "Look what the wind done blew in this morning." Nancy was Big Momma's relief supervisor whenever Big Momma was off.

Jazzy, Maya, and Cha Cha strolled into the dining room and helped themselves to the buffet-style breakfast, which included a choice of bacon, sausages, scrambled eggs, pancakes, oatmeal, and cereal. Ashanti was already up and dressed and eating at the main table in the dining room.

"Maya, do you smell that?" Jazzy asked, tapping Maya on the leg and motioning her head in Ashanti's direction.

"I sure the fuck do," Maya replied.

"Maya, watch your language," Nancy said to her.

Nancy was the total opposite of Big Momma. She was in her early forties, but she had her shit together. Married to an attorney, Nancy had a house in Queens, a master's degree in psychology, and her three kids were all doing well in school. With her caramel skin color and naturally long hair, she looked like she could win any beauty pageant that she entered.

Maya didn't answer Nancy.

"Cha Cha, do you smell that too?" Jazzy said to Cha Cha.

Cha Cha immediately caught on and jumped right in. "I sure do. It smells like snitch to me."

The three girls started laughing, as did some of the other girls in the dining room.

"Look at little Miss Snitch over there eating her oatmeal," Cha Cha said. "Who the hell eats oatmeal, other than babies and old people?"

Ashanti looked up at her.

"Yeah, I'm talking about you," Cha Cha said. "Little Miss Snitch—that's your new name from now on."

Nancy shouted, "Cha Cha, that's enough. Now, all of y'all, get your food and sit down."

"I'll eat whatever I feel like eating. And what you need to do is not be all in my business and worried about what I'm doing every minute of the day," Ashanti fired back at Cha Cha.

All of the girls in the dining room were shocked because everyone knew that Cha Cha had a mean hand-game and would two-piece any bitch in a heartbeat.

"I know Little Miss Snitch ain't talking reckless." Cha Cha put her food down and walked over toward Ashanti.

Immediately Nancy stepped in and stood in front of Cha Cha, who was still in her slippers and pajamas.

"I don't want to hear another word," Nancy ordered. "Cha Cha, leave Ashanti alone, and you go eat your food."

"I ain't no snitch." Ashanti stood up, reached over Nancy, and threw her bowl of hot oatmeal right in Cha Cha's face.

Ashanti's bold move caught everybody off guard, including Nancy. Cha Cha yelled out in pain because the hot oatmeal felt like it was burning her skin.

Before anyone could react, Ashanti went around Nancy and caught Cha Cha with a straight right hand punch to her grill. When Cha Cha fell backwards, Ashanti rushed her and continued to punch her in the face. Then she pushed Cha Cha, and in the process, knocked over most of the trays of food.

Finally Maya and Jazzy came to Cha Cha's aid, grabbing Ashanti and pulling her off Cha Cha. Thankfully for Ashanti, Nancy was able to check Jazzy and Maya before they could throw any punches. There were always a couple of supervisors during the day shift at The Waverly. It wasn't like the night shift, where there was usually only just Big Momma. So in no time two other supervisors rushed into the cafeteria to restore and maintain order.

"Call me a snitch again and see what the fuck happens!" Ashanti told Cha Cha.

"Fuck you! You had to snuff me, but if you fight me straight up, I'll wax that muthafuckin' ass!" Cha Cha said, wiping off the oatmeal and food that was on her. Cha Cha was clearly embarrassed that she had allowed Ashanti to catch her off guard like that, but she was definitely more angry than embarrassed.

"Enough!" Nancy screamed at the top of her lungs.

"Y'all punk-ass bitches ran off like little pussies and left me out there to get locked up, and now I'm a snitch? Bitches, please," Ashanti barked. Ashanti was showing a lot of heart, and all of the other girls in The Waverly definitely were respecting her gangster. Jazzy knew that the little dining room skirmish was probably going to give Ashanti some props in the eyes of the other girls in the group home.

Ashanti, Jazzy, Cha Cha, and Maya continued to trade verbal jabs at each other until the supervisors had fully managed to restore order. It was safe to say that breakfast was pretty much ruined from that point forward, and most of the girls left the dining room and went either back to their rooms or hung out in the living room and watched television.

Ashanti felt good about her victorious scuffle that she had just had, while Cha Cha seethed with anger and she was more than determined to get revenge on Ashanti.

Maya eventually made her way to downtown Brooklyn, where she interviewed with the work-study office and filled out a bunch of paperwork and took different online aptitude tests. By the time she was finished at the work-study office and was making her way back to The Waverly, it was a little after eleven in the morning.

One thing was for sure, she definitely didn't expect to see what she saw when she got back to the group home.

CHAPTER 14

Two Suffolk County police cars and one unmarked police car were parked in front of The Waverly when Maya got back. One cop car was empty, and the other cop car had two cops sitting in the front seats, while a handcuffed Ashanti sat in the backseat of the patrol car looking like she was on the verge of tears.

Maya immediately went inside and up to her room, where she saw Jazzy and Cha Cha standing in the hallway, and inside their bedroom were cops, Big Momma, and other supervisors from The Waverly.

"What's going on?" Maya whispered to Jazzy and Cha Cha.

"Little Miss Snitch told the cops that we have all kinds of stolen merchandise in our room from boosting," Jazzy explained.

"They been in there twenty minutes so far, and they ain't find shit. And they won't find shit," Cha Cha said. "I swear, as soon as all this shit is over, I'm going to put Ashanti through hell, like she never imagined."

"So why is Ashanti sitting outside in handcuffs?" Maya asked.

Jazzy and Cha Cha both weren't exactly sure, and that was one of the reasons they were both extremely nervous at that moment.

Ten minutes later the cops were done searching the girls' room, Big Momma came outside into the hallway to talk to the girls.

"They didn't find nothing, right?" Jazzy knew not to keep major stolen items in their room for long, so she wasn't too worried about the cops finding anything that they had failed to get rid of. But she was worried about the cops finding Cha Cha's weed stash.

Big Momma shook her head no, and then she asked the girls to walk with her so that they would be out of earshot.

"The only thing they found was a bunch of stolen clothes in Ashanti's room," Big Momma explained. "Her dumb ass went and told on y'all, thinking that they wouldn't check her room too. All she did was bring more trouble on herself."

"She is so dumb!" Cha Cha said.

Jazzy and Maya laughed at how Ashanti had managed to bring more trouble on herself without even trying.

"But there is a problem, though," Big Momma cautioned.

"What happened?" Jazzy whispered.

"An off-duty cop said he was assaulted when he was trying to arrest Ashanti. He ended up getting hurt, and so now they looking to pin that on the three of y'all."

Maya shook her head, wondering what else could possibly go wrong in her life.

Jazzy pleaded her case to Big Momma and swore that nothing like that even remotely happened.

"Well, I don't know what to tell y'all. All I know is, they getting ready to bring y'all out to Long Island and put y'all in a lineup. Just hope like everything that the cop doesn't ID y'all because, if he does, there is gonna be a problem."

Cha Cha blew air out of her lungs, looking as angry as she ever looked. She didn't say anything out loud, but she vowed right there on the spot to make Ashanti pay dearly for what she was putting them through. Cha Cha was really starting to despise Ashanti. And one thing about Cha Cha, when she had enemies, she became very creative in thinking up ways to destroy and humiliate them.

Big Momma couldn't talk much longer to the girls because the cops were ready to leave. The two detectives briefly spoke to Maya, Jazzy, and Cha Cha and explained to them that they had to place them under arrest, why they were being arrested, and that they were going to take them down to the precinct in Long Island for questioning and have them take part in a lineup.

Maya, Jazzy, and Cha Cha were all placed in handcuffs and escorted to the empty police car waiting for them in front of The Waverly. When they made it outside, they saw all of the group home girls standing by and watching and asking them what happened, but they ignored them and didn't respond.

"You see she won't even look in this direction," Cha Cha said to Jazzy and Maya, referring to Ashanti, who had her head down while she sat in the back of the other police car.

Maya didn't reply because, out of the three girls, she was definitely the most worried. Cha Cha was also worried, but she talked as if she wasn't the least bit afraid.

Jazzy said to Maya and Cha Cha, "Assaulting a police officer? These charges won't stick because we didn't do nothing to him. All we did was wiggle free from him and pushed him off, but as far as we knew, he was just some random dude in the store who was trying to grope and rob us. You feel me?"

Cha Cha and Maya both nodded their heads yes to Jazzy. They knew that they all had to have the same story to tell or else they would look like liars and thieves who had just come out to the suburbs to rob, steal, and be disruptive.

After the long drive to the precinct, the girls were all escorted into separate rooms, where they were each going to be questioned separately. Big Momma and another supervisor had followed the cops to the precinct because they had to be there as guardians of the girls.

As soon as Ashanti was escorted into the police station, everyone heard Ms. Daniels yell, "Now tell me one good reason I should not kick your muthafuckin' ass!"

"Why are you even here?' Ashanti replied with an attitude.

"I'm here because you are a fuckin' liar, and I'm trying to protect your trashy ass!" Ms. Daniels replied.

Ashanti shook her head and didn't say anything else to her mother.

Eventually all of the girls were questioned, and all of their stories were pretty much the same. They had all said that they were never in Long Island on the day the officer was assaulted, when Ashanti was caught attempting to shoplift. The story that they told was exactly what Big Momma had advised them to say.

As it turned out, Maya, Jazzy, and Cha Cha must have had a guardian angel on their side because the video footage from the mall was not clear enough to show the girls' faces with clarity. But what really saved them was the fact that the police officer and the security guard were both not able to pick Jazzy, Cha Cha, and Maya from out of the police lineup.

And seeing that Ashanti's room was the only room where the cops found stolen merchandise, it made her out to be a liar, and that too worked in Jazzy's, Maya's, and Cha Cha's favor. So the cops, not really having much of a choice, had to release the three girls.

Ashanti wasn't as fortunate. Although the cops didn't lock her up again, they did question her at length, trying to determine if she had any connection to any of the established boosting rings operating out on Long Island.

Although the cops were willing to release Ashanti, they were forced to charge her with assault on the off-duty police officer. They couldn't drop those charges, since her story didn't pan out and didn't allow them to charge Jazzy, Cha Cha, and Maya with the assault.

Ashanti was released into her mother's custody and allowed to return to The Waverly, but she was scheduled to go to court within the next month. The Suffolk County district attorney was willing to drop the shoplifting charges against her, but he was determined to do his best to prosecute Ashanti for the assault charge.

"Even when I send your little ass away and try to get you straightened out, you find a way to stay in trouble," Ms. Daniels screamed on Ashanti as they headed back to The Waverly.

"Now I got to try and come up with money to pay a lawyer to try and keep your ass out of jail."

"Donna, don't do me no favors," Ashanti rudely said to her mom.

Without hesitation, Ms. Daniels took her hand off the steering wheel and smacked Ashanti. "Say something else!" She dared Ashanti.

"You hit like a little bitch!" Ashanti barked on her mom.

Her words enraged Ms. Daniels so much, she steered the car off to the shoulder of the Southern State Parkway, where she parked on the grass and proceeded to beat Ashanti's ass.

Cars whizzed by on the parkway as Ms. Daniels went to work on Ashanti.

"You feel like a real mom now?" Ashanti asked while her mother beat on her. "You didn't raise me properly, and now it's my fault, right?" Ashanti purposely kept on badgering her mother. As her mother hit her repeatedly, she didn't flinch and just sat there and took the beating.

"Keep talking shit!" Ms. Daniels said to her daughter, as if she was some woman she was fighting in the street.

"Keep talking shit? OK, I have the worst mother in the world. All she does is beat on me and kick me to the curb whenever she can. Why did I have to be cursed with her as my mother?"

WHACK! WHACK!

Ms. Daniels was getting madder and madder as Ashanti spoke words that stung her. At that point she started throwing elbows, catching Ashanti twice in the mouth and causing her bottom lip to swell up like a balloon.

Ms. Daniels was breathing heavily from all of the blows she'd been dishing out. Finally, Ashanti decided to shut her mouth, and Ms. Daniels was able to resume driving.

Ashanti didn't look in her mother's direction. She looked straight ahead in a blank stare at the cars on the parkway.

Five minutes later Ashanti pulled out her cell phone and sent Bobby a text message asking him if she could see him later.

Bobby replied, *No doubt. Is everything alright?*

A partial smile came over Ashanti's face, even though her lip was swollen and she was in pain. She replied, *Nah. All kinds of drama. I HATE MY MOTHER!!! I'll fill you in later when I see you. She just beat my ass over some dumb shit.*

"Who the fuck you texting?" Ms. Daniels barked at Ashanti.

Ashanti rolled her eyes. "A friend," she responded, since she didn't want her mother to snatch her cell phone from her.

Bobby responded, *Wow!*

Ashanti texted right back, *It's all good though.*

A few minutes went by and Ashanti got worried because she didn't get a reply back from Bobby so she sent him another text. *You know I want some more of that dick! So don't be stingy with it :)*

Bobby immediately answered, *Oh I gotchu. Don't worry.*

Ashanti smiled. She then texted Bobby and asked him if he could meet her at The Waverly in an hour, and he said yes. The way Ashanti figured, she was going to be back at The Waverly within the next half hour and she doubted that her mother was going to stay more than ten minutes. So she felt that would give her twenty minutes to freshen up and then bounce with Bobby. She couldn't wait to see him.

Being able to leave with Bobby also meant that Ashanti wouldn't have to hang around The Waverly and deal with Jazzy, Maya, and Cha Cha and their bullshit. She knew Cha Cha was going to be gunning for her and trying to get revenge for the breakfast beat-down she'd dished out on her, and she just wasn't in the mood for the drama.

Ashanti's plan worked out perfectly. Twenty minutes after her mother dropped her off, Ashanti was showered and dressed. She was looking good and smelling good as she exited The Waverly. Ashanti looked as if she didn't have a care in the world as she purposely walked past Cha Cha, Jazzy, and Maya, who were sitting in the living room watching TV.

"Look at Little Miss Snitch," Cha Cha said, trying her best to provoke Ashanti. "Think she so cute with her shades."

Ashanti had already dialed Bobby's phone number when Cha Cha had made that comment to her.

"Hey, Bobby. You ready?" Ashanti spoke into the phone extra loud, so everyone could know who she was talking to. "Oh, you outside already? OK, I'm coming out right now."

Ashanti purposely turned her head and looked in the girls' direction and didn't smile or say anything to them. She knew she didn't have to say anything because her action spoke for itself. Regardless of what Cha Cha and the girls thought about her, they had to know that she had it going on, since Bobby was always checking for her.

"I really cannot stand that bitch," Cha Cha said to Jazzy and Maya.

Jazzy said, "I got something for her ass. Yup, I definitely got something for her. And I bet you she ain't gonna be walking around here all high and mighty after I get through with her. Just watch."

CHAPTER 15

As it turned out, Maya was hired by Chase Bank to work as a teller. She had to endure and pass a four-week training course before being placed in a local bank to work. And seeing that Maya truly enjoyed math and working with numbers, the training course proved to be very easy for her, and she passed it with flying colors. For Maya it was the first time in a long time that she had accomplished a goal that she had set for herself, so she genuinely felt a sense of pride.

Chase Bank was very accommodating to Maya, placing her in a bank at Restoration Plaza, located inside of a Bedford-Stuyvesant shopping mall, which was within walking distance of The Waverly.

Maya thought the job and location were both perfect, but the only drawback was, she had to actually go in to work to get a paycheck. Initially the branch had hired her to work only two days a week, Monday and Thursday, from 10 a.m. to 6 p.m., so they could evaluate her performance before increasing her hours.

While Maya was completing her training course at the bank and starting her new career as a bank teller, Jazzy stayed busy being Jazzy, masterminding new boosting scams that she and Cha Cha carried out perfectly.

Over the four weeks of hitting low-end stores and then selling the merchandise on the Internet, Jazzy and Cha Cha were able to stack a little over six thousand dollars.

Jazzy was very loyal and made sure that Maya understood that all of the money was her money as well, and that it was all going into the pot they were building up to move out of The Waverly together.

"This shit is really for the fuckin' birds!" Maya said to Jazzy and Cha Cha as they walked to the check cashing place to cash Maya's two hundred and five-dollar paycheck. "All that fuckin' work and slaving and dealing with them dumb-ass customers, and all I bring home is two hundred and five dollars? And what the fuck is FICA? Why the hell are they always taking money out of my check? I paid them when I was doing the training."

During the training session Maya had been receiving six hundred-dollar paychecks before taxes, but now that the training was over and she was only working sixteen hours a week, she wasn't taking home nearly as much money.

"FICA is so you can get food stamps if you ever quit," Cha Cha incorrectly explained to Maya.

"This shit is crazy." Maya shook her head as she walked into the check cashing place. She handed the girl her paycheck. It cost Maya five dollars to cash the paycheck, and so she was left with two hundred dollars.

"This shit is embarrassing. And this is why muthafuckas don't work! Who the hell can live off of two hundred dollars? And then they try and pull the slick shit, saying you have to use direct deposit. Fuck all that direct deposit bullshit. The only reason they want you to use direct deposit is so they can know exactly what you do with your money," Maya explained.

"Oh, hell no! Don't mess with that direct deposit bullshit, and don't open up no bank account at Chase," Jazzy said. "Them niggas will rape you every month with all kinds of fees, and then when your account goes negative, you'll owe them money, and then boom! They'll start taking the money you owe them right from your paycheck."

Jazzy was cool with Maya not taking part in the boosting. In fact, she had insisted that Maya not join them even on her days off. She didn't want Maya to risk getting arrested and then losing her job. They needed Maya to have a regular job, just so they would look good on paper when they started hunting for apartments.

Jazzy did require that Maya pool all of her paycheck earnings with the money that they were stacking from boosting. And it seemed like almost overnight the girls had managed to stack close to eight thousand dollars.

"We have to chill now," Jazzy told Cha Cha and Maya while they sat on the front steps of The Waverly.

"I know we wanted to get to ten grand, but I just get this gut feeling that if we keep pressing our luck, we're gonna get bagged, and then we'll have to fight a case in court like that dumb little snitch bitch right over there," Jazzy said, pointing to Ashanti.

Ashanti was exiting Bobby's car after a lunch and movies date. She came walking toward the girls in her signature look, which included tight shorts, high heels, and designer sunglasses. Bobby had treated Ashanti to a pedicure and a manicure, and the girls instantly took notice.

"Don't move. Don't let that bitch walk in. Let her ass climb through a fuckin' window," Jazzy said as Ashanti approached the steps leading to the front door.

Right after Bobby pulled off, Ashanti reached the edge of the steps and just stood there with her hands on her hips, waiting for her three nemeses to move so she could enter the building.

"So fuckin' childish, I swear," Ashanti said underneath her breath, loud enough for Jazzy, Cha Cha, and Maya to hear. She was determined not to ask them to move out of her way.

"Tell me one good reason why I shouldn't bust your ass?" Cha Cha said to Ashanti.

Ashanti sucked her teeth, and then she decided to just walk up the steps and push her way into The Waverly.

"Bitch must have forgot that I already beat her ass once." Ashanti brushed past Maya, who she took as the weakest of the trio.

"Watch where the fuck you walking," Maya said to Ashanti and nudged her.

Ashanti had been walking around with a blackjack inside her bag just in case some drama broke out and she had to use it on the three girls. Immediately she reached in her bag, grabbed her blackjack, and swung it at Maya, but Maya was quick, moving out of the way just in time.

WHACK!

Jazzy didn't hesitate to punch Ashanti square in the face.

Ashanti then turned and swung the blackjack, hitting Jazzy on the arm with it.

"Ahhhh fuck! You bitch!" Jazzy screamed out. She didn't know what Ashanti had hit her with, but it hurt like hell.

Cha Cha quickly positioned herself behind Ashanti and put her in the full nelson wrestling hold while Maya went to work on Ashanti, punching on like her she was a punching bag.

Nancy heard all of the commotion and came to the door and broke up the fight with help from one of the newly hired security guards.

Ashanti, who wasn't hurt too badly, quickly hid the blackjack.

"Test me if y'all want to, but I'm telling y'all now, if y'all get into one more fight, all of y'all will be out of here the next day. I promise you that!" Nancy warned the girls.

"But, Nancy, I was just coming home from a date, and they wouldn't let me—"

Nancy cut Ashanti off in the middle of her sentence. "I don't give a fuck who started what or how it started. I'm sick and tired of playing referee and breaking up fights from you four. But, like I said, test me and see if y'all won't be out of here faster than your heads can turn."

The girls all calmed down. They knew Nancy was no Big Momma, and that she didn't play. Nancy would definitely follow through on her word and get the girls kicked out if they didn't listen to her.

"Ashanti, go to your room or to wherever you were going. And Jazzy, Cha Cha, and Maya, y'all better leave her alone. Just stay out here and sit on the steps like y'all were doing." Nancy turned and went back inside with Ashanti indirectly following right behind her.

Jazzy, Cha Cha, and Maya calmed down and continued to talk and finalize plans on when they were actually going to move. Maya only had two weeks left at The Waverly, so the girls didn't have the luxury of time on their side.

They had decided that the next day, which was a Wednesday, they were going to start placing calls and inquiring about apartments for rent they saw on Craigslist. But in the meantime the girls decided to really treat themselves to a celebration dinner for having just about reached their goal of ten thousand dollars.

To celebrate, they decided to take a train ride to Manhattan and treat themselves to the expensive Mr. Chow Chinese restaurant. They figured that they had worked hard and deserved to spoil themselves just a little bit.

The three girls went inside and took showers and got dressed, and they told Nancy that they were heading to Manhattan but would definitely be back before curfew.

Nancy told them, "Well, I'm leaving early. In about an hour Big Momma will be here. Just make sure that y'all get back here before curfew, and for God's sake, leave Ashanti alone."

The three girls assured Nancy that there would be no more trouble coming from them, and then they left and headed out to their celebration dinner.

CHAPTER 16

As soon as Jazzy, Cha Cha, and Maya walked into Mr. Chow, the white male host said to them, "Good evening, ladies. Do you have a reservation?"

The girls all looked at each other sort of confused.

"Uh, yes, we do. I actually called the other day," Maya said, trying to sneak a peek at the list of names on the host's clipboard.

"OK, great. Can I get your name?"

"Uh, yes, actually I had called from my job. I work for Chase Bank, and we're supposed to meet my boss here tonight for dinner. I forgot if I gave you my name or his name. Check for Maya."

As the man scanned his list of names, Maya saw a name that said Javier and the number for next to it.

"It may also be under Javier. That's the name of my boss," she lied and said.

"Yes. Javier, party of four." The host smiled and then placed a check next to the name and asked the girls to follow him.

Jazzy and Cha Cha smiled because they knew that Maya had just lied her ass off to get them into the restaurant.

The host seated them, and then he told them he would have

Javier join them as soon as he arrived.

"OK, thank you," Maya replied.

"Maya, you are crazy," Jazzy said as they sat down and chuckled amongst themselves.

"Let's just hurry up and order because, as soon as Javier gets here, there's gonna be a problem," Cha Cha said.

Maya reassured them that they didn't have to worry, since Javier was a popular name. And if Javier were to show up, all she was going to say is that there must have been some kind of mistake or duplicate names and that her boss Javier was still on his way.

Shortly thereafter a waiter arrived at the girls' table. "Hello, ladies," he said and handed each of them a menu. "Can I start you off with some water? Sparkling or bottled?"

Jazzy and Cha Cha looked confused.

"Sparkling will be fine for all of us. Thank you," Maya said.

The waiter nodded his head and then walked off.

"Would y'all stop with that look that says y'all ain't never been nowhere before?" Maya said to Jazzy and Cha Cha.

"And how the fuck do you know what sparkling water is? When did your ghetto ass ever have sparkling water?" Jazzy asked.

"I know, right? She get a little corporate job, and now she's all sophisticated and shit," Cha Cha added in fun. "I'll have the sparkling water and a spot of tea," Cha Cha said in an old, rich, white-lady voice. She took hold of an empty glass and acted as if she was drinking from it, her pinky finger sticking out prominently while holding the glass.

Maya and Jazzy both laughed.

The waiter then came back with a brand-new bottle of sparkling water and opened it. He poured a glass for each of them and then placed the bottle on their table for them to have to themselves. "Can

I start you off with any appetizers?" he asked.

The three of them looked at their menus, and then once again Maya spoke up for them.

Smiling at the waiter, Maya said, "If you don't mind, can you recommend something for us? We usually like to take the suggestions of the waiters whenever we eat at a restaurant for the first time."

"Oh, sure. I didn't know this was your first time," the waiter said with a foreign accent. He smiled, and then without even asking, he took the menus from the girls while they were still looking at them. "I will take care of you, don't worry. You will trust my choices. I will start you off with appetizers that you will all love," the waiter said, and then he hurried off in the direction of the kitchen.

"I ain't all with the rich crowd, but I can tell we about to get hustled," Jazzy said.

"Huh?" Maya replied.

"Those menus ain't have no prices next to the food, and then did you see how quick he snatched them menus out of our hands? He about to come back with the most expensive shit he can find on that menu. You watch," Jazzy explained.

"So what! We ballin'. This is a celebration for us getting ready to get our freedom from The Waverly," Maya said.

Cha Cha then spotted two celebrities in the restaurant. She saw the baseball player Derek Jeter seated with a white lady and having dinner, and she also saw Hot 97 radio personality Angie Martinez with some black dude.

"Fuck them!" Jazzy said. "They ain't nobody!"

"I should go ask if I can take a picture with them, and then I'll send it out on Twitter." Cha Cha stood up, all star-struck.

"Cha Cha, sit your ass down," Maya said through clenched teeth.

"You can't do that in here! They'll throw us out on the street faster than you can blink."

Cha Cha sucked her teeth. "See, that's why all I need is some fuckin' Red Lobster and I'm good. I can't take all these high-end rules and regulations."

The waiter then returned with two big platters of food and a bed of lettuce. One platter of food had some brown-looking meat that was sliced and chopped up very thin, looking almost like scrambled eggs. And the other platter contained lobster tails.

"You will love this, I promise." The waiter then explained to the girls how they should eat the food with their lettuce.

The girls looked at the food as if they had just been served something from another planet.

Maya took the lead. When the waiter walked off, she scooped out some of the meat and put it inside some lettuce and made a wrap with the lettuce and ate it.

Cha Cha and Jazzy looked at her like she was crazy.

"I ain't eating that shit. That's supposed to be chicken, but to me the shit looks like rabbit. I ain't ever seen no chicken that looks like scrambled eggs," Jazzy said.

Right at that moment, the hostess arrived and explained to the girls that Javier had arrived but that he was already with a party of four. He then asked them, were they sure they had a reservation.

"Of course, we're sure." Maya then looked over toward the entrance and explained that she didn't know that Javier, but that her boss Javier was on his way.

The host looked heated, and at the same time, he didn't appear to know how to handle the situation.

"We already eating, so just find them another seat." Cha Cha tried some of the lobster.

The host shook his head and walked off. He would have thrown the girls out of the restaurant, but their food had arrived, so if he threw them out, then nobody would pay the bill.

"If we was white, he wouldn't even be bothering us," Maya said and she continued to eat.

Eventually the girls all came to enjoy the food that the waiter had brought to them, and they gobbled it all up. The chicken that looked like eggs turned out to be the girls' favorite dish. The main course they loved as well, particularly because they were more familiar with the General Tso's chicken and chicken lo mein.

Overall the girls loved the food, but the only drawback was that they were too young to drink liquor and the waiter would not budge and as much as they begged him to, he refused to accept their bribes and he held his ground and didn't bring them any alcoholic drinks.

Close to an hour and a half later the waiter brought the bill and the girls were shocked when they saw that it was close to five hundred dollars.

"See! What the fuck did I tell you? I knew we was getting hustled," Jazzy said as she examined the bill.

"We could have went right to the Chinese restaurant in the hood and had chicken wings and French fries and we would have paid all of twelve dollars for the three of us." Cha Cha sucked her teeth.

"Look at this shit!" Jazzy vented. "Maya, you and the sparkling water. That water was twenty dollars per glass! I ain't never been raped like this before."

The three of them complained, but eventually they paid the large bill. They were so disgusted by the price tag, they didn't leave the nice, cordial waiter any tip.

"Was everything OK?" the waiter asked the girls after bringing them their change. He was clearly nervous that he wasn't getting his industry standard tip of close to a hundred dollars.

"Everything is all good, but y'all need to get some fuckin' prices and put it on them menus. Y'all can't just be robbing people like this. You just fucked all three of us with no Vaseline!" Jazzy said it loud enough that all of the other customers sitting nearby heard her, and they were shocked by her vulgarity.

When the girls left the restaurant, they didn't feel like getting on the train. The train was too slow in the evening time and they were feeling tired, so they decided to just hail a yellow cab back to The Waverly.

Mr. Chow was pretty close to the heart of Manhattan, so when the girls walked out of the restaurant, they had no problem hailing down a cab. The three of them piled into the back and told the Arab driver where they were going to.

"I can't believe we paid all that money, and I don't even feel full," Jazzy said.

"I know, right!" Cha Cha chimed in.

"It's all good though. I mean, it was a celebration. And it's not like we spent our last dollars on that food," Jazzy said.

Cha Cha and Maya agreed with Jazzy, and they didn't really sweat the restaurant any more from that point forward.

It didn't take long for the cab driver to reach the Brooklyn Bridge and cross into Brooklyn.

"Yo, that's where we need to get an apartment at," Maya beamed, pointing to a brand-new high-rise condo building on the corner of Flatbush Avenue and Gold Street.

"I know this white man that lives there, and he was saying that they have a gym, and restaurants in there and the whole nine yards. And the view of the Manhattan skyline is crazy," Maya added.

"What rich white man you been fuckin' and ain't tell us about?" Cha Cha quickly spoke up and said.

Maya laughed. Then she explained that the instructor for her class when she was training for the teller position lived there, and on their breaks he would shoot home, and that on one occasion he had invited three of the trainees to his apartment for lunch.

Cha Cha looked at Jazzy and twisted her lips.

"What?" Maya smiled, stretching out her arms, holding both of her palms upward.

"Let me find out you fuckin' a white man," Jazzy said.

"I'm not." Maya laughed.

"Mmm-hmm," Cha Cha added, and they all laughed.

"The rent is probably like three grand a month in there. We'll get evicted if they even rent to us," Jazzy said.

"Well, it ain't nothing wrong with dreaming big," Maya replied.

By this time the girls had reached The Waverly and paid the cab fare. After they exited the cab, they walked toward the entrance and saw Ashanti sitting on the front steps with Bobby.

"Don't say nothing to her ass. Just walk right by her," Maya said.

They got closer to Ashanti and Bobby, and Ashanti was staring hard at Cha Cha. Cha Cha saw that Ashanti was staring at her, but she figured the best way to get under Ashanti's skin was to ignore her and only acknowledge her man Bobby.

Bobby smiled and said hello to the girls as they approached. Maya and Jazzy said hello in return.

"Hey, Bobby." Cha Cha stopped in front of him and placed her hand on his shoulder. "Bobby, when is your next game?"

Jazzy and Maya were surprised that Cha Cha had said something, so they stopped to see where things were going to go.

"None of your fuckin' business!" Ashanti said.

"Babe, chill. It's all good." Bobby said and turned toward Cha Cha. "I'm getting ready to head out of town to this Nike basketball camp."

"Oh, the ABCD camp?" Cha Cha asked.

"Yeah. How did you know?"

"Well, do you know this dude named Josh Jones from Newark?" Cha Cha asked.

"Yeah, JJ? That's my man," Bobby said.

"Oh, really? Well, I think he's going to that camp, so that's how I knew of it."

"That's what's up. It's a small world. Word."

"We should link up one day," Cha Cha said to Bobby.

Ashanti's blood was boiling because she felt Cha Cha was disrespecting her in a major way.

"No, the fuck *we* shouldn't. Now, if you don't mind, can you please ska-beat-it? We were in the middle of a private moment," Ashanti said to Cha Cha.

"OK, so good luck at camp. I hope you do well." Cha Cha then extended her hand to Bobby for a handshake. After he shook her hand, she walked up the steps and into the lobby of The Waverly.

Maya and Jazzy were laughing at how disrespectful Cha Cha had been by not even acknowledging Ashanti but still carrying on a conversation with her man.

After having what they thought was going to be their laugh for the night, the three girls went up to their room, where they noticed that their door wasn't locked and was slightly ajar.

As the girls approached their room, Jazzy said, "See, this is why we have to get the fuck outta here. I'm so tired of these supervisors just walking up in our shit whenever they feel like it. And they could at least lock the door when they leave."

Jazzy then pushed open the door, and all three girls couldn't believe what they saw. Their entire room had been completely trashed. Lamps were turned over, the mattresses to their beds had been flung on the floor, and all of their clothes were out of the closets and on the floor. All of their dresser drawers were open, and the contents had been dumped on to the floor.

"I'm going to jail for murdering that bitch tonight!" Cha Cha said in reference to Ashanti. Her words interrupted the shock the girls were experiencing.

"Wait, hold on." Jazzy grabbed Cha Cha and prevented her from running downstairs to whip Ashanti's ass.

Jazzy cleared out some space on the floor so she could open up a folding chair. After the chair was opened, she stood on it and then reached up inside the drop ceiling and searched for the Nike shoebox that she used to stash the money they'd been saving for their new apartment. Immediately she started to panic when she didn't feel the shoebox.

"That bitch got our stash!" Jazzy screamed, the veins popping out of her head from anger. She wanted to make sure the money was actually gone, so she started to lift up all of the drop ceiling tiles, feeling for the shoebox. "That shit better be here," she said nervously.

Cha Cha joined in and started to search the drop ceiling tiles with Jazzy, but it was to no avail.

"Y'all don't have to look no more," Maya said in a dejected tone after she located the empty Nike shoebox on the floor. She picked it up.

Cha Cha was so mad, she repeatedly punched the wall, putting three small holes in it.

"Yo, let's step to that bitch right now," Cha Cha said.

"Ashanti, didn't do this," Maya said.

"How the fuck you know she didn't?" Cha Cha asked.

"Because she wouldn't have been sitting outside that calmly if she did."

"This could have been Ashanti, it could have been Trina, or Tiny could have came back up in here and got us. It could have been Big Momma, it could have been one of the security guards. Hell, it could have even been Nancy and her goody-goody ass!" Jazzy said.

"So what the fuck we gonna do?" Cha Cha asked.

At that moment they had no answer to that question. But the girls did know that, when it came to money, nobody could be trusted, so everybody at The Waverly was a suspect. And they planned to get revenge on whoever had violated them like this.

CHAPTER 17

Jazzy, Cha Cha, and Maya went looking for Big Momma to see if they could get some answers about who broke into their room, but Big Momma was nowhere to be found. This was weird to them because Big Momma was definitely at The Waverly before they went to Manhattan for their celebration dinner.

"This had to have happened before I got on duty," Nancy told the girls after she walked up to their room to look at everything first hand.

"Well, didn't they upgrade the security after the shooting? Look on the videotapes and see who came and who left, so we can narrow it down to who the fuck did this shit to us," Jazzy said.

"Watch your mouth, Jazzy," Nancy warned.

Jazzy gave Nancy a look to kill, but she kept her mouth shut.

"As far as the videotapes, we had cameras on the upper floors near the bedrooms, but we had to disconnect the cameras due to privacy issues, and we only have them operating mainly at all of the entrances to the building," Nancy explained.

All of the girls shook their heads in disbelief, and then they listened to Nancy as she told them that all she could do was call the police and have them fill out a police report.

After Nancy walked off to go call the police, Jazzy said, "It was that fat miserable bitch, Big Momma, who got us."

Cha Cha and Maya thought to themselves for a moment, but they couldn't come up with a motive that Big Momma would have to want to rob them.

"She robbed us, so her fat ass can eat Big Macs and French fries all day long! I'm telling y'all, it was that bitch, and I swear on everything, I'm confronting her ass tomorrow when she gets here," Jazzy said.

"How can you say it was definitely her? Nancy could be the culprit just as well as Big Momma!" Maya reasoned. "And we still didn't narrow down Ashanti and the other girls."

"I know it was Big Momma because she's MIA. How the fuck she disappear on the night we get jacked? How could she do that if she's leaving her shift early? Ain't no way she would risk getting fired unless she had a good enough reason to jet," Jazzy explained. "And that bitch is greedy for money! I'm telling you she did it."

"What the fuck are we going to do now?" Maya started to pick up some of the clothes from on the floor.

"Maya don't touch anything until the cops get here," Cha Cha warned.

"You know the cops aren't going to do a goddamn thing when they get here," Maya replied, and she continued to clean up the disaster.

Jazzy and Cha Cha sat in silence for a few minutes until Ashanti and one of the other girls in The Waverly walked past their room. Ashanti did a double take after passing their room, and after she saw the ransacked room, she let out loud laughter.

Cha Cha got up and walked into the hallway. "What the fuck is so funny?"

Ashanti didn't respond, but she kept laughing as she walked away.

"Keep laughing and see if I don't come down to your room and fuck you up," Cha Cha yelled.

Nancy arrived back at the girls' room just as Cha Cha slung her threat at Ashanti. She didn't say anything to Cha Cha, but her look alone spoke volumes. The girls knew she was running out of patience with them.

"The cops will be here soon. I spoke with Big Momma, and she said that she did her usual sweep of the entire building right before she had to leave early, from what she remembers, there was nothing out of the ordinary," Nancy said, clipboard in hand.

The girls all looked at each other, but they didn't say anything.

"I have to write up an incident report and turn it in to the state, so the first thing I need to know is what exactly was stolen from the room?" Nancy asked.

"Just money," Jazzy quickly replied with an attitude.

"How much money?"

No one said a word.

"Don't everybody all speak at once."

"Well, I know I had just about saved all of the money from my job since I started working, and that's all gone now," Maya said.

"OK, so how much was that?" Nancy asked, ready to scribble it down on her notepad.

"Twenty-five hundred," Maya replied.

"And me and Cha Cha both had five hundred apiece saved up, and now that's gone," Jazzy added.

"So there was thirty-five hundred dollars in cash in this room?"

The girls knew not to say that there was more than that, so they all nodded their heads yes.

Nancy looked at them with suspicion, but she didn't say anything as she wrote on her clipboard.

"We were saving so we could, I mean, so I could get an apartment next month," Maya told Nancy.

Nancy shook her head. "Maya, you're working at a bank now, so why would you have that kind of money just laying around and not put it in the bank? And I'm sure every chance that you got you have been telling everybody in here just how much money you had."

"I didn't tell anybody anything," Maya replied.

"Well, I don't know what to tell you all, other than chances are really good that that money is gone forever, unless somebody steps up and confesses to stealing it, and we all know that that isn't happening."

Maya said, "See, this is why I can't wait to get out of here. Nancy, forgive me for being rude, but it is so fucked up living in here. It's like we on some kind of plantation or some shit. I'm so tired of it. We always getting violated in some kind of way, and nothing is ever done about it. The cops are on their way here and for what? Just so they can tell us the same thing that you just said?"

There was nothing Nancy could say, other than tell Maya that she understood where she was coming from and that she would make sure to question all of the girls in The Waverly to see if anyone knew anything.

Before long, the cops did arrive and were out of there almost quicker than you could blink. It was just as Maya had said it would be. In all of five minutes, the cops had filled out a police report and told the girls that there was nothing more they could do. And then, they left.

When the cops and Nancy were gone, Maya broke down and started crying out of frustration.

"Maya, don't worry about this. We'll be alright," Jazzy said in an attempt to comfort her friend.

"No, you and Cha Cha will be alright. Me, I'm literally gonna be ass out in a minute, and what the fuck am I gonna do? Where the hell am I gonna go? I'll have to go to a fuckin' shelter. See, shit like this is exactly why bitches end up selling they pussy for these pimp-ass muthafuckas. What other options are there? Like who can fuckin' live on two hundred a week? And now Chase is telling me that they about to move me to some other branch way the hell out in Great Neck, Long Island. By the time I pay for taking the Long Island Railroad out there and pay for lunch, what the hell am I gonna be left with? A hundred fuckin' dollars a week? Urrgghhhh!"

Jazzy sat next to Maya on the floor and put her arm around her as tears fell from Maya's eyes.

"What the hell did we do to deserve this life and to be living up in this shithole? It's just not fair! Everybody takes so much shit for granted. And it's like with me and you and Cha Cha and with basically all of the girls up in here, all we want is just to be a part of a normal fuckin' family," Maya said, tears streaming down her face.

"I wouldn't care if I just lived with one parent in the worst projects in the city. That would still be better than being up in here knowing that not one blood relative, or anybody for that matter, loves you enough to say, 'Nah, Maya, you family, come stay with me. You don't have to be up in no group home and exposed to all kind of crazy shit.'"

As tears streamed down Maya's face, Jazzy and Cha Cha were both quiet. Although Jazzy and Cha Cha both had exteriors that were tougher than leather, on the inside they were your typical insecure and vulnerable teenage girls who just wanted to be loved and to give love in return.

"Maya, whatever doesn't kill us, it'll only make us stronger," Cha Cha said.

"Yeah, I know that. But you know what? I'm tired. I'm tired of surviving off of clichés like that. I'm just tired in general. Like, why at eighteen years old do I have to worry about where I'm gonna live and how I'm gonna pay my rent? I'm not even old enough to legally drink or gamble, but I have to worry about taking care of adult shit and fending for myself. Life is crazy. For real for real."

Cha Cha and Jazzy both were quiet. They knew it was best to just let their friend continue to vent.

Maya stopped crying and wiped away her remaining tears. "You know what I was thinking about the other day? I was saying to myself that I could deal with living in a group home, and I could deal with aging out of the group home and all of the shit that comes with that. I could live with all of that and struggle as much as I had to struggle, and I wouldn't even complain if I just had one family member who would simply tell me every once in a while that they loved me. That's all I want, is for somebody to tell me that they love me. I mean, is that too much to ask or to want?"

Maya looked as if she was about to get emotional again, but she held herself together.

"Maya, I feel you and all," Cha Cha said. "But on the real, when you fall down off your bike and scrape up your knees, you just have to get back up, dust yourself off, and start pedaling again. The scars on your knees will remain there forever, but you can't let nothing stop you from dusting yourself off and getting back up on that bike and going toward your destination."

Jazzy said, "Exactly! And, Maya, you ain't gonna have to worry about selling your pussy just so some pimp can take care of you. This robbery shit was fucked up, but like Cha Cha said, we just have to dust ourselves off and keep on going. I got a plan, don't worry."

Jazzy did have a new plan for the girls, and as the three of them straightened up their room to its normal state, they all made a vow right then and there that they would start over and do whatever they had to do to rebound from this huge setback.

Although the three of them felt thoroughly violated, they knew that as long as they had each other's back that there wasn't anything they could not rebound from. They were accustomed to living the hard-knock life, and they knew that when life gave you lemons, it simply meant that it was time to make lemonade.

CHAPTER 18

The day after the girls' room had been vandalized, Jazzy found herself in New York's Public Library in Harlem. She had gone to the library to use the Internet, and she didn't want to use any of the computers at The Waverly, nor did she want to use any of the computers at the local Brooklyn libraries. Jazzy wanted to order GHB, the date rape drug, and she wanted her tracks to be covered and untraceable on any of the computers local to her, just in case her plan didn't work out the way she thought it would. Before she went to the library, she walked to the local supermarket and purchased a prepaid American Express card that she would use for the GHB.

Jazzy ordered the GHB and had it sent to her aunt's house in Queens. She told her aunt to expect a package to be delivered within the week and asked her aunt to call her when the package arrived. While Jazzy was executing this part of the plan, she made sure not to tell any of it to Maya or Cha Cha.

Four days after she ordered the GHB, it arrived at her aunt's house, and she traveled on two trains and a bus to make it to the tree-lined street in Laurelton, Queens. Her aunt lived on 229th Street in a beautiful Tudor-style house with a manicured lawn, right across the street from an elementary school playground.

As Jazzy made her way to the front door of the house, she couldn't help but wonder what it would have been like to have grown up in a house like the one her aunt lived in. She paused and looked at all the little kids running and laughing and having so much fun as they played with each other on the playground. Jazzy smiled, daydreaming, imagining that the window above her aunt's front door was the main window in her bedroom—a bedroom that she didn't have to share with anyone. She pictured what her bed would have been like and how she would have decorated her room.

Jazzy knew, had she grown up in such a tranquil environment as her aunt's house she probably would have never learned to boost or known anything about boosting. She wouldn't have learned how to roll a blunt at twelve or how to apply a condom to a dick at age thirteen.

Jazzy slowly shook her head. The smile left her face as she returned to reality. She looked over her shoulder one more time at the kids with their parents on the playground, and then she walked to her aunt's front door. Just as she was about to ring the doorbell, she saw a handwritten note taped to her aunt's door.

The note said:

Hello Jazzy, sorry that auntie couldn't be here to see you. I had to run to New Jersey for something and I won't be back until tomorrow. If you look inside the mailbox you will see the package that came for you. I hope all is well.

Talk to you soon.

Auntie

Jazzy immediately thought back to what Maya had said the other night in their vandalized room about all she wanted was for somebody to tell her that they loved her.

Wow! She couldn't even bring herself to say something like, with love, from Auntie. Jazzy retrieved the small cardboard box from the mailbox. She took hold of the package and laughed to herself for being so naïve to think that her aunt was going to be waiting to meet her with open arms and greet her with a freshly cooked lunch or something hospitable like that.

Jazzy walked away from the house and back toward Merrick Boulevard, so she could catch the bus and head back to the E train. When she was a block away, she decided to turn on 137th Avenue so she could walk up 228th Street, where there was a store. And when Jazzy headed west on 137th Avenue, her mouth fell open when she saw an all-black Range Rover with vanity New York license plates that said ACHIEVER.

All of the good feelings quickly exited Jazzy's body, and she made an about face and turned back around and went right back to her aunt's house.

I don't want shit from your ass, you dumb bitch. Parking around the corner just so I wouldn't think you were home. Oh my God! I swear.

Jazzy made it back to her aunt's house and repeatedly rang the doorbell like she was a lunatic.

Jazzy yelled, "Auntie, I know you in there. Open up the door. We need to talk!"

Her aunt was in fact home but didn't dare come to the door. She sat in the comfort of her air-conditioned bedroom and watched game shows on the Game Show Network. She also wondered how Jazzy knew she was home.

Jazzy went to the side door and repeatedly rang that doorbell and banged on that door. But she got no answer. She rang both the front and the side doorbells for nearly ten minutes, and she also banged on both doors, but she got no answer. So she went across the street and asked one of the moms in the playground if she could borrow a pen, telling them she would give it right back to them.

Jazzy took the pen and marched back across the street, and on the same note that her aunt had left for her, she scribbled the following message in capital letters.

MRS. "ACHIEVER" YOUR NIECE DIDN'T WANT ANYTHING FROM YOU. I ONLY CAME FOR MY PACKAGE. BUT SINCE YOU AND MY MOTHER BOTH DON'T HAVE TIME FOR ME, ALL I'LL SAY IS FUCK YOU AND FUCK MY MOTHER TOO! HAVE A NICE "ACHIEVING" LIFE. STUPID BITCH!

After Jazzy scribbled that on the note, she went across the street and handed the lady her pen back and thanked her. Jazzy's anger wasn't evident to the mothers on the playground, but on the inside her blood was boiling. She wanted her aunt to feel the hurt she was feeling.

Jazzy walked back across the street to her aunt's house and picked up one of the beautiful brick stones that her aunt used to accentuate her manicured lawn. The heavy brick was more like a heart-shaped stone the color of a red rose. With all of her might, Jazzy tossed the stone right through her aunt's front window.

The sound of shattering glass crashing to the ground and the heavy stone landing on the hardwood living room floor startled Jazzy's aunt. She jumped to her feet, thinking her ghetto-ass niece and some of her thuggish friends were trying to break into her house. Jazzy's aunt suddenly forgot about the note she had written and came racing upstairs to the living room. She looked around to see what had happened and couldn't believe her eyes when she saw her beautiful expensive bay window completely ruined.

Jazzy could see her aunt in the living room through the hole in the window. She flailed her arms and repeatedly called out to her aunt to get her attention. Her aunt finally walked right up to the window, and when she saw Jazzy, she wanted to choke the shit out of her.

"Back from New Jersey so soon?" Jazzy asked.

Her aunt knew she was busted, but at that point she didn't care. She raced to her front door and snatched it open. "You little bitch! What the fuck is wrong with you?" her fifty-year-old aunt screamed.

"The same thing that's wrong with you and my mother! That's what's wrong with me!"

"You gonna pay for this window!"

"I ain't paying for shit!"

WHACK!

Jazzy's aunt slapped her so hard, she saw stars.

"Say something else smart, and I'll beat your ass into a coma!"

"You're a fuckin' liar, and you're selfish just like my piece-of-shit mother!"

WHACK!

Jazzy's aunt slapped her so hard a second time, she fell to the ground, and her aunt started to kick and stomp on her. Thankfully for Jazzy, her aunt was wearing house slippers, so it helped lessen the blows.

Almost instantly two of the mothers from the playground came running to Jazzy's aid. They prevented her aunt from putting her in that coma as she had intended.

Jazzy was seeing stars, and her ears were ringing, like a microphone placed too close to a speaker.

"Miss, is everything OK? This really isn't necessary," one of the mothers said to Jazzy's aunt. "You can handle this another way."

"Mind your fuckin' business," her aunt screamed as the two ladies restrained her.

Another lady came to Jazzy's aid and helped her up.

"All this because I caught her in a lie," Jazzy said.

"You ain't catch me in shit! And I don't have to explain nothing to your ghetto ass!"

"Oh, I'm ghetto now? So what the fuck does that make you?"

"I'm OK. Really, I'm good," Jazzy's aunt explained to the two ladies restraining her.

One of the ladies threatened to call the police if her aunt didn't calm down.

"Nobody in the family can do anything with this child, and that's why her ass is in a group home now. You see what she just did to my window?"

Suddenly the women's perception of Jazzy and the whole situation changed.

Jazzy had regained all of her wits and was still in fight mode, but she figured there was no sense in trying to force someone to see their own ugliness and selfishness.

Jazzy spat at her aunt's feet. "The only reason I'm in a group home is because of whores like you and my mother, who fuck every Tom, Dick, and Harry but don't want to accept the responsibility of raising the babies that y'all make."

"You're exactly right, and that's why back then and even to this day I tell my sister that she should've just aborted your black ass!"

"Oh, miss, come on now. That wasn't necessary," one of the ladies said to her. "Be the bigger person."

Jazzy was feeling completely deflated, but she wasn't going to let her aunt see that or know how she was feeling. She shook her head and looked at her aunt.

"I'll be the bigger person," Jazzy said, before walking off and making her way back toward Merrick Boulevard so she could catch the bus to the train and make it back to Brooklyn.

"And you gonna pay for this window! You better believe that!" Jazzy's aunt yelled, determined to get the last word in.

Jazzy did eventually make it back to The Waverly. She had accomplished her mission for that day by retrieving the GHB. But the day's events with her aunt had drained her emotionally, and when she got back to her room, all she felt like doing was getting in her bed and staying there. She was in no mood to plot with Maya and Cha Cha. The plotting would have to wait until at least the next day. For the time being, she just wanted to be left alone with her thoughts. She also didn't want anyone to ever see her cry. She pulled the bed sheet over her face and put her pillow over her head, and then she let the tears roll out of her eyes.

CHAPTER 19

With the money that Big Momma had stolen from the girls she was able to get completely caught up on her rent and still pay one month of rent in advance. Big Momma had also been dying to get some new furniture, so she bought herself a brand-new 56-inch flat-screen television and a new loveseat and sofa.

Big Momma had also gone clothes shopping with some of the money, treating herself to fifteen hundred dollars' worth of new outfits, including a designer sweat suit and an expensive pair of Nike running shoes to match. That was the outfit she wore on her first day back at work since breaking into the girls' room and robbing them. She was working the night shift.

"I got a fish dinner from Rockaway Fish House, if you want some," Big Momma said to Maya after knocking on her bedroom door.

Maya stepped away from her computer and went and opened up the bedroom door. She saw Big Momma standing there all dipped out in her new clothes and smelling good. Big Momma had also purchased Beyoncé's new fragrance and had sprayed a bit too much of it onto all parts of her body.

"Hey, Big Momma," Maya said, after opening the door. "No, thank you. I'm good. I just ate the garbage food they had up in here."

"You sure? Maya, you know how they pile the food on over there at Rockaway Fish House. One dinner can damn near feed three people. And you know I'm on a diet, so I don't need to be eating all this by myself."

Maya smiled. "I'm sure I don't want none. But thanks anyway for offering to share."

"I got collard greens and baked macaroni and cheese to go along with the fried fish."

"Big Momma, I'm good, really." Maya was starting to get annoyed, wanting to get back to Facebook.

Big Momma had been feeling extremely guilty for taking the girls' money, and at the same time, she was also scared as hell that she might get caught, since one of the security guards had seen her coming out of the girls' room on the night she'd ransacked and robbed it.

"So let me ask you—Did they find out who broke into your room? I couldn't believe that when Nancy called me and told me what happened."

Big Momma was glad that Maya was alone in the room simply because she was easier to manipulate and not as street-smart as Cha Cha and Jazzy, who would have smelled the guilt on Big Momma a mile away.

Maya just looked at Big Momma with a look that said, *"Come on now. Are you serious?"*

"So I guess that means no?"

"Big Momma, you know don't nobody give a fuck about shit around here. The cops came in here with the biggest attitude, and they were so annoyed that we actually called them about the robbery. It was like pulling teeth just to get them to write a police report."

Big Momma was happy, but she didn't show it.

"That is so fucked up, but I think as soon as they send someone down from the state to review the tapes, it will get somebody on tape leaving here with something that they stole from y'all," Big Momma said, trying to sound believable.

"Nope. Not happening. Because whoever it was that robbed us, they knew what they were after. And the only thing that they took was cash, so there won't be anybody on camera carrying a laptop or a bag of clothes or anything like that. And there aren't cameras up here near the rooms, so it's a wrap. That money is gone, and there ain't no sense in worrying about shit we can't change," Maya said.

"You're right about that." Big Momma replied. "What the hell is wrong with people?"

Maya wanted to be done talking, so she made her way back over to her computer.

Big Momma didn't get the hint to leave Maya alone. "So how much money did they take from y'all?" she asked after fully stepping into the girls' room.

"Big Momma, you don't even want to know." Maya sighed. "It was a lot. It was the money we was gonna use to get up outta here and get an apartment with."

"No way!" Big Momma said, trying to sound like she was in genuine disbelief.

"Big Momma, no offense, but like I said, it don't make no sense in worrying about shit that we can't change, so I really don't want to keep rehashing this story. So, if you don't mind, can you leave me alone now? I'm about to use this new Facebook chat thing they got."

"Oh, OK. No problem. This food is calling my name anyway, so I was just about to leave." Big Momma turned and walked toward the door to leave. Then she stopped. "And listen, Maya, like I've always told you before in the past, out of all of the girls who have ever come through The Waverly over the years, you're the one who, if I had a daughter, I would want her to be like."

"Awww! Big Momma, I love when you tell me that," Maya said. Big Momma's words really made her feel good.

"And I say that to say, don't be stressed out about aging out of here and having to leave with no place to go." Big Momma then went and closed the door, and she started to whisper just loud enough for Maya to hear her. "Don't be stressed out because, if you need somewhere to stay, you're more than welcome to come live with me rent-free until you get yourself situated."

"Oh my God! Big Momma, are you serious?" Maya asked in disbelief.

"Shhhhh!" Big Momma said to Maya, making sure she kept her voice down.

"Yes, I'm serious," Big Momma whispered.

Maya got up from the computer, opened the door, and ran over to Big Momma and hugged her really tight.

"Oh my God! Big Momma, you don't even know. It feels like the weight of the world has been lifted off my shoulders," Maya said, tears forming in her eyes.

"I could only imagine." Big Momma then warned Maya not to say anything to anybody because she knew that it was against The Waverly's policies for Maya to come live with her.

"Trust me, my lips are sealed! You don't even have to worry about that," Maya said.

"Alright. So we'll sort everything out over the next few days because it don't make sense for you to be waiting to the last possible day to start moving your stuff out of here."

"OK, we'll talk it through," Maya said with a smile.

Suddenly, Facebook didn't matter to Maya anymore. She was relieved that she didn't have to resort to her plan B. Maya hadn't told Cha Cha or Jazzy, but secretly her plan was to go and work for Diamond's, the strip club that Tiny and Trina worked out of. It was something that she was very reluctant to do, but with the money she would make she could rent a cheap motel room until she got things sorted out.

Big Momma wasn't too fond of sharing her space with anyone, but by opening up her home to Maya, it made all of her guilt go away. In fact, she even felt justified in taking the girls' money.

"You know what? My appetite just came back. I think I will take you up on that offer for some food," Maya said.

Big Momma smiled a fake half-smile because the way she looked at it, she had already done her good deed for the day by telling Maya she could stay with her. At that point after Maya had turned down her original offer to share the food, Big Momma had already had it in her mind that she was going to tear it up all by her lonesome.

"Oh, now you want some? Well, you can have some, but I can see we already need some kind of understanding because, when you move in with me, you can't be eating me outta house and home, thinking that food is free like it is up in The Waverly. Big Momma works too hard to put food on the table."

"Well you know that I still have my job at the bank so I'll be able to buy my own food."

Big Momma and Maya both exited the room and made their way down to the dining room, where they split the fish dinner. Maya was in a good mood, and Big Momma was feeling that more than likely she wasn't going to get caught for the theft, so she was also in a good mood.

Big Momma being in a good mood was the perfect setup for Jazzy to execute her GHB plan. Jazzy walked in on Maya and Big Momma as they ate their food and asked Maya if her and Big Momma could have a moment alone to talk in private.

Maya nodded her head yes. Then she put her food down and walked out of the room so that Big Momma and Jazzy could talk business.

"Big Momma, I really need a favor," Jazzy said to her after sitting down.

Big Momma felt as if she had already doled out enough favors for the day, but she still heard Jazzy out. When Jazzy was finished talking, Big Momma told Jazzy she would cooperate.

In the grand scheme of things Big Momma had a lot of power at The Waverly, and she could help the girls out with almost anything.

"OK, but listen, I don't want no more than twenty niggas up in here, and I mean that shit!" Big Momma said to Jazzy.

"I promise. No more than twenty." Jazzy smiled and walked out of the dining room. She now had the permission she needed to pull off her GHB plan so that her, Cha Cha, and Maya could once again start stacking their paper.

CHAPTER 20

Jazzy waited until the last possible moment to tell Cha Cha and Maya her plan simply because she didn't want them to get cold feet and back out. But once she had cleared things with Big Momma, she had to fill them in on the plan.

After Maya had finished eating with Big Momma, she returned to her room and found Cha Cha and Jazzy sitting in the room. Cha Cha had a sinister look on her face, so Maya immediately knew something was up.

"What are y'all up to?" Maya asked.

Jazzy had already filled Cha Cha in on the plan, and since Cha Cha wasn't as long-winded as Jazzy was, she took the initiative and started telling Maya what was up.

"It's GHB time tonight, baby!" Cha Cha smiled as she held up the bottle to show Maya what she was referring to.

Cha Cha had been itching to get back at Ashanti ever since the two of them had their fight and Ashanti had snuffed her with the bowl of hot oatmeal.

"GHB?" Maya took hold of the bottle of pills and examined them. "What is this?"

"It's a date rape drug," Cha Cha said eagerly, while Jazzy looked on, smiling from ear to ear.

"So why do we need this? What am I missing?" Maya asked.

"We're gonna slip it into Ashanti's drink later tonight. The pill will immediately dissolve," Cha Cha explained. "She's not going to know, and after she finishes drinking whatever it is she's drinking, we're going to take her up to our room and charge niggas twenty dollars apiece to fuck her brains out."

Maya thought to herself for a moment, and then she examined the bottle one more time. She opened the bottle and looked at the pills.

"What?" Jazzy could sense Maya's hesitation before she even said anything.

"Y'all are buggin' the fuck out. Here." Maya handed the bottle of pills back to Cha Cha. "I ain't with this shit. I'm sitting this one out."

"What? Maya, come on," Jazzy said in a disappointed tone. "You know how we roll. We roll like a unit."

"Listen, boosting clothes, stealing shit, and selling drugs, all those hustles have their place. But this shit right here, this is just wrong y'all, and we can't do this shit. This is taking things too far."

"Maya, after all we been through together, we're inches away from the goal line and you're not going to help us score the winning touchdown?" Cha Cha asked.

"This winning touchdown involves rape and possible murder. Hell, no. I'm not with this."

"Murder?" Jazzy said. "Ain't nobody getting murdered. What are you talking about?"

"We slip that shit into Ashanti's drink, and she drinks it and passes out. OK, cool. But tell me what the fuck happens if her ass doesn't wake up in the morning. We all know that the minute these grimy-ass street dudes get knocked for something totally separate, they are gonna start singing to the police about these three girls in The Waverly—us—who let them fuck their friend Ashanti for twenty dollars, and now Ashanti is dead, and they think they can help the cops solve her murder. Then, the next thing you know, the three of us is doing football numbers up in Bedford Women's Correctional Facility."

"Maya, you sound like an old-ass housewife or some shit," Jazzy said. "The bitch ain't gonna die from the shit. All it will do is knock her ass out, and she won't be able to remember anything. This stuff has been around for years. It's safe."

Maya sat there silently and she didn't say anything.

"Well, fuck it! If she don't want to be down with it, that's cool. But, Maya, you ain't getting none of the money we make off of this," Cha Cha said.

"That's fine," Maya quickly replied, knowing she had already secured a place to stay with Big Momma.

"That's fine?"

"Yeah, that's fine," Maya added with emphasis.

"They about to toss your ass up out of here any day now, and you sitting around all nonchalant like you got time on your side," Cha Cha said to Maya.

"I'll be alright."

"You'll be alright?" Jazzy asked, suspicious.

"Yes, I'll be alright."

Jazzy was now beyond frustrated. More than just making the money, she wanted to get at Ashanti like this, so she could leave her humiliated beyond recovery, and Maya was throwing monkey wrenches in her plan. The way Jazzy had mapped things out in her mind, out of the three of them, only Maya would be able to get close enough to Ashanti to spike her drink without arousing Ashanti's suspicion.

"Maya, the only way you'll be *alright* is if your ass had something to do with our room getting vandalized and you're sitting on stolen stacks right now," Jazzy said with a sharp tone.

"You're joking, right?"

"No, Maya. I'm dead-ass serious. Whenever bitches who are supposed to be close to you start fronting on you like this, then their ass becomes suspect, and you're looking mad suspect to me right now."

"And to me too!" Cha Cha added.

"Really? Jazzy and Cha Cha, I mean, really? Like, for real, for real, y'all both know me better than that."

"That's right," Jazzy said. "We do know you, and the Maya we know would be down with this plan in a heartbeat, and she also would have told us how it was that she was so confident that she was going to be alright on her own, with no stash and no place to stay."

"I'm gonna be alright because I already decided to strip at Diamond's," Maya lied.

"What?" Cha Cha asked in disbelief.

"You heard what I said."

"So, Maya, you would rather let some grimy-ass muthafuckas throw dollar bills at you, instead of getting shit on your own?" Cha Cha asked.

Maya was quiet, and she looked angry.

"You doing that just so you could prance around half naked? What you think? You gonna meet a baller who will wife you?" Jazzy asked. "That's like whoring yourself out."

"Maybe. If so I'll have somewhere to stay, and someone to take care of me. And y'all better not start judging me because all of us in here done laid on our backs and opened up our legs for money before, so don't be acting like I'm the devil all of a sudden."

"We ain't judging you, but it's like you just gave up hope or some shit," Cha Cha said.

"Ya think?" Maya replied sarcastically.

Everybody in the room was quiet, consumed with their own thoughts.

Maya's mind was racing. She knew that from then on out it was going to be hard as hell for Jazzy and Cha Cha not to believe that she didn't have anything to do with the money going missing. After all, out of everybody in The Waverly, Maya had the biggest motive to steal simply because she was the one in the most desperate state.

"You don't have to go the stripper route, exploiting yourself for nobody," Jazzy said, breaking the silence.

Maya continued to pile on to the lie. "It's not like that's all I'm gonna be doing. I'm gonna still be working for the bank and then doing bachelor parties and shit like that on the side until I can restack my paper."

"Maya, I don't want to say you're stupid, but your ass is stupid! First of all, there ain't no security except for false security when you're dealing with that stripper money. You see how broke Tiny and Trina used to be. We made more money boosting than they did and yet we weren't sticking bottles up our pussy and letting dirty niggas fuck us after a lap dance. And what if a nigga beats the shit outta you, then what?" Cha Cha said.

"I don't know!" Maya yelled. "But what I do know is that both of y'all are seventeen and neither one of you has aged out of this system, so you don't know what it's like or what I'm facing. So don't sit up here and judge me for doing what I feel like I gotta do!"

Jazzy and Cha Cha both didn't have a comeback, so they remained quiet.

After about two minutes, Maya calmed down. She knew she had to say something to get Jazzy and Cha Cha to believe that she was being sincere.

"And how are y'all gonna get niggas up in here to fuck anyway? You know they got cameras all around ever since that shooting," Maya said in a low tone.

"I already spoke to Big Momma," Jazzy said. "I cleared everything with her, and she told me that she knew how to manipulate the cameras so that it could point in opposite directions. Big Momma looks out for us when she has to. You know that, Maya. We run this place when she's in here alone."

The room went quiet again for a few moments.

"OK, so what do I have to do?" Maya asked.

But before Jazzy and Cha Cha could respond, she spoke up again and laid it out for them as to what she was and wasn't going to do. "No, matter of fact, this is the deal. All I'm doing is, I'll slip the drug into Ashanti's drink, but after that, I'm not helping y'all bring her back up to the room, and I'm not taking any of the money in my hand from any of these dudes that pay to fuck her. After I slip the drug into her drink, it's all on y'all," Maya said. "If that bitch dies, I don't know nothing."

Jazzy and Cha Cha both smiled.

"Maya, that's all I wanted you to do in the first place before you ran off on this Mother Teresa thing," Jazzy said. "And the bitch ain't dying, so stop saying that."

"Mother Teresa?" Maya shot back.

"Yes, Mother Teresa," Jazzy replied.

"Last I checked, Mother Teresa was some real holy-roller bitch. I was just in here talking about being the hottest stripper New York's ever seen. That's a big difference from Mother Teresa." Maya chuckled to herself.

Jazzy and Cha Cha both chuckled too.

"Fuck you. You know what the hell I meant," Jazzy said to Maya in a playful tone.

"And for the record, I want my cut of the money," Maya added, trying her best to save face.

"We got you, don't worry," Cha Cha said.

"Yeah, we got you. And as far as the stripper shit, Maya, that ain't happening. Just give me some time, and I'm telling you, I'll get us back to where we was at money-wise," Jazzy said.

"Trust you?" Maya asked.

"Yes, just trust me."

CHAPTER 21

Ashanti, tired of the constant fighting and bickering between herself, Jazzy, Cha Cha, and Maya, was doing her best to avoid them. Whenever she left her room, she was usually leaving The Waverly altogether to go and hook up with Bobby. Her and Bobby seemed like they were really genuinely starting to fall in love, and it was as if they couldn't get enough of each other. And whenever Ashanti wasn't with Bobby, she usually stayed in her room and would lay in her bed and use her iPad for just about everything.

It was Maya's job to slip the GHB into Ashanti's juice. But the problem was, the only real opportunity the girls had to drug Ashanti's juice was at breakfast time or lunch because those were the only times Ashanti would leave her room. Lately she hadn't been eating dinner at The Waverly because she was always out with Bobby.

On this particular night, the night that Jazzy wanted to enact her GHB plan, Ashanti was nowhere to be found at dinner time. Jazzy was getting worried that things weren't going to go down. But just before curfew, Ashanti came strolling into The Waverly, seemingly in a really good mood. Usually whenever Ashanti returned from hanging with Bobby, she'd be in high spirits simply because Bobby showered her with love and attention and made her feel special.

"Is that Ashanti that just walked in here?" Big Momma yelled from inside her office. "Ashanti, come here for a minute."

Big Momma was too fat and lazy to get up off of her ass to go to Ashanti, so Ashanti came into her office. "What's up, Big Momma?"

"Your mother called about an hour ago. She wanted me to remind you that she'll be here in the morning to pick you up for your court date. She said, 'Be ready to go at seven thirty because of all that traffic heading to Long Island.' She doesn't want y'all to be late."

"Uggghhh! OK," Ashanti said. "This shit is so annoying, and these charges are bullshit."

"Well, your mother told me she is confident with the attorney that she got for you, and she thinks the judge will throw the case out tomorrow."

"She really said that?"

Big Momma nodded. She reached into her box of Entenmann's crumb cake, cut herself a big slice, and took a bite of it.

"You just going to sit there and eat that and not offer me none?" Ashanti smiled, knowing Big Momma never shared her Entenmann's with anybody.

"Girl, you know this is my crack! I don't part with my Entenmann's. You know that," Big Momma said with her mouth stuffed, white powder on her lips and cheeks.

Ashanti smiled and nodded her head, and she turned to leave Big Momma's office.

"Make sure your ass is up and ready in the morning," Big Momma said in a muffled voice. After swallowing the crumb cake, Big Momma gulped down a glass of milk. "Ashanti, you hear me?"

"I'll be up and ready to go. Don't worry." Ashanti then made her way out of Big Momma's office and through the living room and up to her bedroom. Along the way she saw Maya sitting in the living room watching TV, but they didn't say anything to each other. Ashanti wondered where Jazzy and Cha Cha were.

Maya knew that Ashanti was more than likely retreating to her room for the night, so she had to do something if they were going to pull off the plan. She got up from the living room couch and quickly made it up the steps that led to the second floor, catching up to Ashanti just as she was about to enter her room.

"Ashanti," she called out.

Ashanti's hand was on her room's doorknob. She stopped in her tracks, wondering what the hell Maya wanted with her. Ashanti didn't say anything; she just looked at Maya and waited for Maya to speak.

"We getting ready to order some pizza from Papa John's. You want something?" Maya asked.

Ashanti looked around to make sure Maya was speaking to her, and even though no one else was around, she still asked Maya, "You talking to me?"

"Yes, I'm asking you, Ashanti."

"What's the catch?"

"Ashanti, there isn't any catch. You want some pizza or not?"

"Well, I'm sure by *we*, you mean you, Jazzy, and Cha Cha, so thanks for offering, but I'll pass." Ashanti then went into her room and closed the door in Maya's face.

Maya paused for a moment, and then she knocked very lightly on Ashanti's door.

"What now?" Ashanti asked, after opening the door.

"I just wanted to ask you, how is your case going?"

Ashanti looked Maya up and down and rolled her eyes.

"Ashanti, listen, I don't know if you know this, but I'm eighteen now and I aged out of The Waverly, so any day now I'll be getting put outta here."

"Yeah. So?"

"So I'm just saying I want to leave with us on good terms, so if it means anything, I want to apologize if I did anything or said anything to you that was disrespectful."

Ashanti looked at her and twisted her lips. She just slowly nodded her head, but there was a big part of her that knew not to trust Maya.

Maya extended her hand to Ashanti, who reluctantly reached out and shook it. Then there was this awkward silence.

"Well, if you want some pizza later on, just come downstairs and get some. My treat." Maya smiled.

Ashanti wanted to smile but she kept a poker face and just nodded her head.

Maya then turned and walked away.

"Good luck out there," Ashanti said to her.

A puzzled Maya turned and looked at her.

"I'm sayin', when you leave The Waverly, good luck."

"Oh, that's what's up." Maya then continued to walk off.

At that point Maya felt pretty good that she had set Ashanti up perfectly. Even though Maya had turned down her offer to join them for pizza, she knew that once the pizza arrived and she personally took it to Ashanti's room, she would more than likely accept it. And that was just what Maya planned on doing.

The only problem was, Maya was now having second thoughts about drugging Ashanti. In that brief interaction with Ashanti, and with Ashanti wishing her luck, she realized that Ashanti wasn't that bad of a person, and in fact was just like her, Jazzy, and Cha Cha.

Maya went to her bedroom, where Jazzy and Cha Cha were. She knew she couldn't show any signs of weakness, or they would seriously think that she had something to do with their room being robbed.

"So what happened?" Jazzy and Cha Cha both eagerly asked.

"We gonna get her. The way I set it up was by saying we're getting ready to order Papa John's."

"And she went for that?" Jazzy asked.

"No, she was hesitant and said that she would pass. But then I got her to talk regular talk, and she wished me luck on aging out and all of that. So I know if I order the pizza and then bring it to her room, she'll take it. And when I bring it to her room, I'll come with a two-liter of Coke. And that's how I'll slip the GHB into her drink."

"Perfect! I love it." Jazzy then instructed Cha Cha to go online and order the pizza.

Maya said to Cha Cha, "Ashanti loves bacon, so order a whole pie with bacon toppings."

Cha Cha also ordered a pie for Big Momma, and after she was done placing the orders, Jazzy asked Maya if she was sure she would be able to pull it off.

"Jazzy, I got this. Start spreading the word."

Jazzy immediately called one of her home boys that she had spoken to earlier in the day and told him that everything was official, that it was going down in about two hours, and she asked him to start rounding everybody up.

Jazzy then went to Big Momma's office to remind her that they were gonna be having boy company. But when she got to Big

Momma's office, she found Big Momma sound asleep and snoring. Big Momma had crumbs all over her and frosting on her lips from the crumb cake she was eating. It took Jazzy about three minutes of pushing and shaking Big Momma to get her to stop snoring and wake up.

"Jazzy, you better have a good fuckin' reason for waking me up," Big Momma said, after opening her eyes. Her body didn't move at all as her eyes locked in on Jazzy.

"We ordered pizza, and it's on its way. We got you a large pie and a two-liter of cherry Coke. Sausage and pepperoni, right?"

Big Momma sat up. "Yeah, that's what I like. Papa John's, I hope, and not that cardboard-tasting disgusting-ass Domino's Pizza. And please tell me that you ordered some Buffalo wings! Can't nobody eat pizza without Buffalo wings."

"Oh, no doubt. We got you, Big Momma. We know how to take care of you. It'll be here soon. And, oh yeah, our company is coming over in an hour or so, so don't forget to do what you gotta do with the cameras."

Big Momma told her OK, and then she reminded her that she didn't want more than twenty dudes in the house.

Thirty minutes later, the pizza arrived. Maya immediately went up to Ashanti's room with the pizza, a two-liter of Coke, and a couple of Styrofoam plates and cups. She knocked on Ashanti's door, and Ashanti opened it and saw her standing there with the pizza.

Maya didn't wait for Ashanti to invite her in and walked in right past her and placed the food and drinks down on Ashanti's desk.

"Babe, let me call you back," Ashanti said to Bobby, who she had been talking to on her cell phone. "I told you I didn't want any pizza," she said to Maya.

"Girl, get over here and eat some of this pizza. I got bacon on it, and I know you like bacon. Where is Ciara? I got a plate and a cup for her too," Maya said, referring to Ashanti's roommate.

"Maya, why are you being so nice to me all of a sudden?"

Maya took two slices of pizza and handed the pizza to Ashanti, who put two slices on a plate for herself.

"Where is Ciara?" Maya asked again.

"She went outta town for something. She won't be back until next week," Ashanti said, after reluctantly taking hold of the pizza.

Maya had already had the GHB inside one of the plastic cups, so when she started to pour the Coke, nothing looked out of order or suspicious.

"And, to answer your question, I'm being nice because I'm tired of all of this tension between my homies and you."

"Well, *you* and your homies got issues."

"Ashanti, let's forget about all the bullshit."

Ashanti ate some of her pizza, looking at Maya and waiting for her to say why she was really there. "Maya, what do you want from me? Just be straight up with me."

Maya handed her the cup of Coke, and Ashanti took hold of hit and drank some.

"I don't want nothing. I didn't come here to ask you for anything, and I won't ask you for anything tomorrow, or next week, or next month, or next year." Maya took a bite of her pizza and drank some of her Coke.

Ashanti drank some more of the soda and ate some more of the pizza.

"You gonna talk to me before I leave here."

"Talk to you about what?"

"Your case, your new man. Just relax and talk."

Ashanti drank some more of the soda and shook her head and smiled.

"OK, you want me talk? Well, my mom is coming here in the morning, and I have to go to court. I'm hoping the case gets thrown out tomorrow. And as far as Bobby goes, that nigga loves my ass! He be acting like he ready to marry me and shit." Ashanti said.

Maya figured the GHB was starting to kick in, causing Ashanti to loosen up.

"That nigga Bobby loves this pussy right here." Ashanti grabbed her crotch. "Yo, the other day I tossed that nigga's salad, and he almost lost his mind. Yo, you ever seen a nigga scream like a bitch during sex? All you gotta do is toss a nigga's salad and they can't handle that shit." She started laughing.

Maya ate more of her pizza and drank more Coke. She watched as Ashanti drank more soda and barely ate any of the pizza. She knew that the GHB was kicking in because Ashanti was starting to talk way too much and was going off on so many different tangents.

"But, for real, I think Bobby was used to just messing with skank hoes or something. 'Cause all I know is he ain't never have no pussy as tight as mines. All he talks about is how he can't believe how tight my shit is. It's like I was cursed with good coochie or something." Ashanti laughed again.

Before Maya could say anything, Ashanti started talking about something completely different.

"OK, be honest, Maya. That day in the dining room, didn't I beat Cha Cha's ass?"

Maya smiled and nodded her head.

"Oh shit! You are here on some real love shit." Ashanti ran up to

Maya and gave her a hug.

"If you had lied and said no, then I would have known you was full of shit." Ashanti laughed and put the big red plastic cup of Coke to her head.

Ashanti finally paused for a moment. She had this glossy-eyed look, staring at Maya.

"What?" Maya asked.

"I ain't never tell you this, but you a pretty-ass bitch. You know that?" Ashanti started laughing again. It was almost as if she was drunk as hell, but GHB was relaxing her and causing her to lose all of her inhibitions.

"You're prettier than I am, Ashanti."

"Well, I know that, but I'm just saying you ain't so bad. I mean, your shape can't fuck with mines, and you don't have that good dick-magnet shit like I do, but you know, you all good though." Ashanti went and sat down on her bed.

"You want some more pizza?" Maya asked.

"No, I'm good. I just want some more of Bobby. I want that muthafucka right now," Ashanti said, and then she lay down on her bed.

At that point Maya knew it was just a waiting game. In a matter of minutes Ashanti was gonna be out cold and clueless to what was happening around her and to her.

Ten minutes later when Ashanti was unresponsive, Maya ran off to go tell Jazzy and Cha Cha that the GHB had worked. And just like she had said, Maya took no part in the plan, letting Jazzy and Cha Cha handle everything from that point. Maya's only hope was that Ashanti would eventually wake up from the GHB. She wouldn't be able to live with herself otherwise.

CHAPTER 22

"Yo, she's out cold!" Maya said in a loud whisper to Jazzy and Cha Cha after she burst into their room to let them know that she had completed her end of the deal.

"Where's Ciara?" Cha Cha asked.

"She's out of town for the week," Maya replied.

Jazzy and Cha Cha didn't say anything else to Maya. They quickly left their room and made their way down to Ashanti's room, where they found her fast asleep on her bed.

"Ashanti." Cha Cha called out her name, but she got no answer in return.

"You get her feet and legs, and I'll grab her from underneath her arm pits," Jazzy said to Cha Cha.

Within seconds Jazzy and Cha Cha had Ashanti's limp body hoisted off the ground, and they were carrying her down the hall to their room. Most of the girls from the group home were still downstairs in the living room watching TV, but two girls were inside the common second-floor bathroom, so Jazzy and Cha Cha had to be careful that no one saw them.

"Put her on your bed, because I don't want no sex juices on my bed," Maya said to her roommates.

Jazzy and Cha Cha put Ashanti on Jazzy's bed. Jazzy lightly tapped her on the cheek to see if she would wake up, but Ashanti just continued to sleep.

"We have to take these sheets somewhere later on today and dump them," Jazzy said to Cha Cha, and she began to unbutton Ashanti's shorts. "This bitch ain't even wearing no panties."

Cha Cha laughed. "She must have known she was going to be fuckin' tonight."

Jazzy fully took off Ashanti's shorts and folded them and put them in the corner of the room.

Ashanti normally kept her pussy hair completely shaved. But she had started to let her pubic hair grow back just a little bit because Bobby had told her that he likes pussy with hair on it. Ashanti's pussy hair wasn't bushy at all, so the girls were all able to notice a huge tattoo of Chinese letters that Ashanti had tattooed right near her pussy.

"I wonder what the fuck this shit says," Cha Cha said out loud. She grabbed her cell phone and was about to take a picture of Ashanti's pussy, so she could find out later what the Chinese words meant.

"Cha Cha, put that fuckin' camera away! What the hell is wrong with you? You trying to send us to jail?"

A disappointed Cha Cha reluctantly put the camera away.

"And we have to make sure that for every nigga that comes up in here we check them for cell phones because we don't want nobody taking no pictures or videotaping anything," Jazzy said while pulling Ashanti's shirt over her head. She then unclasped Ashanti's bra and removed it. Ashanti's body was now fully exposed. Except for the little bootie socks that she had on her feet, she was butt-ass naked.

"Her body ain't even all that," Cha Cha said out of envy.

It was obvious that Ashanti was blessed not only with good looks but also with a gorgeous body. It seemed as if she didn't have an ounce of fat on her body. She had no stretch marks and no signs of any cellulite. Ashanti's arms were toned, and so were her legs. And every time she inhaled and exhaled, her six-pack became visible. Ashanti's body was in shape the way it was due to her days of running track and being a cheerleader.

"I still say that y'all are bugging with this shit." Maya got up and went downstairs to the living room.

The first person she ran into was Big Momma, who motioned for her to come into her office.

"Close the door," Big Momma said. "I was just about to come up to your room before the company that y'all invited over gets here."

Maya instinctively became nervous. "Why? What happened?" Maya asked.

"I'm getting ready to step out for a few hours. But listen, promise me that y'all will have everybody up out of here by three o'clock in the morning, and that there won't be no music at all," Big Momma stressed in a loud whisper. "And no more than twenty niggas! You hear me?" Big Momma added before Maya could even answer.

Maya promised her that she would follow all of her directives.

"Big Momma, let me find out you got a late-night booty call lined up." Maya smiled.

"Girl, please. I'm not thinking about no dick right now. I'm taking a cab up to Empire City Casino in Yonkers."

"There's a casino in Yonkers?"

"Yeah, girl! It's kind of new. It hasn't been around for too long, and all they have is slot machines and craps," Big Momma said, sounding very passionate.

"Oh, so you going to get your gamble on?"

"Yesssir!" Big Momma replied with excitement.

"Personally, I hate slot machines, and I don't even understand craps, but everybody keeps telling me that the slot machines be paying out big if you get there after two in the morning."

"Really?"

"I know three people who won money up there so far, so it's the real deal." Big Momma stuffed the last slice of pizza from the pizza pie into her mouth.

"Well, hopefully you'll win big," Maya said.

"Hopefully? Maya, this is money in the bank." Big Momma gathered up her keys and her pocketbook.

Maya laughed.

"My cab is here. I'll be back at five in the morning, OK?"

"OK, I'll hold everything down."

Big Momma then instructed Maya on how to rotate the two main cameras back to their normal position.

"After everybody leaves, you have to make sure you rotate them cameras back to the correct position and make sure that you keep the lights off in the front yard. The camera has to record total darkness. I'll turn them back on when I get back." Big Momma rushed out of her office, so she could get inside her cab and take the forty-minute ride to Yonkers.

Maya took in all of her instructions, and as soon as Big Momma was out of sight, she hurried upstairs and told Jazzy and Cha Cha that Big Momma had left for the casino and that they had The Waverly to themselves.

"Say word?" Jazzy said.

"Word. She said she would be back around five in the morning," Maya explained.

Jazzy was ecstatic. She quickly got her cell phone and sent out a text to her boy.

It's on and poppin' as of right now! And there is no limit anymore, TELL EVERYBODY!!!

Jazzy's boy immediately called her as soon as he got the text message because he didn't understand exactly what she meant. He thought she meant that there was no limit to the number of nuts they could bust for twenty dollars. But Jazzy explained to him that she was referring to the cap being lifted on only twenty dudes being allowed to fuck.

Jazzy had promised her homeboy a ten percent cut of whatever she made, so he had a real incentive to help spread the word. And her homie did a damn good job because within a half an hour there was a line that started at Jazzy's and Cha Cha's room and snaked down the steps, through the living room of The Waverly, and out the front door. The line was easily thirty guys deep—most were young inexperienced thugs—and it seemed like it was growing.

Maya didn't want to get involved, but she stayed downstairs to help maintain order, so she could keep her word to Big Momma. Jazzy stayed just outside the door to their room, so she could collect the money from all of the guys and hold on to their cell phones while they fucked. And Cha Cha stayed inside their room to make sure that none of the dudes did anything too crazy.

It actually worked out well that Cha Cha stayed inside the room because all of the other girls in the group home automatically assumed that Jazzy and Maya were pimping Cha Cha and that she was the one inside their room getting a train ran on her.

Jazzy knew that Ashanti always bragged about how good her pussy was, so she charged a hundred dollars for whoever wanted to be the first person to fuck her. And within seconds Ashanti had dudes offering up the hundred dollars. She took the first offer from this dude named Courtney, who had just come home from jail a little less than two weeks earlier.

After Courtney and so many other dudes had so eagerly agreed to pony up the one hundred dollars, Jazzy started wondering if the twenty-dollar price tag was too low. But at that point there was nothing she could do because the word was already out that the price was twenty dollars.

Courtney fucked Ashanti, while Cha Cha looked on, happy as hell to see Ashanti's limp body getting used and abused. Courtney had turned Ashanti on her stomach and fucked her from the back.

Courtney had a jailhouse muscular body with the tattoos and all, and the gangster street look that Cha Cha loved. Cha Cha suddenly found herself getting turned on as she watched Ashanti get fucked, but she knew she had to stay focused.

Courtney was fucking Ashanti so hard, Cha Cha thought he was going to break the bed. But after about five minutes of pounding the shit out of Ashanti, Courtney pulled his condom-less dick out of her and sprayed come all over her ass and back.

"Damn! That shit was good!" Courtney said as he stood up, his body glistening with sweat, and his big dick swinging in the wind.

Cha Cha had to really try hard to stay focused because she had never been that close to muscle and dick and not have any of it. She got a wet towel and wiped the come off Ashanti, so that the next dude coming in to fuck wouldn't be turned off.

Right after Courtney got dressed and left, Jazzy sent in guy number two.

And that was the routine for the next four and a half hours straight. And when it was all said and done, Ashanti had unknowingly been fucked by fifty-five of the grimiest Brooklyn dudes imaginable.

The scene in Cha Cha's room looked like a gang-bang scene straight out of a porno movie. Some of the dudes used condoms, others didn't. Some busted inside of Ashanti's pussy, others pulled out and busted on her titties, her ass, and her face. Through it all, Ashanti was out like a light.

The only time Ashanti flinched was when a couple of the dudes fucked her in the asshole. But even that wasn't enough to wake her.

When all of the guys had left, Maya returned to their room and opened up all of the windows and sprayed Lysol nonstop, until she was certain that the entire room was disinfected from any kind of germs.

After Jazzy and Cha Cha put Ashanti's clothes back on her, they carried her back to her room and put her in her bed. Then they took a bottle of Hennessy and spilled a little of it on her bed sheets. Then they poured some of it in two cups and left the two cups on Ashanti's desk.

Jazzy then put some of the Hennessy in her hand and splashed it on Ashanti's mouth as Ashanti lay in her bed.

But to really make things convincing, Jazzy opened up her own mouth and stuck two fingers all the way to the back of her mouth and forced herself to vomit, depositing it on to Ashanti's bedroom floor. Then she and Cha Cha exited the room, making sure to leave the bottle of Hennessy behind.

When they made it back to their room, they laughed their asses off as Cha Cha, in great detail, told exactly how each dude fucked

Ashanti. For them, it wasn't really about the money. That was chump change. The humiliation is what they were after.

As they laughed, they rounded up all of the towels and bed sheets they had used and put them inside of a large black garbage bag that they were going to take miles away and put inside of a dumpster.

Jazzy and Cha Cha both felt an enormous sense of accomplishment. Maya didn't feel the same jubilation. She felt bad for Ashanti and wondered how she, Jazzy and Cha Cha had turned out to be so damn sheisty.

CHAPTER 23

Big Momma returned back from the casino at a quarter to six in the morning, her heart pounding from nervousness. She was praying that no one from the six to two shift had shown up for work early. Big Momma handed the cab driver seventy dollars, which was all the money she had left, and hustled out of the cab and into The Waverly.

She looked around on the first floor, and everything seemed fine. She put the lights and the security cameras back to their normal positions and settings, and then with heavy, laborious breathing, she went upstairs to make sure everything was good. After catching her breath, she sighed a huge sigh of relief after realizing the place hadn't been wrecked in her absence and there were no violent incidents.

Big Momma now had time to reflect on the seven hundred dollars she had blown at the casino. She was certain that the slot machines had been rigged. Had she been at Atlantic City, she would have won money. She vowed to never step foot inside any other casino that wasn't located in either Atlantic City or Las Vegas.

Although Big Momma had been gambling with the money she had stolen from the girls, she still thought seven hundred dollars was a big loss, and it made her feel depressed.

Usually, whenever Big Momma was feeling depressed, she would stuff her face with all kinds of junk food. She made her way to the kitchen to get some food, but before she could find anything worthwhile to eat, Nancy walked in.

"Oh my God!" Big Momma grabbed her heart. "You scared the shit outta me."

"I'm sorry." Nancy laughed.

"What are you doing in here so early?" Big Momma said to Nancy. "You don't come in until this afternoon. I was expecting to see Charlotte or Yvette."

"Oh well, you know Maya is leaving us next week. So a social worker is coming by this morning to talk to her, and I wanted to be here when she got here."

Big Momma nodded her head, but she didn't believe that was the only reason Nancy was there. She knew Nancy was there to snoop on her.

"So how did the night go?" Nancy asked.

"Everything was quiet." Big Momma's heart continued to pound, and her palms got sweaty.

Nancy didn't say anything, and her silence was torture to Big Momma.

"But I did allow the girls to have some company after curfew last night," Big Momma added.

"You did what?"

"I let the girls have company last night after curfew," Big Momma said in a matter-of- fact tone.

"Big Momma, are you crazy?"

"Nancy, it's Maya's last week, and they just wanted to have a little farewell get-together. And with all the shit these girls have to go through in their lives, letting them have a farewell get-together is the least we could do for them."

'Nancy frowned, shaking her head in disagreement. "Well, that's on you. As far as I'm concerned, we didn't even have this conversation."

Big Momma walked out of the kitchen and went into her office, where she had a stash of Nilla Wafers. She started eating and didn't stop until she had eaten the entire box.

Twenty minutes later, Big Momma was still in her office. She had no idea that Ashanti's mother had arrived to pick her up for her court date, and she didn't find out until Nancy came into her office and closed the door behind her.

"Big Momma, you know I don't even curse, but please tell me what the fuck were you thinking last night?" Nancy said.

"Nancy, calm down please. I mean, there wasn't no incidents, so what difference does it make?"

"No incidents? Well, then do you mind coming up to Ashanti's room and explaining to her mother why there is a open bottle of Hennessy in her daughter's room and vomit on her daughter's floor?"

"What?"

"You heard what I said. And guess who is having a hard time waking up for their court date?"

Big Momma got up from her desk and went upstairs to Ashanti's room. Thinking fast and hard for an excuse, she didn't know what to say. Big Momma walked into Ashanti's room and gasped at the sight.

"Ashanti, wake your ass up!" Ms. Daniels looked at Big Momma. "Were you on duty last night?"

"Yes, and I think I can explain this," Big Momma said, thinking quick on her feet, Nancy standing right behind her.

Nancy and Ms. Daniels both looked at Big Momma and waited for her to speak.

"This has to be a result of that basketball player she's been seeing. Usually only guys drink Hennessy, and she was with him yesterday, and he dropped her off. And now that I think about it she went straight to her room last night and didn't come out, not once. She was probably feeling sick from the liquor as soon as she walked in here." Big Momma's hands were trembling from the lies.

"What basketball player is this?" Ms. Daniels asked.

Both Big Momma and Nancy explained to Ms. Daniels who Bobby was and how he was projected to go straight from the high school to the NBA, and all of the girls were going crazy over him.

Ms. Daniels shook her head, looking at her daughter in disgust.

Nancy said, "I think she might have alcohol poisoning. We should probably call an ambulance."

"No. Nope. Hell no. Let that little heifer lay right there and suffer," Ms. Daniels said.

Nancy had the biggest heart in the world and it was eating her up inside to know that Ashanti's mother really could have cared less about her daughter at that moment.

"We're all women here, so I know you both smell what I smell," Ms. Daniels said.

Big Momma and Nancy didn't have any idea what Ms. Daniels was talking about because all they could smell was liquor and the slight stench from the vomit on the floor.

Ms. Daniels didn't wait for Big Momma or Nancy to reply. "That little bitch was too drunk to even take a shower after letting that nigga nut all up in her pussy."

Nancy was shocked by Ms. Daniels vulgarity, but Big Momma

didn't mind it because she knew Ms. Daniels wasn't going to try and hold her personally responsible for her daughter's condition.

"That's why these young girls don't need to be out here fuckin'. They don't even know simple shit like how to make a nigga use a condom." Ms. Daniels then started to repeatedly tap Ashanti on her cheeks, trying to wake her up.

"Ashanti, get up so we can get out of here and go deal with this case," Ms. Daniels said.

Big Momma and Nancy were still remaining silent.

"I can't believe that she done blacked out and got the nerve to have it smelling like a cheap bar up in here. Nancy and Big Momma, I am so sorry and so embarrassed. I mean—"

"No, no, Ms. Daniels, you don't have to apologize or explain anything," Big Momma said.

"Yes, I do, because I just want it known that I definitely raised my daughter better than this. I mean, I don't know what else to do with her. She just seems to keep getting worse."

"All you have to do is be there for her and make sure that she knows you love her," Nancy said.

Ms. Daniels gave Nancy a dirty look and shot back, "I am there for my daughter, and she knows that I love her. Thank you very much."

"Drinking and having sex is just Ashanti's cry for attention from you," Nancy replied.

"Oh, now who died and made you Dr. Phil?"

"Ms. Daniels, I'm just saying—"

"You just saying what?"

Big Momma was sitting back enjoying every minute of what was going on. At that moment Ashanti's body began to move a little bit while she was in the bed.

"Wake your ass up so we can go." Ms. Daniels slapped Ashanti on her ass as hard as she possibly could.

Nancy screamed, "Ms. Daniels, don't hit her like that!"

"Don't tell me how to raise my daughter!"

Nancy chuckled, sarcastically. "Apparently you need somebody to tell you."

"What? Bitch, I don't know who the hell you think you're talking to, but I'm not one of these little group home girls. I'm a grown-ass woman, and if you say some disrespectful shit like that again, I will knock you the fuck out!"

Nancy had a temper, but she didn't want to risk losing her job. So she just walked out of the room and went downstairs.

"Ms. Daniels, please try not to pay her any mind. And if it means anything, I think you're an excellent mother. I always tell Ashanti, if I had any daughters, I would want them to be just like her," Big Momma said, in her ass-kissing mode.

"Thank you." Ms. Daniels tried to calm down.

"Listen, if you want, I will be here after my shift ends, and I'll make sure that Ashanti is OK. This way you can meet up with her lawyer, and maybe he can speak on Ashanti's behalf and she may not even need to be there," Big Momma said.

Ms. Daniels thought to herself for a moment and realized that Big Momma's suggestion was actually a good one. "OK, I would appreciate that. But please tell Ashanti to call me as soon as she wakes up."

"I sure will."

As soon as Ms. Daniels left the room, Big Momma went to work and started to clean up the vomit. She got rid of the Hennessy by pouring it down the sink and throwing the bottle in the garbage.

While Big Momma was cleaning, Nancy came back up to Ashanti's room holding something in her hand.

"You wasn't even here last night, were you?" Nancy asked Big Momma.

"What are you talking about?" Big Momma asked, her faced frowned up.

"I'm talking about this Empire City Casino sweepstakes ticket that I see was validated at one in the morning and it was right next to an Empire City Casino cup of soda that has your lipstick on it."

Big Momma walked up to Nancy and snatched the ticket out of her hand. "You need to mind your fuckin' business," she said.

"And you need to do your damn job!"

"I was here all night. All you have to do is check the security cameras," Big Momma said, hoping that Nancy wouldn't call her bluff.

Nancy shook her head and looked at Big Momma. She rolled her eyes and walked out of Ashanti's room.

Big Momma wasn't too worried because she knew Nancy's bark was bigger than her bite. She also knew that Nancy wouldn't rat her out because the State could say enough is enough and then shut down The Waverly entirely, which of course would mean that she would be out of a job.

Big Momma's shift ended at seven that morning, but she didn't leave The Waverly until after four that afternoon. She had stayed that long because that was the time that Ashanti had awaken from her hibernation.

Ashanti woke up feeling extremely groggy and out of it. She had a pounding headache and couldn't remember anything from the night before.

"Girl, you better not *ever* get drunk like that again! You hear me?" Big Momma screamed on Ashanti.

"What are you talking about?" Ashanti asked, trying to sit up in her bed.

"I'm talking about, I don't want to be up in here cleaning up your vomit and pouring out your bottle of Hennessy while you're lying in your bed passed out drunk!"

"Oh my God! Are you serious?" Ashanti asked in a very low voice. Her eyes began to dart back and forth around the room. She felt odd and couldn't get a handle on her thoughts.

"Yes, I'm serious. And you missed your court date because we couldn't wake you up! Call your mother right now, because she was here and she wasn't too happy."

"Nooooo!" Ashanti howled. She held her face in both of her hands and slowly ran her hands down her face and exhaled.

Big Momma handed Ashanti the phone, so she could call her mom and find out what happened with her case. And while Ashanti feared what her mother would tell her, it wasn't her mother's words that concerned her the most. She was more concerned with what in the hell had happened to her the night before. Why was her asshole and her pussy hurting and feeling sore like she had just delivered a twelve-pound baby?

CHAPTER 24

Cha Cha couldn't wait for Ashanti's next date rape night. She and Jazzy were both pleased about the way things had turned out, and they were even more pleased when they found out that Ashanti couldn't bring herself to wake up for her court date. But what really took them over the top with laughter and the sense of accomplishment was seeing Ashanti walking gingerly around The Waverly and wincing in obvious pain from her sore ass and sore pussy.

Ashanti's last memory prior to being drugged and raped was spending time talking to Maya, so of course when she saw Maya, she stopped her and asked her about the previous night.

Maya laughed as she told Ashanti, "Yo, word up, you were talking so reckless! You were talking mad shit about how good your pussy is and how much Bobby likes fuckin' you. And you were talking about how you had whupped Cha Cha's ass. All kind of random shit was coming out of your mouth nonstop."

"Are you serious?" Ashanti asked in both horror and disbelief.

"Dead-ass."

"That is so weird because I don't remember any of that."

"Of course, you don't. Your ass was so tore up from the floor up."
Maya laughed again.

"What do you mean?"

"What I mean is, you were drunk as a skunk!"

"This is really scary because I don't even remember having a drink.
Man, I swear I am gonna fuck Bobby up when I see him! I know he got
me drunk to the point where I blacked out, and then he fucked me on
some freaky shit. I'll be the first one to tell you that I loves me some
dick, but I don't like a nigga taking advantage. You feel me?"

Maya nodded.

"And I've been blowing up Bobby's phone since like six o'clock
tonight, and of course, his punk ass ain't picking up."

Maya didn't respond to Ashanti's last comment and told her she
had to leave and that she would see her later. Maya really did have
to go because it was getting late. Jazzy had been telling her that she
wanted to talk with her and Cha Cha, so she could tell them her new
master plan.

As soon as Maya walked into their room, Jazzy handed her three
hundred dollars. "That's your cut from last night," Jazzy said.

Maya counted it and smiled.

"We made eleven hundred, but Big Momma was riding my ass
because Nancy was riding her ass. So I gave her two hundred dollars
today just to shut her ass up," Jazzy explained.

Maya nodded her head. She wanted to say something sarcastic
about Big Momma, but she held her tongue. If everything went
according to plan, she would soon be living with Big Momma, and she
didn't want to come across as a hypocrite later on.

"The money from last night was good money, but obviously we
can't drug Ashanti every night and expect to eat off of that. So I was

thinking that we might as well look at this as a one-time hit," Jazzy said.

"Not really," Cha Cha chimed in and said. "We just couldn't do something like that every night, and we probably wouldn't be able to do it here at The Waverly. But if we got creative and had a party somewhere at somebody's house or at a hotel or something like that, all we would have to do is invite Ashanti, and we would be good money."

Jazzy shook her head no and smiled. "Believe me, I can't stand Ashanti, so I'm with you on the way you're thinking. But we have to think about things strictly from a money standpoint. That's what I've been doing for a while now. I have a new master plan to tell both of y'all about."

Maya and Cha Cha looked at Jazzy and nodded their heads, giving Jazzy the permission to go ahead and tell them her new master plan.

Jazzy got up and went to her closet and took two pieces of paper from the pants pocket of her jeans. Both pieces of paper were about half the size of regular loose leaf sheet of paper, and both sheets of paper had writing on it that said the same thing.

Maya and Cha Cha read the handwritten note. Cha Cha smiled after reading it, but Maya didn't.

The note read:

Don't Panic. Remain calm and you will not get hurt.

I have a gun pointed right at you.

Give me all of the money that you have.

"Don't tell me you're not with it, Maya," Jazzy said in response to Maya's lack of enthusiasm.

Maya didn't say anything.

"This is how we're gonna get paid the quickest."

Maya said, "But there's a lot of things you probably didn't even think about that could go wrong."

"Exactly! And that's why the three of us are here right now. So we can talk this thing through. Ain't none of us ever robbed a bank before, and you're the one who works in a bank, so you know the ropes."

Jazzy's master plan was to go to the bank branch that Maya worked at and hand Maya a note demanding money. Maya would load a bag with money and hand it to Jazzy, who would walk out of the bank with the loot. Jazzy thought it would be easier than taking candy from a baby.

"We could pull this off," Maya said. "But FBI and bank investigators will ride my ass until they catch us. They know that the majority of bank robberies are usually due to inside jobs."

"And if they ride your ass, all you gotta do is deny shit," Jazzy said.

Maya was still hesitant.

"Maya, listen, cops and the feds aren't gods. The only way they catch muthafuckas is because people got big mouths. I ain't saying shit, and Cha Cha wouldn't say shit, so how the hell could you get caught?"

"How much do you think you're going to get?" Maya asked.

"As much as we possibly can," Jazzy replied.

"Well, I'm saying, sometimes I'll only have ten grand in my drawer at my station, so it's not like we're gonna walk away with six figures."

"Cha Cha, would you be mad if we walked away with *only* ten grand?" Jazzy asked.

"Hell no, I wouldn't be mad! Sheeiiit! That's all the money we would need to get up outta here, and it would put us back to even."

"Yeah, and it could also put our asses in a federal penitentiary."

"Maya, what the fuck!" Jazzy screamed. "You was fronting on the GHB shit with Ashanti, and now you fronting on this too?"

"I'm not fronting. I just don't want y'all to think it's as easy as it looks on TV."

"OK, I get that. But just tell me what it is I don't know," Jazzy said in frustration.

"There's something called dye packs. So if you come pass me the note, they train us not to panic and to place the money in a bag for you. But we're supposed to also place a dye pack inside of the bag of money. And what will happen is, the dye pack will eventually explode, and there will be this red dye all over the money, and we wouldn't be able to use it anywhere because nobody is going to take money that looks like it was dipped in red paint. That would make the whole robbery a big waste of time."

Jazzy thought to herself for a moment. She took the note from Maya, got a pen, and added the words: *NO DYE PACKS!!!* She handed the note back to Maya.

"I'll add that to the note, and the problem is solved. What's the next hurdle?"

Maya sighed and informed Jazzy that she was trained to activate the silent alarm with her foot, and that once she activated it, a cop could be on the scene within two minutes.

Jazzy nodded her head and looked at her watch, keeping silent. Her silence lasted for two whole minutes. She broke the silence to make her point.

"You see how long that was?" Jazzy said. "That was two minutes right there. That's nothing to overcome, because it will take all of thirty seconds for you to load the bag with the money, and it will take me at most, sixty seconds to walk out of the bank and to get in the stolen car that Cha Cha will be waiting outside in, and we'll be up outta there within two minutes."

Maya nodded her head in agreement to show Jazzy and Cha Cha that she wasn't resisting the plan.

"What else?" Jazzy asked.

Maya thought long and hard, careful not to come across as a coward.

"Well, the other big obstacle is the bulletproof glass partition that the banks put between the teller and the customers. It's impossible to get a bag of money underneath the partition, but that's not a problem because they moved me out to Great Neck, Long Island, and they don't have any partitions out there."

"Exactly!" Jazzy smiled. "See, you think I don't pay attention, but I remember you telling us about that when they first transferred you out to Long Island. And, believe it or not, but that's when the idea really jumped off in my mind."

Maya told them that it could work, but she felt that they should first do a dry run before they did the actual robbery. The dry run was going to let them know if the disguises that Jazzy and Cha Cha were going to wear were going to be effective enough, and would also give Cha Cha a chance to learn the getaway routes, and Jazzy could time exactly how long it would take for her to walk from the teller and out of the bank to the getaway car.

"A'ight, cool. So we'll do the dry run on Thursday," Jazzy said. "I'll come inside the bank and act like I need two rolls of quarters. And from the time I hand you twenty dollars for the quarters, that's when I'll start timing everything to make sure we stay under the two-minute mark."

Maya had a lot of reservations about the scheme, but she didn't say anything in opposition to it.

"So then Monday will be the real deal," Jazzy said to both of them.

"Monday it's on and poppin'," Cha Cha said with a smile.

Jazzy rubbed her hands together like she was about to sit down at a dinner table and indulge in a tasty meal. All three girls gave each other a pound, and Jazzy ended the meeting with a smile.

CHAPTER 25

"Babe, I was out of the country playing in tournaments," Bobby tried to explain to a very angry Ashanti. "And my phone doesn't work outside of the United States. That's the only reason I didn't call."

Ashanti screamed into the phone, "Muthafucka, I don't give a fuck! You still need to explain to me why the fuck did you get me so drunk to the point where I passed out."

Bobby took his phone away from his ear, held it out, and looked at it to make sure it was Ashanti he was talking to. "Ashanti, you are really buggin' right now because, on the real, I have no idea what the hell you are even talking about."

"Urrgggghhh! Yo, I swear you make me so fuckin' sick!" Ashanti screamed.

On the other end of the phone, Bobby was silent, not knowing what to say. He was starting to wonder if Ashanti was bipolar or had some other kind of mental illness.

Ashanti walked out of her room and went into the hallway. She walked into the bathroom and made sure that she was the only one inside. While still on the phone, she reached her hand inside of her shorts and started to scratch her crotch area. She then spoke into the phone in a low and angry whisper.

"And, muthafucka, I'm telling you right now. When I see you, it is on, and I'm whupping your ass. You fucked around and gave me the crabs, you dirty-ass, grimy-ass son of a bitch!"

"What?"

"You heard what the fuck I said."

"Ashanti, now you are really talking like you lost your goddamn mind."

"I'm gonna lose my foot in your goddamn ass! That's what I know!" Ashanti replied.

"So this is what all this crazy talk is about." Bobby chuckled into the phone. "I see what the hell is going on now. You was out there whoring around and you messed around and caught the crabs, and now you putting on this big song and dance to make it seem like this is all on me!"

"This is all on you! You're the only one that I've been fuckin'!" Ashanti screamed loud enough for everyone inside The Waverly to hear.

"Well, then you explain to me how is that you have the crabs and I don't!"

"Bobby, you are so full of shit! I swear that you are. And how convenient it was for you to just up and disappear on me, and now you tell me some bullshit about your phone not working overseas. Nigga, you disappeared because you was getting treated for the crabs!"

Bobby sighed into the phone and then he chuckled to himself again. "And you know what's crazy?" he said to Ashanti. "I was really, *really* starting to feel you and really starting to feel this whole relationship thing, and I was thinking how I didn't need all the groupie love and attention I was getting because I had you."

Ashanti was annoyed as she listened to Bobby. She started scratching her pussy area because the itching was so intense.

"No, muthafucka! What's *really* crazy is your ass had too much damn *groupie love* and you caught the crabs from one of your groupies and passed that shit on to me!"

At that point Bobby was mentally exhausted and felt like he had nothing else to say to Ashanti and her psycho ass. "Ashanti, I'm hanging up."

"If you hang up this phone, you better fuckin' lose my number," Ashanti yelled into the phone, totally not caring that she was throwing away a potential NBA lottery ticket by essentially kicking Bobby to the curb and telling him to get lost.

Bobby was starting to really feel Ashanti, but he had way too much going on for himself to stress over one chick, regardless of how bad she was or how good her pussy was. He knew there would be thousands of other chicks who looked better than Ashanti, who had better pussy than Ashanti, and who would be willing to drop their panties quicker than Ashanti, but wouldn't be nearly as crazy and ghetto as her.

"See, this is what the fuck I get for fuckin' with a group home bitch!" Bobby said, and then he hung up the phone on Ashanti.

"Fuck you, Bobby!" Ashanti screamed into the phone. She wanted to get in the last word in, but Bobby had already beat her to the punch.

Ashanti began scratching her pussy again. It seemed to her like the itching would never end. She left the bathroom and went back to her room to get a towel, so she could take a shower to try and provide her with some temporary relief from the itching.

As soon as she walked out of the bathroom, she bumped into Cha Cha, who saw Ashanti scratching her crotch as if she was looking for gold.

Ashanti didn't care that Cha Cha saw her scratching. She wasn't in the mood for no rah-rah bullshit with Cha Cha, so she quickly walked right past her without even acknowledging her.

Cha Cha had seen the way Ashanti was scratching her pussy and couldn't help but laugh at her. She knew right away that Ashanti had probably contracted some kind of STD on the GHB night.

Cha Cha turned and called out, "Ashanti."

"Not now, Cha Cha. I don't have time for games." Ashanti kept walking to her room.

Cha Cha was genuinely going to offer whatever help she could to Ashanti, but since Ashanti brushed her off, she didn't press the issue. She went to her own room and got ready for bed, since she was tired and it was already late on a Sunday night and there really wasn't much else to do.

Jazzy and Maya were downstairs in the living room hanging out with the rest of The Waverly girls watching TV. Cha Cha thought about going downstairs and telling Jazzy and Maya about Ashanti's scratching episode, but she decided against it.

Cha Cha wanted to stay focused, and she also wanted Jazzy and Maya to stay focused. In less than twenty-four hours the three of them were going to attempt to pull off the bank robbery, and they couldn't afford for anything to go wrong.

Tomorrow it's on! Cha Cha thought after she changed into her night clothes and lay in the bed. She was just hoping that everything would go off as smoothly for them as the dry run had gone.

CHAPTER 26

The next morning Maya woke up, and Jazzy and Cha Cha were sound asleep. Maya was thinking about calling in sick and not going through with the bank robbery. She just didn't have a good feeling about it and wanted to back out and tell the girls that she didn't need to do it because Big Momma had offered up her apartment to her.

Although she didn't want Jazzy and Cha Cha to be walking around thinking that she was the one who set their room up to be burglarized, she felt in her heart that it was just smarter to lose their friendship than do fifteen years in jail for some bank robbery.

"Why you up so early? I told you Cha Cha would drive you out there," Jazzy said in a groggy voice from underneath her bed sheets, startling Maya.

"You scared the shit out of me. I thought you were still asleep," Maya said to Jazzy, avoiding her question.

"Nah, I was up. I was just laying here thinking and going over everything in my head."

Maya didn't say anything as she continued to get dressed for work.

Jazzy sat up in her bed. "Are you going to ride out to Long Island with us in the stolen car?"

"I'm going take the iron horse," Maya said, thinking quick on her feet. "Whether something goes wrong or not, they are going to question me and want to know every little detail about my day and my typical routine. So if I always take the railroad to work and then out of all days, the day that the bank gets robbed, I don't take the train, they may know something is up."

"Riiiiight," Jazzy replied with a smile. "You're thinking. I like that."

Jazzy called out Cha Cha's name to wake her up to get ready. Cha Cha had already stolen the car they were going to use and had it hidden on a residential block in their Bed-Stuy neighborhood.

"OK, so I'm leaving," Maya said to Jazzy.

Maya looked every bit like a professional woman with her dark blue dress slacks on and her light blue Chase Bank button-up, short-sleeve shirt.

"Keep thinking things through. And if there is anything we missed and you feel it might trip us up, just hand me back the note when I slide it to you, and I'll know what's up and walk right back out the bank."

Maya was glad that Jazzy had just given her an out. "Everything will be fine. Don't worry."

Maya was hoping that the armed security guard was going to be working that day and not the regular toy cop security guard who only had a nightstick and handcuffs. If the armed security guard was there, she wasn't going to go through with it.

An hour and a half later when Maya got to work, she realized that the toy cop man from Nigeria was on duty, so she wouldn't be able to use the "armed guard" excuse. So at that point she just blocked everything out of her mind and decided to focus on her job and being friendly to her co-workers and to the customers. The last thing she wanted was to come across as if she was on edge about something.

Maya had fifteen minutes before her ten-to-six shift started, so she went inside the break room and had a free donut and some coffee. She struck up a conversation with one of the other tellers, asking her how her weekend was.

"Oh, we took the kids to our weekend home up in the Poconos," the middle-aged white lady said, a smudge of red lipstick stuck to her top row of teeth. "They really love it up there. And what about you? How was your weekend?"

Maya knew there was nothing she could say that the white lady would have been able to relate to, so she just played it off and said the first thing that came to her mind.

"Oh, my weekend wasn't nearly as exciting as you and your family's weekend. I just basically lounged around and relaxed all weekend and watched movies."

The white coworker seemed as if she was about to really engage Maya in a conversation, which was something Maya didn't want any parts of. Maya abruptly told her that she had to get to her teller station because she wanted to make sure that she didn't have any problems logging on to her computer.

When Maya got to her station, she sat there and realized that, including the customers and the employees, she was the only black face in the entire bank. Jazzy and her ghetto ass was going to stick out like a sore thumb. At that point she figured that there was nothing she could do about anything. She was just going to suck it up and go through with it.

Maya opened up her teller station and began servicing customers. Seeing it was a Monday morning, the bank was more crowded than usual. Maya didn't mind the bank being crowded because it made her day go faster.

Before Maya knew it, it was close to eleven thirty, and Jazzy walked into the bank. The only reason she recognized Jazzy was because she knew what Jazzy looked like and because she was expecting her to show up. But Maya was surprisingly shocked by how good Jazzy's disguise was. Jazzy had black hair, but she had on a brown wig with long, straight hair that came down to her shoulders and designer sunglasses, which did a really good job of shielding her face, which was made up with MAC makeup, making her look like a super model. Jazzy also had on a pencil lined skirt with matching high heels and a real nice designer blouse, an outfit that Maya had never seen her in before.

Jazzy acted as if she was filling out a withdrawal slip, but she was really trying to time it so that the line could clear up and she could go directly to Maya to be serviced. But people kept coming inside the bank, so Jazzy got on line and waited patiently.

Fortunately, the bank-robbing gods were on Jazzy's side, and by the time she got to the front of the line, Maya had no customers and called Jazzy over.

"Welcome to Chase." Maya smiled. "How may I help you today?"

Jazzy returned Maya's smile with a smile of her own, and she didn't look nervous at all, her bright red lipstick glistening from the sunlight that graced the bank.

"Oh, I would just like to make a withdrawal." Jazzy placed her large designer handbag on the counter and kept her right hand inside it. With her left hand, she slid Maya the note, along with a withdrawal slip, all the while keeping a smile on her face.

"A withdrawal?" Maya asked prior to reading the note. "I will be glad to help you with that today." Maya then looked down at the note and tried to act a little startled by quickly popping her head up and looking at Jazzy.

"I would like all large bills, and can you can give me back the note and the withdrawal slip," Jazzy said to Maya, talking loud enough only for her to hear. Jazzy made sure that she continued to look pleasant.

Maya reached down to her money stand, which was loaded with stacks of money in thousand-dollar increments. She grabbed stacks of hundred, fifties, and twenties and placed them on the counter. And Jazzy quickly scooped up the stacks with her left hand and put them inside her bag.

Meanwhile Maya had activated the silent alarm after she had handed Jazzy the third set of money stacks.

After Jazzy bagged the seventh set of money stacks, she said, "I think that will be all for today. Thank you, sweetie, so much for your help. It's been a pleasure."

Jazzy then turned and walked out of the bank quickly, her heels click-clacking very loud on the floor and the sound echoing throughout the bank. Jazzy heart was pounding a mile a minute as it had been from the time she'd walked into the bank. At that point she was desperately wishing that she had worn sneakers instead of the pumps she had on.

Jazzy thought to herself, *Hurry up, Jazzy. You only have about thirty seconds.* For some reason, Jazzy's walk to the exit of the bank seemed to take much longer than her walk inside had taken her when she'd first arrived. The suspense was killing Jazzy, and she couldn't wait to see the sunlight hitting the sidewalk.

"Excuse me, miss," a tall white man in suit asked Jazzy. "May I have a word with you?"

Jazzy had no idea that the white man was just a bank employee whose job was to solicit customers and try to offer them low interest rate loans before they exited the bank.

Jazzy was certain that the white man had realized that the alarm had been triggered and was on to their robbery scheme. So with all of the energy and might that she could muster up, she pushed the white man in his chest as hard as she could and started running to the exit.

"Ahhhh!" the man screamed. He stumbled backwards, tripped over a small trash can, and fell on his ass. He ended up banging the back of his head on the tiled bank floor, and all of his colored low interest rate loan brochures went flying in the air.

The predominantly rich white Jewish customers in the immediate vicinity, all gasped and looked on in horror at what they thought was a fight.

"Help me! He's trying to rob me!" Jazzy screamed to the six-foot five, blue-black, baboon-looking African security guard, hoping to distract him for a split second, and it worked.

Jazzy felt like she was going to faint from fear. When she made it to the sidewalk, she realized Cha Cha wasn't where she was supposed to be.

"What the fuck?" Jazzy really started to panic. She looked around and finally saw Cha Cha making a U-turn and heading back toward the direction of the bank but on the opposite side of the street.

Jazzy darted into the street with her high heels, and she almost slipped and fell. Cars blew their horns at her and swerved to avoid hitting her. One man rolled down his window and cursed at Jazzy.

"Get in! Get in! Get in!" Cha Cha yelled to Jazzy.

Jazzy ran around the front of the car, ripped open the front passenger's door, and jumped in. Before Jazzy could even close the car door, Cha Cha had sped off.

"Yo, I'm so sorry! But there was a cop who had made me move when I was parked in front of the bank, and I didn't want to argue with him and then have him see you running out of the bank."

Jazzy was trying to catch her breath and talk at the same time. She explained to Cha Cha that everything went smoothly, until right at the end when she had to push the tall white man to the floor.

As the girls were just about to get on to the Long Island Expressway, they could hear police sirens coming from what sounded like all directions.

"Yo, we hot as hell. Let's not get on no highways, no expressways, or anything like that. Let's just find a mall parking lot or something and pull into it, and we'll sit and wait until rush hour before heading back to Brooklyn."

Cha Cha took Jazzy's advice and maneuvered through the back streets of Great Neck, Long Island, with its pristine million-dollar homes. It took them about five minutes before they found themselves on busy Northern Boulevard, where they spotted a Pathmark supermarket and pulled into the parking lot.

"Holy shit!" Jazzy screamed. She was finally able to exhale and fully let out all of the nervous energy pent up inside of her. "When I tell you, I was shitting bricks! Yo, I ain't never lied. I thought my heart was about to jump through my chest or something."

She then reclined her seat and turned up the air conditioning in the car. Then she reached inside her handbag and started to take out the stacks of money.

"Cha Cha, can you believe this?" Jazzy asked as they both looked at the perfect crisp bills. "A few stressful hiccups at the end, but this bread definitely makes all the stress worth it!"

Cha Cha and Jazzy didn't even have to count out all the money because it was still in denominated money bands. They couldn't believe they were sitting with fourteen thousand dollars of stolen money. Although they couldn't really believe their eyes, they knew the money was as real as it gets.

As they sat and waited for the five o'clock rush-hour traffic, they couldn't help but wonder how things had turned out on Maya's end, and how things would ultimately turn out for the three of them in general.

CHAPTER 27

By the time Maya made it back to the group home, it was close to ten o'clock at night. Jazzy and Cha Cha had been worried about her, but they didn't want to take any chances and call her. Jazzy and Cha Cha had been sitting outside on the front steps of The Waverly when they saw Maya walk through the gate. They both ran over to her and hugged her.

"Oh my God!" Jazzy said. "What happened to you? We didn't know what to think."

"Yo, shit was crazy! It was like less than a minute after you got out of the bank, it was flooded with police. At first I just knew they had caught y'all and we were all about to go to jail." Maya laughed.

Jazzy then told her, "Maya, word up, son. I was seconds from shitting on myself. I come outside the bank, and Cha Cha wasn't nowhere to be found! I was like, what the fuck? I'm holding all this stolen cash. I was panicking my ass off. And you say you thought we were going to jail? At that moment I *knew* that my black ass was going to jail." Jazzy burst out laughing.

"But then I showed up on some Batman and Robin shit, and Jazzy got in the whip, and we pulled off. And since we figured the highways and expressways would be hot with cops, we decided to just go to a mall parking lot so Jazzy could take off her disguise and then chill until rush hour, so we wouldn't get knocked on a humble."

"That's the best thing y'all could have done because they had helicopters, bloodhounds, and the whole nine."

"Bloodhounds?" Jazzy asked, a huge smile on her face.

"Muthafuckin' bloodhounds trying to track down your scent. It was so wild; they shut down the bank for the rest of the day. All the news stations were there, the feds were there and all that."

Jazzy was getting ready to ask something, but Maya cut her off and started laughing out loud.

"Jazzy, why the hell you knock Mr. Anderson on his ass like that? He is the nicest man in the world. He had the biggest speed knot on his head from hitting the ground."

Jazzy started laughing. "I didn't know who he was, so I just reacted as if he was a cop trying to arrest me."

"All he does is push loans on people. And your ass just knocked him to the ground and sent his papers flying in the air." Maya continued to laugh.

"Yo, but the funny shit was when I was yelling, 'He's trying to rob me!'"

Cha Cha, Maya, and Jazzy all laughed at what had gone down. They knew they were fortunate that they hadn't been caught.

Jazzy said, "So we came off with—"

"Fourteen grand!" Maya said, sounding very excited.

"Exactly! How did you know?"

"They had to count my drawer, so the bank could have an accurate amount of how much they lost."

"Oh, OK," Jazzy said. "So, me and Cha Cha were saying, what we should do is split the money three ways of course, but after we split it, each of us should be responsible for hiding their money on their own. This way we can avoid having all of our money in the same spot and then getting robbed like we did last time."

"I agree," Maya replied. "And you know once these bitches up in here see that it was my bank branch that got robbed, they're gonna start putting two and two together and figuring that we came off with the loot from that robbery."

The girls were lucky because, up to that point, no one in The Waverly had watched the news or even heard about the robbery.

Maya sighed. She told Jazzy and Cha Cha that this federal agent had questioned her for two hours straight, and when she thought he was done, he came back to her an hour later and questioned her again.

"He was trying to see if your story changed anywhere along the lines," Cha Cha stated.

"I know exactly what he was doing, but the muthafucka was annoying. And he really was pissing me off with his stank hot-ass breath."

"So from the questions he was asking you, what do you think? Do you think we should be worried?" Cha Cha asked.

Maya shook her head. "I don't think so. I think the fact that I pushed the alarm while you were still in the bank may have saved my ass. I mean, as long as we hide the money real well, then we should be good. We just have to wait a couple of weeks before we start spending the cash."

Jazzy and Cha Cha both agreed with Maya.

"Oh, yeah, the thing that really had him riding my ass was the fact that I didn't have a copy of the note you had passed to me. He was trying to make it seem like I just handed you the money and I wasn't really robbed."

"Fuck him!" Jazzy said, "Tell his ass to go play back the videotape if he doesn't believe you."

"I don't have to tell him that because they already played that tape backward and forward about a hundred times, trying their best to get a clearer shot of your face."

Jazzy explained, "We never discussed fingerprints. So on the ride over it dawned on me that all our prints were all over that note. That's why I stressed to you that I wanted both papers back. I knew you would peep why."

"It's all good. I mean, I figured that's why you had taken it. But they can question me all they want to because they ain't never getting anything outta me."

The three of them continued to talk about all of the aspects of the robbery, and before they knew it, it was past their curfew. So they went inside their room, and they continued to talk amongst each other until the wee hours of the morning.

One thing that became evident as they spoke was all three of them decided that since they had more than enough money to float them, they figured that it only made sense for them to take a break from their hustling ways for a while. They realized they'd been pressing their luck and didn't want to get greedy and end up in jail.

They also agreed that they were going to seriously start looking for their three-bedroom apartment that upcoming Monday. They were more than ready to kiss The Waverly goodbye.

CHAPTER 28

Maya was off from work, so she planned on sleeping until at least noon. It was only ten in the morning, and she, Cha Cha, and Jazzy were sound asleep in their room when Big Momma came at their door with a thunderous knock.

"Maya, get up!" Big Momma yelled through the locked door. "There's somebody here to see you."

When Big Momma got no answers from the girls, she used her master key and let herself into their room.

Maya opened her eyes as she continued to lie in the bed. The first thing that came to her mind was, *Why in the world is Big Momma wearing leggings, showing all of her cottage cheese rolls of cellulite?*

"Maya, you didn't hear me knocking? I said someone is here to see you."

"I heard you, but I just woke up. Who is it? Is it someone from the state?" Maya thought a social worker had brought her discharge papers.

"No, it's some white federal agent dude."

Maya's heart immediately started beating. She sat up in her bed wondering, had the cops somehow caught her in a lie. Did any kind of fingerprints come back that linked Jazzy to the bank robbery? She didn't know what to think.

"OK, tell him I'll be right there." Maya nervously got up and put on her robe and slippers.

Big Momma shook her head, wondering what Maya had gotten herself into, as she walked out of the room. What bothered Big Momma the most was, she knew in her heart that Maya must have gotten some illegal money from some new scheme and didn't kick any of the money back to her. Big Momma knew that had to be why a federal agent was knocking at her door so early in the morning.

Big Momma smiled and said to the FBI agent, "She'll be right down."

The nerve of that selfish-ass bitch! Big Momma thought to herself. After offering to let Maya stay with her in her apartment rent-free, the least Maya could've done was hit her off with a little something.

"If you don't mind me asking, but can you tell me what's going on?" Big Momma said to the agent.

The agent looked to be about fifty-five years old. He was tall and slim with salt and pepper hair and he had on a nice suit. Big Momma could tell he was a seasoned veteran.

"Well, yes, I'm sure you've heard about the bank robbery that took place yesterday out on Long Island. Well, Maya was working at the time of the robbery, and I just want to ask her some questions," he said.

Big Momma nodded her head, her blood pressure instantly shooting up from anger and resentment.

"Here you go, ma'am." The agent handed Big Momma his card. "I'm agent Scarpetta."

"Oh, thank you," Big Momma replied. "I'll enter your name and contact information into our logbook."

Big Momma walked a few feet to her office and she put agent Scarpetta's card on her desk, but she didn't bother to log anything. Her only thoughts were on trying to figure out how she could get the girls away from The Waverly for a few hours so she could search their room for the stolen money. She was convinced that the girls were involved in the robbery that took place simply because Maya hadn't mentioned anything to her about her bank branch being robbed.

Just then Maya came down the steps in her black terrycloth robe and her black house slippers.

"Hello, Maya," Agent Scarpetta said.

"Good morning," Maya responded, no enthusiasm at all. She couldn't believe that Agent Scarpetta was there to see her so early in the morning after he had interviewed and questioned her for hours the previous day.

"Do you have some place that we can talk?" Agent Scarpetta asked Maya.

"We can talk right here," Maya responded with an attitude.

Mr. Scarpetta nodded his head, and then he asked Maya to go over the events of the bank robbery one more time.

"You know, not for nothing but this is the third time you have me telling this same story, and it's really getting annoying. This is like harassment or something. I mean, is everybody in the bank getting questioned like this, or am I just special because I'm the only black person working in that branch?"

"Maya, this has nothing at all to do with you being black. The only reason I am here is because over the years I've found that right after a crime, a person's adrenaline is flowing and they could be in shock or feeling spooked from the crime and their emotions can affect their ability to remember certain details. So usually after a day or so I've seen situations where people remember things they didn't remember the day before."

Maya looked at him and rolled her eyes.

"Well, guess what? There ain't anything new that popped into my head."

Agent Scarpetta looked at her and nodded his head. He was more convinced at that point that Maya had something to do with the robbery than he was the previous day.

"OK," Agent Scarpetta said to Maya, "I understand how you feel and what you're going through. And you have my card, so if there is anything at all that comes to your mind that you think I might need to know, call me right away."

"Can I go back to sleep now?"

Agent Scarpetta looked at her with some disbelief, and then he looked at his wrist watch. He didn't say anything in response, so Maya walked off and went back upstairs to her room.

The agent walked over to Big Momma's office and asked her how many girls stayed at the group home. He had seen about three girls sitting around when he'd first arrived and was wondering how many in total stayed there.

"Well, we have eight girls who are here on what we call a permanent basis, and we have four who are here on a temporary basis," Big Momma explained.

"And what about Maya? Is she permanent or temporary?"

"Oh, Maya is permanent. But she turned eighteen years old, and at eighteen you age out of the system. So any day now she will be forced to leave here."

The agent nodded his head. He knew right then and there that he had just uncovered a motive for Maya to take part in the robbery.

"Let me ask you, if you don't mind. How does Maya get along with everyone? How is she with the staff and with the other young ladies who live here?"

"Maya isn't a problem at all. I mean, relatively speaking, of course," Big Momma replied, trying to sound educated and articulate.

"Who is she close to? And is there anyone here that you would say she doesn't get along with?"

"Well, she is close with her two roommates, Jazzy and Cha Cha. And as far as who she doesn't get along with"—Big Momma paused and thought for a moment—"other than a young lady named Ashanti, Maya gets along pretty well with everybody. And even with Ashanti, it's almost a situation of, who gets along with Ashanti, if you understand what I mean?"

"I do understand." He stood in contemplation. "Would it be OK to speak to a couple of the girls for five minutes or so?"

"Sure. Not a problem."

"Is Ashanti around?" Agent Scarpetta asked.

Big Momma nodded her head. "I'll go and get her for you."

As Big Momma went off to go get Ashanti, Maya had already awaken Jazzy and Cha Cha and told them that the FBI agent was snooping around at The Waverly.

"What did you tell him?" Jazzy asked.

"I didn't tell him shit, other than I was tired of him thinking I had something to do with the robbery just because I'm black."

"You didn't say that," Cha Cha said with a chuckle.

"I swear on everything that I did."

The girls thought to themselves for a moment and figured that

Agent Scarpetta was going to come and talk to Jazzy and Cha Cha as well. Jazzy and Cha Cha weren't too concerned though, because they had already rehearsed what they were going to say. They were at The Waverly all day yesterday. They figured that, if it came down to it and if their alibi came into question, Big Momma would back them up.

"Well, I'm gonna go downstairs and get something to eat," Jazzy said. "I don't think we should all just be holed up in our room. If the agent is snooping around, then we want to make sure to come across as normal as possible."

Jazzy threw on some clothes and went downstairs and made her way into the dining room. She popped a blueberry muffin into her mouth and then poured herself a bowl of Rice Crispies cereal that she drowned in sugar before adding some milk to the bowl.

Two other girls were in the dining room at the time, but Jazzy didn't hang around to chit-chat. Instead she went into the living room with her cereal, and she sat down and started watching TV. She saw the white FBI agent standing off to the side of the living room but paid him no mind.

"Hey, good morning, Big Momma," Jazzy said.

Big Momma acknowledged Jazzy, but she was more concerned with introducing Ashanti to Agent Scarpetta.

Ashanti initially had a standoffish attitude toward Agent Scarpetta because she didn't know why he was there or what he wanted with her. But after about two minutes or so, Jazzy saw Ashanti and the FBI agent go inside Big Momma's office, while Big Momma stayed in the living room.

Jazzy walked over to Big Momma. "What's that about?" she asked.

Big Momma replied, "You tell me."

Jazzy immediately detected some stankness in Big Momma's tone. "Tell you what?" Jazzy asked.

Big Momma cut her eyes and stared at Jazzy. "Nothing, Jazzy. I got work to do." Big Momma pushed past Jazzy and walked toward the rear of the building toward a room that contained office supplies.

Jazzy couldn't make heads or tails of Big Momma's mood. She tried to block out Big Momma, and as she ate her cereal, she slowly crept close to Big Momma's office. Big Momma's office door was open, and Jazzy tried her best to eavesdrop on the conversation between the agent and Ashanti.

"Oh, your mother works in the 103rd Precinct?" the agent said to Ashanti. "Years ago, in the early eighties, I started out with the NYPD as a clerk, and that was the precinct that they had me in. But then I took the test to become an FBI agent, and here I am."

"Which one do you like better?" Ashanti asked.

Ashanti was clearly feeling comfortable with the agent, which made Jazzy want to vomit as she listened to the agent tell Ashanti why he liked being an FBI agent better than working for the NYPD.

"So you said that it's Jazzy and Cha Cha who are the closest with Maya?"

"You ever heard the term *virgin-tight*?" Ashanti asked.

The agent was caught off guard by Ashanti's question. He'd turned red before responding. "I hadn't heard that term in a while, but I'm familiar with it."

"Well, put it like this—They are tighter than a nun's pussy."

Jazzy wanted to wring Ashanti's neck.

The agent noticed that Ashanti kept scratching her crotch area and asked her if everything was alright.

"Yeah, I'm OK. Just these fuckin' bed bugs up in here," Ashanti said, embarrassed.

"Well, here's my card. Tuck it away somewhere because you never know when you might need it. And if you ever feel you need me for anything, don't hesitate to call me."

Jazzy walked past Big Momma's office to make her way back to the dining room. She turned her head and looked inside Big Momma's office, but neither the FBI agent nor Ashanti saw her walk by. But Jazzy was able to see Little Miss Snitch taking hold of the FBI agent's card.

After Jazzy poured herself some more cereal, she went back upstairs to her room and told the girls that they might have a problem. Jazzy didn't like the way things were starting to line up, with an FBI agent snooping around the premises, Big Momma seeming to have some kind of attitude, and Little Miss Snitch running her mouth.

Jazzy knew that she, Cha Cha, and Maya had some brainstorming to do.

CHAPTER 29

The day after the FBI agent interviewed Ashanti, Big Momma pulled Maya aside at the start of her shift, so she could talk to her and see if she could figure out for sure if the girls had actually stolen money from the bank.

"I didn't want to talk out in the open in front of everybody, so that's why I asked you to walk outside with me," Big Momma stated.

"Yeah, that's cool. It feels good out here anyway. No humidity, just like I like it."

"Girl, tell me about it. I can't take too much more of these humid days we been having. My thighs are already rubbing together as it is, and then with the humidity, I start sweating, and you should see the rash that breaks out on my inner thighs."

Maya was totally turned off by just the thought of Big Momma's nasty rash.

"Well, anyway, I wanted to know if you want to come by tomorrow and see the apartment. I'm taking off tomorrow, so I figured that would be a good time to show you around."

Maya didn't want to tell Big Momma that she wasn't going to need the apartment anymore because Big Momma would easily put two and two together and figure out that she must have made a come-up with that bank robbery for real.

"Oh, OK, yeah. Tomorrow is no problem, but I just won't be able to get over there until after I get off work at six. So I'll make it over there around eight o'clock. You live in Prospect Heights, right?"

"Yeah. Right where they're building that new stadium."

"OK, I'll get the exact address from you later on."

"So you like this new job of yours?" Big Momma asked.

"It is what it is."

"Well, I guess that means no."

"They just need to pay me more money, they need to get me in a branch closer to Bed-Stuy, they need to get me off of this bullshit-ass, cuts-through-my-entire-day, ten-to-six shift, and then I might be alright, and I might actually like the job. And ever since the bank got robbed the other day, it's like my supervisor done lost her damn mind. I swear, she be acting like we back in slavery times. But that bitch gonna fuck around, and I'm gonna slap the shit outta her."

Big Momma laughed. "You so crazy."

"I'm dead ass."

Big Momma changed the subject. "Yeah, listen, I been wanting to talk to you about that whole robbery thing."

Maya just looked at Big Momma and wondered if she was wearing a wire or something and trying to set her up.

"Talk to me," Maya replied, trying her best to be short and to the point with her words.

"Be honest with me," Big Momma said. "You had something to do with that bank getting robbed, didn't you?"

"Hell no! Are you crazy? Big Momma, you know if I was that stupid to do something like that, you would have been the first one I told. Shit! Your refrigerator and your freezer would have been packed with steaks, shrimp, and lobster because I damn sure would've taken a sister grocery shopping before moving in with you." Maya tried to be as convincing as possible, just in case she really was being recorded by Big Momma.

"You sure, Maya?"

"Big Momma, yes, I'm sure. And now you're scaring me. See, this is why this whole work thing ain't for me. Look at all the stress I'm going through on account of this job—FBI agents are questioning me, you looking at me sideways now. This shit is crazy."

"Well, I'm just asking because I want to be sure I did the right thing by telling the FBI guy that Cha Cha and Jazzy were here at The Waverly. Because if later on they prove otherwise, then my ass could be in a sling for perjury or some shit like that. So, in other words, if I'm lying and covering for y'all, the least y'all could do is tell me what's really good."

Maya had no idea that Big Momma had voluntarily spoken up on Jazzy and Cha Cha's behalf and offered up an alibi for them to the FBI agent. She realized that Big Momma did actually have a valid point, but she kept her mouth shut and didn't tell Big Momma a thing about the robbery.

"Big Momma, you're good. You don't have nothing to worry about, as far as me and any bank robberies."

"Well, I know one thing, and that's that you and your two roommates are about to have some problems in a minute."

"Why? What are you talking about?"

"Well, all I know is the FBI agent spoke to me briefly yesterday after he had spoken with Ashanti, and he asked me, was I one hundred percent certain that Jazzy and Cha Cha were here at The Waverly on the day of the bank robbery. It was like he was stressing to me to make sure I was telling him the truth, so I asked him what reason I would have to lie to him for. And, without blinking, he told me that my story wasn't matching with what Ashanti had told him. Ashanti told him that she saw Jazzy and Cha Cha leave The Waverly, and she even described exactly what they were wearing and everything,." Big Momma had dry-snitched on Ashanti.

"Are you serious?"

"Yes, I am," Big Momma replied. "I think Ashanti is after the ten thousand dollars in reward money."

Maya shook her head, but she didn't say anything in reply. Maya's wheels were turning and so were Big Momma's.

Big Momma's wheels were definitely spinning more than Maya's. Big Momma was convinced that Maya wasn't being straight up. Maya was acting way too cool for someone who had supposedly been falsely accused of taking part in a bank robbery and also the prime suspect. Big Momma was determined to find that stolen loot.

"Ashanti won't get no reward money because we ain't have shit to do with that robbery."

"OK, so then tomorrow we're good?" Big Momma asked, trying to end the conversation.

"No doubt."

"Alright, so round up your crew and go somewhere, because the exterminator is about to come and spray for all these roaches we been seeing lately. He was saying that he may fumigate all of The Waverly, and if he does that, then the whole building would have to be empty before he starts."

"Oh, so we all have to leave?" Maya asked.

"Yeah, just for two hours for everything to air out."

Big Momma didn't have to tell Maya twice. Maya rounded up Jazzy and Cha Cha and they left The Waverly and went to Junior's Restaurant on Flatbush Avenue to get some cheesecake. On the way there, Maya filled Jazzy and Cha Cha in on everything Big Momma had told her.

Cha Cha looked at Jazzy, and they both shook their heads.

"What?" Maya asked them.

Jazzy said to Cha Cha, "Tell her."

"Big Momma is really becoming a big pain-in-the-ass problem."

"Why? What happened?"

"She's the one that got us for that money when our room supposedly got robbed," Cha Cha said.

"Get the fuck out of here!"

"She had to have gotten us. OK, so you remember Shonnie that was like three grades ahead of us and she graduated the year we came into high school?"

"Yeah, of course, I remember her."

"Shonnie told me that Big Momma had been paying her mother a couple of dollars to wait at Big Momma's crib for different deliveries. And she said that Big Momma has been getting all kinds of new shit. She got a huge flat-screen television, an iPad, new stainless steel appliances, a new bedroom set, new hardwood floors, and she bought all kinds of new clothes," Cha Cha explained.

"What! And let me guess," Maya said. "All of this new stuff came *after* our room got robbed."

"Yessir!"

Jazzy jumped in and said, "We know how much Big Momma is making at The Waverly, and she couldn't afford all of that new shit on her salary. Income tax time been passed, so she didn't buy all of that stuff with her income tax check. And there ain't no dude in her life, so all of that stuff had to come from *our* money."

"Well, Big Momma was telling me earlier that, if I didn't have anywhere to go once I got out of here, I could stay with her for a week or two. And today she asked me to come by her crib and look at everything, so I could have an idea of how big her apartment was. So definitely tomorrow when I get there I can see for myself if everything Shonnie's mother is saying is true."

"Maya, it is true! Big Momma is a snake!" Cha Cha said.

"She's a damn good snake," Maya added. "And here I was thinking that Big Momma was looking out for us by telling me what Ashanti had been saying to the FBI agent."

Jazzy said, "Man, fuck that! I bet you it's Big Momma's fat ass that's telling the feds all that they want to know. Her ass is probably trying to collect that reward money."

"All I know is that Little Miss Snitch and huge, fat-fuck, gotta go."

"You can't trust a snake or a snitch," Maya added.

"Yup, and that's why both of their asses is getting ready to get up outta here," Jazzy said.

CHAPTER 30

Big Momma looked under every nook and cranny, but she didn't find where the girls had hidden their money. Pissed off, she wanted to trash their room, but she knew she couldn't do that again.

Jazzy had cut open one of her pillows, hid the money inside, and sewn the pillow closed again. Maya had done a similar thing. Only, she had cut open the lining of one of her winter coats, where she hid her money, and sewn the coat closed again. And as for Cha Cha, she decided to walk around with her money on a twenty-four-hour basis, even sleeping with it.

After the exterminator left and the girls were let back into The Waverly, word had started to get around that Ashanti had the crabs. Apparently Ashanti's roommate had suspected it because of her excessive scratching.

Maya and Cha Cha thought it was the funniest thing in the world. Jazzy knew that Ashanti had more than likely caught the crabs from one of the guys who had paid them to fuck her the night she was drugged. Jazzy figured that if stories started circulating about Ashanti having the crabs then stories of her getting fucked by a slew of Bed-Stuy dudes could also start circulating, and in the process get Jazzy and her crew busted.

So the next morning Jazzy went to Walgreens and purchased some over-the-counter ointment to help clear up Ashanti's crabs.

Jazzy knocked on Ashanti's bedroom door. Ashanti opened the door and saw Jazzy standing there.

"What the fuck do you want?"

Jazzy looked inside Ashanti's room and noticed that her roommate wasn't there, which was good because she didn't want to embarrass Ashanti.

"Knock off the rah-rah shit because I didn't come here for any of that."

"So, like I said, what the fuck do you want?"

"It's obvious that you have a little problem, and I wanted to help you out." Jazzy handed Ashanti the medication.

Ashanti took hold of the medication and looked at it. Then she looked at Jazzy. She was in an awkward position, pissed off and embarrassed. Ashanti's crotch started itching, and she desperately wanted to scratch it, but she held off.

"Listen, I know somebody else who had the same thing that you got, and she used this, and it worked," Jazzy said, making sure not to use the word *crabs*.

At that point, embarrassment won over Ashanti, and her anger subsided.

"Does it work?" Ashanti couldn't stand it anymore, and right there on the spot, she started scratching her pussy.

Jazzy wanted to laugh, but she held it in. "I wouldn't be handing it to you if it didn't work."

"Thank you."

"You're welcome. Let me know how it turns out." Jazzy then turned to walk away.

"Hey," Ashanti said to Jazzy before she got too far away. "How did you know I needed this?" Ashanti was wondering if Bobby had started spreading rumors about her.

"Ashanti, you been scratching worse than a dog with fleas. It was obvious."

Ashanti couldn't help but smile from embarrassment. "I guess I did look pretty fleabag-ish."

Jazzy nodded her head. "Just use that, and you'll be alright. Because you could wash ten times a day and it won't do you any good unless you apply that ointment to properly kill everything off."

"OK."

As Jazzy walked off, Ashanti really started to think to herself that maybe Jazzy and Maya and even Cha Cha weren't really all that bad.

Ashanti locked her door, took off her clothes, and read the instructions on the box. She then opened up the ointment and generously applied the cream to her crotch area.

Jazzy felt like her mission had been accomplished. She wanted Ashanti to start letting her guard down, so she could set her up. Jazzy knew all she had to do was be patient and give things a couple of days. She figured that as soon as Ashanti was cured of the crabs, she would be forever grateful to her.

After Jazzy had given Ashanti the crab cream, she went back to her room, and she, Maya, and Cha Cha waited until later that evening to get at Big Momma.

At ten o'clock Jazzy went back to Walgreens and bought four

pints of vanilla Häagen Dazs ice cream and a pint of rum raisin for Big Momma.

When she got back to The Waverly, Cha Cha and Maya came down out of their room and met up with Jazzy in the dining room. Jazzy handed Cha Cha and Maya the pints of vanilla ice cream, and they went into the kitchen with it.

Jazzy walked off to Big Momma's office with the rum raisin ice cream. She tapped three times on Big Momma's office door and then let herself in.

"Hey, Big Momma, we bought you something." Jazzy handed a depressed-looking Big Momma the pint of rum raisin ice cream.

Big Momma's face lit up. "Girl, I was just thinking about getting me some rum raisin!" She snatched the ice cream out of Jazzy's hand. Then she reached into her desk drawer, took out a spoon, and started devouring the ice cream.

"Let me tell you. This shit right here, it's better than sex!"

Jazzy was thoroughly amused as she watched Big Momma's eyes roll to the back of her head in pure bliss.

"We just wanted to cheer you up because we noticed you've been down a little bit lately."

"Oh, I've been alright." Big Momma stuffed another spoonful of ice cream into her mouth. "I just been so tired lately."

Jazzy almost slipped up and said something about how nice Maya said Big Momma's apartment was, but no one was supposed to know that she had been there the previous day, just as no one was supposed to know that Big Momma had offered to let Maya live with her.

"Well, maybe you should take a vacation soon. Go on a cruise or something and just relax."

"Go on a cruise? With what money? With these pennies they pay me, the only cruise I'll be on is that cheap-ass Circle Line that takes you to the Statue of Liberty."

Big Momma's little joke wasn't funny, but Jazzy forced herself to laugh. "Oh, Big Momma, you are too funny. Well, anyway, enjoy your rum raisin. Me, Cha Cha, and Maya are going to be in the kitchen making vanilla milkshakes. Do you want one?"

"Do I want one? Is the Pope Catholic?" Big Momma said, her mouth full of ice cream.

Jazzy laughed and told her that she would bring her the milkshake in about ten minutes.

"OK, cool. And y'all make sure y'all clean up all of them dishes in that kitchen. Don't leave that blender dirty. I'm tired of cleaning up after y'all."

Jazzy made it to the kitchen and gave Maya and Cha Cha the thumbs-up sign. Cha Cha immediately went into her pants pocket and pulled out five peanuts that were already out of their shell. She then dropped them into a plastic Ziploc bag and crushed them down with a spoon before dumping them into the blender. She mixed that into the milkshake they were making.

"You sure that's enough?" Jazzy asked.

"Yeah, it's enough. If she's allergic to them shits the way she says she is, then all we need is one single peanut and she'll feel that shit," Cha Cha replied. "And, besides, we don't even want her to be able to taste any peanut flavor at all."

Jazzy agreed with Cha Cha, and she and Maya looked on as Cha Cha finished whipping up the milkshake. They added Nestle chocolate syrup to guarantee she didn't taste the peanuts.

Cha Cha soon filled up four glasses of vanilla milkshake, and she added a straw and a spoon to each glass just to make the presentation look official.

The three of them walked out of the kitchen and headed straight to Big Momma's office. Big Momma had just finished the pint of rum raisin, so the milkshake was like a sight for sore eyes to her.

Big Momma smiled and reached her hand out for one of the milkshakes. "Y'all are right on time with this right here."

Cha Cha handed Big Momma a milkshake.

"I have to warn y'all though that I'm a little lactose intolerant, so in another half an hour we might have to evacuate this building when I start farting up in here."

"That's all good. It'll just help fumigate the roaches," Cha Cha joked.

As Cha Cha, Jazzy, and Maya sipped on their milkshakes, the three of them watched in amazement as Big Momma sucked down her milkshake as if she was in some kind of speed-eating contest or something.

"Who made this milkshake?" Big Momma asked.

Cha Cha smiled and raised her hand.

"You stuck your foot in this thing!" Big Momma said to her. "It tastes better than White Castle's milkshakes."

Cha Cha thanked Big Momma, and then the girls all sat around making small talk, wondering if Big Momma was going to have any reaction to the peanuts.

After about ten minutes, Cha Cha spoke up and asked Big Momma if she wanted another shake.

"No, I'll wait and have another one tomorrow. I'm not feeling too good. I feel like I have to throw up or something. I probably ate all of that ice cream too fast." Big Momma then complained of feeling dizzy.

At that point the girls could see hives starting to break out on Big Momma's arms and neck.

"Ahhh, shit! Jazzy, go and get me the Benadryl from the bathroom medicine cabinet connected to Nancy's office." Big Momma stood up and handed Jazzy the key to the supervisors' bathroom.

"Everything OK, Big Momma?" Maya asked.

"I just need that Benadryl because I'm having one of my allergic reactions," Big Momma said.

Big Momma started to feel a lump in her throat and she started to panic. Her throat was closing up on her, and she felt like she was starting to choke.

"Tell Jazzy to hurry up," Big Momma said, feeling a sense of impending doom.

Cha Cha ran over to the bathroom to meet Jazzy. "She going down," Cha Cha whispered to Jazzy.

"I found the Benadryl, but I'm going to say it wasn't in here." Jazzy stuck the Benadryl in her pocket.

Jazzy and Cha Cha ran back to Big Momma's office and informed her that there wasn't any Benadryl in the medicine cabinet.

"You want me to run to Walgreens and buy some?" Jazzy asked.

Big Momma quickly shook her head no. "We don't have time for that. I need y'all to call 9-1-1 for me," Big Momma barely managed to whisper. She clutched her throat, trying to get more air.

All three girls started to reach for their cell phones but none of them had their phones on them.

Big Momma started to bang on her desk and pointed to the landline phone on her desk, motioning for the girls to use that phone to call 9-1-1.

"Big Momma, you need to sit down and try to relax," Maya said.

But Big Momma was way too panicked to calmly sit down.

Just as Jazzy picked up the phone to pretend to dial 9-1-1, Big Momma collapsed to the floor, and the whole room shook from all of her weight.

Cha Cha motioned to Jazzy as if she was slicing her throat with her index finger. Then she silently mouthed her words, "Put the phone down."

It was clear that Big Momma had passed out, so the girls figured it was best to wait a while before calling an ambulance.

Big Momma had collapsed to the floor at about ten thirty at night, but it wasn't until twelve thirty, a whole two hours later, that the three of them decided to dial 9-1-1.

They knew they were fowl, but Big Momma drew first blood when she robbed them of their money.

Payback is a bitch!

That's what Jazzy, Cha Cha, and Maya all thought to themselves as they heard the sound of the ambulance's siren as it rapidly made its way toward the Waverly.

CHAPTER 31

By the time the ambulance arrived at The Waverly, Big Momma was barely alive. She had a faint pulse, and the paramedics immediately started to perform CPR on her. All of the girls in the group home were in shock as they stood by and witnessed the tragic scene.

Big Momma was either loved or hated by the girls in the group home, but even with the girls who hated Big Momma, it was tough for them not to cry as they watched the paramedics—who had to also call the fire department to help assist them with hoisting her overweight body onto the stretcher. They proceeded to give her chest compressions as they hurriedly sped off in the ambulance to Kings County Hospital.

Jazzy, Cha Cha, and Maya did their best to look just as sad and disturbed as all of the other girls. Maya even managed to shed tears for Big Momma. And while Maya wanted Cha Cha and Jazzy to believe that her tears were just a show, they were in fact genuine. Maya was really starting to feel horrible for what she had allowed herself to be a part of. Maya hated that she was impulsive and then would later feel remorseful for her actions, but she chalked it up as being human.

Jazzy and Cha Cha didn't want to show it or admit it, but deep down inside they were both wondering, if they had taken things too far.

"She's gonna be alright, y'all," Ashanti said to everyone after the ambulance pulled off. "She had a slight pulse, so that's a good thing. God will take care of the rest and see her through this."

Meanwhile, one of the police officers who had arrived on the scene with the paramedics managed to get in touch with Nancy and told her what had happened. A shocked Nancy told the officer she would get down to The Waverly as soon as she could.

As the officers waited for Nancy to arrive at the scene, they started to question all of the girls and ask them what had happened, taking notes during the interviews.

As Maya cried, she told the officer that the only thing she could think of was that there might have been something in the ice cream that Big Momma had just eaten that probably triggered an allergic reaction.

Jazzy and Cha Cha couldn't believe Maya was walking down that road with the cops. But the way Maya reasoned things was that it would have looked more suspicious if the hospital found the peanuts in her system and they pretended not to know of Big Momma's allergies.

"What the fuck is wrong with you?" Jazzy asked Maya after the cop left.

"We had to tell them something," Maya replied.

"No, the fuck we didn't!" Jazzy barked. "We ain't no doctors. We don't know nothing. All we know is that her fat ass passed out. Hell, it could have been a heart attack, for all we know. And a heart attack is more plausible. But here you go with the allergic reaction bullshit."

Jazzy, Cha Cha, and Maya were all in their room. Jazzy wouldn't let it go that Maya had mentioned the allergic reaction theory to the cops.

"Jazzy, you need to calm the fuck down," Maya said. "You're overreacting. It's not like they weren't gonna find out in the hospital what happened to her. And it's not like I actually told the cops that we put peanuts in her milkshake!"

"Shhhhhh!" Cha Cha said. "Both of y'all need to shut the fuck up and stop talking so damn loud. These walls up in here are thin, and y'all both know that. Now let's just play everything cool and see how it plays itself out. We already scrubbed all the dishes in the kitchen. The blender is clean, so there ain't no way that nothing can come back to us. We'll be good on this."

Cha Cha was finally able to calm the girls down while they waited in their room for an update on Big Momma's condition.

In Ashanti's room, she was on her cell phone with her mother and she was telling her what had just happened to Big Momma. But she was also trying to use that as an excuse for her mother to allow her to leave The Waverly and come back home.

"So that big, fat, heart-attack-waiting-to-happen bitch passes out and gets rushed to the hospital, and you're saying that's why you should be allowed to come home?" Ms. Daniels asked Ashanti.

"Yes, Donna. It's horrible up in here, and all kinds of crazy shit is always happening. I just want to leave and come home and be safe before something happens to me."

Ms. Daniels was barely paying her daughter any mind. Unbeknownst to Ashanti, her mom was butt-ass naked on the other end of the phone with a twenty-two-year-old rookie police officer named Xavier. Xavier was also butt naked, and his dick was rock-hard at the moment. And while Ms. Daniels spoke on the phone, Xavier was steady trying to stick his dick inside of her.

Ms. Daniels loved dick more than anything, and just the tip of Xavier's young dick touching her pussy had sent shock waves through her body. She totally forgot she was on the phone with her daughter.

"Donna! Donna! Are you even listening to me?"

"Yeah, I am."

"So can I come home and leave this place?'

Xavier started to kiss on Ms. Daniels neck and then whispered in her hear, "Hang up the phone, babe."

"Ashanti, listen to me. Your ass is too fast, and you're too grown and you ain't been reformed yet. So, no, you can't come home. You're staying there until I know that you're ready to respect me and live by my rules and stop getting in trouble." Ms. Daniels moaned slightly as Xavier slid his dick deeper into her pussy.

Ashanti sucked her teeth. She realized that her mother was with some man. "Donna, I can't even believe you right now." Ashanti wondered which rookie her mother was fucking now.

"Ashanti, I have to go."

"Go and enjoy your green-eyed young dick!" Ashanti hung up the phone.

Ashanti knew her mother was with Xavier because lately that's all she'd been talking about. Every chance she got, she would talk about how Xavier had green eyes and good curly hair, saying she really needed to think about having his baby, so she could have a son with some good hair just like Xavier's.

Ashanti had never actually met Xavier, but he was more important in her mom's life than her own flesh-and-blood daughter. Ashanti also knew that the only reason her mother wasn't going to let her come back home anytime soon was because she wanted to be free to frolic with her young studs.

Ms. Daniels also definitely didn't want her young lovers to be attracted to her daughter, which was a real possibility, considering her boyfriends were so much closer to Ashanti's age than hers.

Ashanti realized that she could easily be at The Waverly for another year, if not longer. So she made up her mind right then and there as she lay in her bed that if she was going to have to stay at The Waverly for such a long period of time, she was going to be at peace with all of the girls in there.

Ashanti knew that Maya and Jazzy had all but extended olive branches to her and she was grateful for that. She figured she would be able to get Cha Cha on her likeable list within the next week or so. And she also figured that the first thing she needed to do was to forget about Agent Scarpetta and stop helping him out by feeding him information to crack the bank robbery case.

The "crabs cream" had really helped Ashanti. And as she continued to lay in her bed and think about all kinds of things, her mind couldn't help but keep going back to Bobby. She wondered if there was any way she could still be a part of his life.

Deep down all Ashanti wanted was peace and happiness. She was determined to start making peace with her enemies and to get Bobby back in her life so she could have the happiness she so desired.

CHAPTER 32

Big Momma had been in ICU from the time the ambulance rushed her to the hospital. And because of the swelling in her air passageways, the hospital had to hook her up to a breathing tube to get her the oxygen she needed. Two days after Big Momma had drunk the peanut-laced milkshake, she took a turn for the worse.

The problem was that Jazzy, Cha Cha, and Maya had waited so long to call the ambulance that the oxygen levels in Big Momma's blood had dropped dangerously low, causing permanent damage to two of her vital organs. Ultimately, this led to her dying in the ICU at Kings County Hospital.

When Nancy broke the news to the girls at The Waverly, there was nothing but tears and long faces. Even Jazzy and Cha Cha admitted amongst themselves that they had taken things too far. They were wishing they had called the ambulance sooner. They realized they had literally murdered Big Momma because they knowingly fed her the poison.

All of the girls gathered in the living room of the group home and started sharing funny stories about Big Momma. And what was evident right away was, most of the stories they told involved food.

Ashanti's roommate said, "Remember that time we all went to Coney Island on the Fourth of July and Big Momma was in the hot dog-eating contest at Nathan's?"

Instantly the room lit up with laughter because everybody who had been around for that trip to Coney Island clearly remembered Big Momma devouring twenty-five hot dogs in five minutes to get the second prize.

"Ketchup and mustard and hot dog pieces were running down her shirt and everything. Ashanti, you should have seen it. Big Momma hadn't even practiced for the contest, like most of the people who enter it do, and she almost won it. It was hilarious when they were replaying clips of her on the news and on ESPN."

Ashanti smiled and said, "I wish I had seen that." Then she added, "What I liked about Big Momma was, she knew how to be straight up and stern with me when she had to be, but at the same time she wasn't a bitch about it, like some people are."

Ashanti was clearly taking a stab at Nancy, who was in the room at the time. Nancy looked at Ashanti but didn't say anything to her.

It was hard for Maya to join in and tell funny stories because she felt like it would be spitting on Big Momma's grave, so she kept quiet.

"Cha Cha, I know you must have some funny stories about Big Momma," Ashanti said.

Cha Cha, feeling very remorseful, was caught off guard. She quickly put aside her differences with Ashanti. In fact she actually smiled at Ashanti.

"Actually, I do have a real funny story. Maya, this was right before you got here. Maybe like two weeks before. And our old roommate Lisa had went out and came back so twisted and drunk that she peed on herself at the top of the steps, and Big Momma ended up slipping in the pee and falling down the full flight of steps!"

Everybody in the room burst out into laughter.

"Yo, it was so funny, because everybody was either 'sleep or in their rooms just chillin', and then all of a sudden you hear this loud sound like a plane crash. It felt like the whole building shook. So everybody comes running out of their rooms to see what happened, and we all saw Big Momma doubled over in the fetal position at the bottom of the steps! It was hilarious." Cha Cha laughed as she recalled the incident.

"OK, OK, I think that's enough stories for now," Nancy said. "Listen, I know this has taken an emotional toll on a lot of you, but I just want to say that we'll get through this and everything and everybody will be alright. But for right now, it's getting late, and I need everybody to retreat to their rooms."

All of the girls sucked their teeth and sighed in disgust. They hated that Nancy followed all the rules so strictly.

"I'll be here, so if anybody wants to talk to me, or if you need a shoulder to cry on, I'm here." Nancy smiled.

All of the girls retreated to their rooms to reflect on things in their own individual way.

Ashanti didn't go to her room; instead she went to Nancy's office to talk to her. "Nancy, I wanted to talk to you, if you have a minute," Ashanti said.

"Sure. What's up?" Nancy asked Ashanti as she stood a few feet across from her.

"Well, I wanted to ask you if one of my friends could come by tonight and see me for a few minutes."

"Ashanti, I don't even know why you're asking me that because you already know the answer to that question."

Ashanti sucked her teeth. "Dang, Ms. Nancy! Why you gotta be so strict all the time?"

"I have to teach all of you to learn to have some boundaries. You won't appreciate it now, but when you get older, I'm sure you will."

Ashanti had made contact with Bobby and desperately wanted to see him so that she could hug and kiss him. She was missing him like she never thought she would. Her crabs were gone, and although she wanted to have make-up sex with Bobby, she didn't want to chance things so soon. But, at the very least, she wanted to see him before he left to go out of town again. And it was by chance that he was even home, simply because the out-of-town tournament had been unexpectedly canceled.

"Ms. Nancy, please. I mean, I really would give anything if you could just make one exception for me just this one time. All I want is fifteen minutes, please," Ashanti begged.

Ms. Nancy held her ground, and Ashanti walked off feeling defeated. At that point all Ashanti could do was call Bobby and tell him straight up that she wasn't going to be able to see him until he got back.

Ashanti dialed Bobby's number, and after the second ring, someone picked up, but it didn't sound like Bobby. Ashanti automatically assumed that it was his coach or somebody, because the person sounded like a white man.

"Hi. Can I speak with Bobby?" Ashanti asked.

"Bobby? Is this Ashanti?"

"Yes, this is Ashanti."

"Ashanti, this is Agent Scarpetta."

Ashanti realized that she had inadvertently dialed the wrong number. Agent Scarpetta was the last person she wanted to speak to.

"Oh, Agent Scarpetta, I dialed the wrong number. I must have dialed your cell phone. I was trying to reach my friend. OK, sorry about that. I have to go," Ashanti said, trying to rush off the phone.

"Wait. It's no problem. It's good that you called. I was going to give you a call in the morning, but while I got you, I wanted to tell you that they upped the reward from ten thousand to twelve, so if you get any more relevant information, be sure to give me a call," Agent Scarpetta said, hoping to entice Ashanti.

Ashanti paused, thinking about how to respond. "I guess you didn't hear about Big Momma."

"Oh, I heard. She's in the hospital. How is she doing?"

"I'm sure she's been better. She actually passed away a few hours ago."

"You're kidding me!"

"I wish I was."

"Oh, that's awful! I'm so sorry to hear that."

Agent Scarpetta was experienced, so he knew when to push things and when to pull back. This was clearly a time to pull back.

"Well, Ashanti, some things in life are obviously way more important than other things. And right now you and all of the girls need to be focused on being there for one another. You don't need to be worried or distracted with calling me. So why don't I give you a couple of weeks, and then I'll give you a call to see how things are going?"

Ashanti shot right back. "Actually, I don't think that's even necessary."

"What do you mean?"

"What I mean is, I had meant to call you and tell you that I had things wrong and I remember everything much more clearly now.

On that day of the bank robbery, Cha Cha and Jazzy both were here at The Waverly all day long."

Agent Scarpetta instantly got bloodshot red because he knew Ashanti was lying. "Are you sure about that?"

"I'm more sure than ever. I'm as sure as I'll ever be."

Agent Scarpetta sighed into the phone. "Well, if that's how you remember it, then that's how you remember it. Give your regards to the staff for me over at The Waverly. If I need anything more from you, I'll give you a call," Agent Scarpetta said.

At that point Agent Scarpetta knew that with Big Momma's passing and with Ashanti recanting her story, the case against Maya, Jazzy, and Cha Cha was bound to go cold and unresolved. Without any concrete evidence to pin the crime on the girls, and without eyewitness testimony to disprove alibis, he knew he would be up shit's creek without a paddle.

Ashanti, on the other hand, felt real good about how she handled that situation. She felt like a huge burden had been lifted off her shoulders. Jazzy, Cha Cha, and Maya didn't know it, but Ashanti had just taken a huge step in making sure there was peace amongst them all.

Ashanti only had one more issue she really needed to tend to, and that was figuring out how she was going to go around Nancy and still see Bobby.

CHAPTER 33

After Big Momma's funeral had ended, everyone who attended came back to The Waverly for the repast. All of Big Momma's relatives had driven up from North Carolina to attend the funeral, and it was easy to see that the fat gene had been passed from one generation to the next. The Waverly had never seen so many fat and big-boned women at one time.

At the repast, people started to loosen up while they ate soul food and drank all kinds of liquor.

Cha Cha walked over to Ashanti with a Styrofoam plate with chicken and collard greens on it, and in her other hand, she had a plastic cup of soda. Cha Cha rested the cup of soda on a coffee table and extended her right hand to Ashanti, who smiled and reached out and clasped her hand.

Cha Cha said to Ashanti, "Life is too short, and we need to squash our beef."

"Since Big Momma died, I've been thinking the same thing." Ashanti held on to Cha Cha's hand. "So we're good?"

Cha Cha nodded her head. She let go of Ashanti's hand and reached down for her cup of soda and drank some. "That hot-ass

oatmeal you threw on me, that was really fucked up, but we're good."
Cha Cha smiled.

"Oh my God!" Ashanti covered her mouth with her hand. She wanted to laugh, but she held it in. "Cha Cha, I am sorry about that. I don't know what happened. I just snapped that day."

"It's all good," Cha Cha replied. "Life is too short, right?"

"Yes, it is."

At that moment Ashanti's cell phone started vibrating. It was a call from a blocked number. At first she wasn't going to pick it up, but then she excused herself from talking to Cha Cha and answered the phone.

"Hello."

"Hey, babe. What's good?" Bobby asked.

"Baby! Oh my God! I didn't think I was going to speak to you for another week or so," Ashanti excitedly replied.

"I know. We just been running around all over the place. We had a sponsor who was paying for all of our flights and hotels and all of that, some rich, white lawyer dude. But come to find out, the dude just got busted for molesting little boys."

"No way!"

"I swear to God. So once that news broke, all of his sponsorship money dried up on us overnight and the team don't want to have nothing to do with him. So we ended our trip early. We're coming back home tomorrow."

"Oh, baby, I miss you so much," Ashanti said into the phone, a ton of passion in her voice.

"I miss you too."

By this time Ashanti's crabs had departed, and her pussy and asshole had snapped back to their pre-GHB condition.

"My shit is so tight and ready for you, it's screaming your name,"

Ashanti said to Bobby.

Bobby chuckled into the phone.

"You laugh, but I'm dead serious. My pussy been twitching and jumping out of my pants for the past week now, but I been saving her for you."

"That's what's up."

"So what time do you touch down tomorrow?" Ashanti asked.

"I think at midnight. We're in France now. I can never get the time zone thing down."

"OK, so no matter what time it is, just hit me up as soon as you land, and I'll figure out some way to see you."

Bobby assured her that he would definitely call her when he landed at Kennedy Airport.

Ashanti ended her call with Bobby on cloud nine. Other than her mother not giving two shits about her, Ashanti was starting to feel like everything was finally going right for her. She was really feeling like she was in a good space emotionally and wanted to stay in that space.

Ashanti went into the dining room and got some chicken from off the table, and as she was standing around eating it, Cha Cha came back up to her.

"I didn't want to interrupt you while you was on the phone, but I wanted to tell you that tomorrow night, me, Maya, and Jazzy are going to this house party on Halsey Street. You can roll with us if want to. It should be kind of live," Cha Cha said.

Without hesitation Ashanti accepted her invitation, not because she was so eager to hang out with them, but more so because she knew she would be able to leave the party and go see Bobby, or have Bobby come meet her at the party.

"But what about Nancy? She be on some other shit," Ashanti said.

"Don't worry about her. We'll leave a half-hour before curfew, and we'll get back when we get back."

Cha Cha didn't care about the rules because it seemed like since all the commotion and drama with Big Momma's passing, things had become slack. The girls were happy that the state hadn't forced Maya to leave although she had aged out but they knew that it was only a matter of time. The following week she was going apartment-hunting with Jazzy and Maya.

"Well, I'll be ready. I'm there."

Ashanti and Cha Cha soon went their separate ways. Cha Cha continued to mingle amongst Big Momma's family members, but Ashanti went straight upstairs to her room and searched through her closet, looking for the perfect outfit to rock the next day.

She wanted something that would make her look good at the party, something with the perfect amount of sexiness, so Bobby would want to rip her clothes off and fuck her as soon as he saw her. Ashanti was in the best of moods, singing one Nicki Minaj song after the next, as she searched through her closet and her dresser drawers. Tomorrow couldn't get there soon enough.

CHAPTER 34

It was a little after nine at night when Ashanti knocked on Jazzy's door and told her that she was ready to leave for the party. Jazzy opened the door for Ashanti and asked her to give her a few more minutes to get ready.

"You look nice," Jazzy said, applying makeup to her face.

"Thank you. You look nice too," Ashanti replied. "Where's Maya and Cha Cha?"

"Oh, they left already, about ten minutes ago. We're going to meet them there. They wanted to stop off at the liquor store, and Cha Cha had to make another stop somewhere. So this new dude Maya is talking to, he picked them up."

"Oh, OK." Ashanti looked around the room, wondering what it would be like to be roommates with her three former nemeses.

"Let's hurry up and go before Nancy comes up here on her drill sergeant bullshit." Jazzy sprayed perfume on her body, and then her and Ashanti left the room and made their way out of The Waverly.

The two of them walked two blocks to a livery cab stand and got inside a cab to take them to the party.

"I thought Cha Cha said the party was on Halsey Street," Ashanti said to Jazzy. "We could have walked."

"Walk? Girl, you see the heels that you got on? I got on heels too. We ain't walking nowhere. And it is on Halsey Street, but it's all the way down toward the end. But we have to make a stop first near Marcy. I have to pick up some money from one of my friends who borrowed a hundred dollars from me. It'll only take a few minutes."

Ashanti didn't say anything in response. She just wanted to hurry up and get to the party because she couldn't wait to see Bobby. Bobby had told her that he would come straight to the party as soon as his plane landed, and then they would leave and go to a motel to fuck. As the cab drove through the Brooklyn streets, Ashanti pulled out her cell phone and sent Bobby a text message. But she made sure to let Jazzy know who she was sending a text message to.

I can't wait to see you. Just letting you know that I'm leaving now for the party. I'll see you later. :) xoxoxo

After Ashanti sent that text message, she put her phone away and smiled, telling Jazzy she couldn't wait to get some dick from Bobby later on that night.

Jazzy ignored Ashanti's comment. Deep down she knew Ashanti was still who she was—a jealous, envious, hating-ass, ghetto bitch.

"You know, when you lend people money and they say they have the money to pay you back, you have to go and get that shit the same day," Jazzy remarked, trying to make sure she kept the conversation on anything other than Bobby.

"Yup, because if you don't, they'll end up spending it," Ashanti replied with a slight laugh.

"Exactly! That's why I'm going to get this money right now."

Jazzy and Ashanti both sat quiet for a moment and then Jazzy spoke up. "We're only like three blocks away," she informed Ashanti.

"I'm cool. It's OK. You want me to wait inside the cab when we get there?" Ashanti asked.

"No, because I can probably get my friend to drive us when I get the money from her," Jazzy replied as the cab sat at a red light. "Can I ask you something that I've been *dying* to ask you?"

"Yeah, what's up?" Ashanti asked.

"How the hell were you getting those clothes out of the store with the security devices still on them? I been racking my brain trying to figure that shit out."

Ashanti chuckled and then she smiled. The old Ashanti would have told Jazzy to go kick rocks. But the new and improved Ashanti, who was now cool with her enemies, decided to just spill the beans.

"It's easy," Ashanti said just as they reached their destination.

Jazzy paid the driver, and the two of them exited the cab.

"Keep talking. I'm listening," Jazzy said. "My friend lives right down the block. We just have to walk down this alley and get to her back door. Let me text her and tell her we're here."

Jazzy sent a text message to both Maya and Cha Cha: *We're walking down the alley right now. Be ready.*

"So you was saying it's easy?" Jazzy asked.

"Yeah. OK, all you have to do is properly prepare your booster bag, and you'll be good. So what I would do is, I would go in a bathroom or somewhere discreet and line the bag with aluminum foil. And I would put all the stolen items in the bag lined with aluminum foil." Ashanti smiled.

Jazzy asked with a confused look, "Aluminum foil?"

"Yeah, the aluminum foil neutralizes the alarm system and it sort of makes like a protective shield around the bag so that the signal from the security devices isn't picked up."

"What?"

Jazzy had been trying her hardest to figure out what Ashanti knew when it came to boosting, and now she had her answer. Now that the mystery was solved, Jazzy felt good because she knew that, once she moved out of The Waverly, she, Cha Cha, and Maya would be able to return to their bread and butter, which was shoplifting, in order to make money to pay their rent.

"Don't go and tell everybody," Ashanti said to Jazzy as the two of them walked down the dark alley.

"I won't," Jazzy told her.

WHACK!

Out of nowhere, Cha Cha emerged from behind a dumpster and cracked Ashanti behind her neck with a Louisville Slugger. Ashanti instantly fell to her knees, too disoriented and too woozy to even scream.

"You thought I was just gonna let that shit slide when your ass snuffed me that day?" Cha Cha asked Ashanti.

WHACK!

Cha Cha swung the baseball bat and hit Ashanti square in the chest, completely knocking the wind out of her.

"You snake-ass bitch!" Cha Cha barked. "We know you was talking to the feds."

Cha Cha then swung the baseball bat four more times at Ashanti's skull, each swing producing splatters of blood.

Ashanti fell face first to the ground. The force of the blows from the baseball bat were so violent and devastating, Ashanti was dead before her face even hit the pavement.

Maya quickly handed Cha Cha and Jazzy a bag of clothes, and the three of them all stripped down to their panties and bra and quickly changed their clothes right there in that dark back alley, making sure to change their shoes as well.

Maya scooped up all of the clothes they had just taken off and put them inside of a huge black industrial-size Hefty garbage bag. She also put the Louisville slugger inside that same garbage bag and tied it closed. The three of them quickly rushed out of the back alley and made their way over to the Bushwick section of Brooklyn. Once they made it to Broadway, they stopped for a second to catch their breath.

Broadway was a busy commercial street in Bushwick with a lot of stores, bodegas, and fast-food establishments, and elevated train tracks that formed a part of the New York City subway system.

The girls found a closed Chinese restaurant with a lot of garbage bags on the curb, waiting to be picked up by a private sanitation company that handled commercial garbage. So they decided to just dump their garbage bag right there.

"Y'all think it's cool to dump it right here?" Maya asked.

Jazzy and Cha Cha both said that they thought it was a good spot. The three of them then hailed down a livery cab and instructed the driver to take them to The Waverly in Bed-Stuy.

By the time the girls made it back to The Waverly, it was a little past ten p.m. They had made it in before curfew, so they knew they weren't going to have any problems with Nancy. And they knew that eventually they would get asked if they had seen Ashanti, and they all agreed that they were going to say that Ashanti had left The Waverly with Jazzy and that the only thing Jazzy knew was that Ashanti had said that she was going to be meeting up with her boyfriend Bobby later that night.

The three sheisty chicks were sure they'd covered all their bases. Now all they had to do was wait and see how things played out.

CHAPTER 35

Before the break of dawn, the police found Ashanti's dead body in the alley. Ashanti's mom was notified. She was heartbroken and full of guilt because her daughter had been asking to leave the group home out of fear that something tragic would happen. The Waverly was also notified of Ashanti's death. Nancy, nor anyone else, could actually believe what had happened.

In order to deflect attention from herself and in an attempt to exploit her daughter's death for financial gain, Ashanti's mom quickly retained one of the best lawyers in New York City. The lawyer called for a twelve noon press conference, where he basically laid out his plans to sue New York State over the poorly run The Waverly Group Home.

"My daughter would be alive at this very moment if they'd just had the proper supervision in that group home," Ms. Daniels said, sitting to the right of her attorney. "At nine and ten o'clock at night you have young teenage girls who can just come and go as they please! That isn't right, and someone in this group home has to be held responsible."

Their press conference had managed to garner a lot of media attention, with all of the twelve noon news broadcasts airing a segment of the press conference. But by the time the five o'clock and six o'clock news aired, there was a much bigger and much more sensational story that everyone was focused on. It was revealed that the young girl found dead in a Brooklyn alley was actually the pregnant girlfriend of high school hoops phenom, Bobby Patterson. Bobby Patterson, dubbed as the next LeBron James, had instantly become the New York City Police Department's prime suspect in Ashanti's murder.

The sports world was on fire with the story, and no one knew what to believe or not believe.

Jazzy, Cha Cha, and Maya sat all day watching the local news, CNN, and ESPN. They couldn't believe how much press Ashanti's murder was getting. But with Bobby Patterson's name being mentioned as the prime suspect in Ashanti's death, they knew they stood a great chance of getting away with murder.

EPILOGUE

Ashanti's autopsy results and DNA tests later determined that the fetus she was carrying wasn't Bobby Patterson's baby, bringing Ashanti's character into question. She quickly got the label of being a loose and misdirected teenage young lady.

But Bobby was never able to shake the allegations that he had something to do with Ashanti's death, which derailed his promising, can't-miss-NBA career. Upon graduating from high school, Bobby, who had been projected by all the NBA scouts to be drafted number one, ended up not being selected by any of the NBA teams. Since there was no statute of limitations on murder, no NBA team wanted to take a chance on drafting him and giving him a huge contract, fearing he might end up in jail for murder one day.

Bobby ended up going overseas and playing professional basketball in Europe. His only hope at redemption and vindication lay in the fact that the DNA from Ashanti's fetus was going to be kept in the CODIS database. If the true father ever went to prison for anything or was ever arrested for any major crimes, then his DNA would match the DNA of the fetus and then that person would likely be able to shed light on Ashanti's murder and possibly clear the dark cloud hanging over Bobby's head.

As for Jazzy, Cha Cha, and Maya, they displayed the ultimate disrespect by continuing to smear Ashanti's name throughout Brooklyn and even at her funeral.

The three of them did, however, reach their goal of moving out of The Waverly. Less than two weeks after Ashanti had been killed, Jazzy, Cha Cha, and Maya moved into a beautiful three-bedroom apartment in the popular Clinton Hill section of Brooklyn, in the heart of everything that is Brooklyn.

It didn't take long for Maya to ditch her job at the bank, and the trio stayed on their grind, doing sheisty shit. The fact that they had eluded arrests for the bank robbery, Big Momma's death, and Ashanti's murder made them feel untouchable.

All of the negative press The Waverly had been receiving caused it to become a bull's-eye. The city eventually condemned The Waverly as unsafe, due to lead paint as well as other building code violations, and the group home was forced to close down. All of the girls were either relocated into foster homes or different group homes throughout the city.

The original founders of The Waverly Girls Group Home promised to clean up and correct all of its violations and vowed that The Waverly would reopen under a new regime in the not-too-distant future.

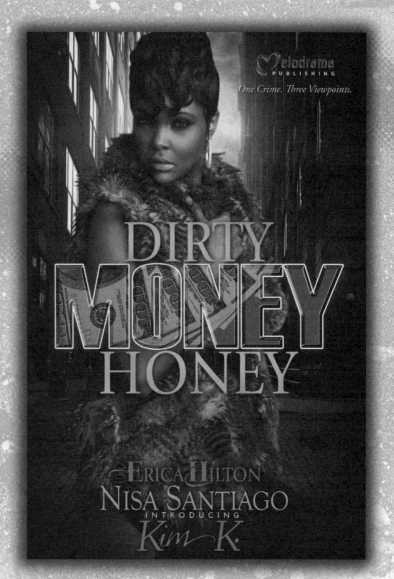

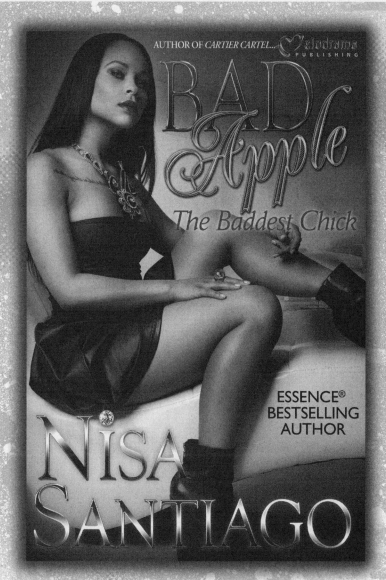

WIFEY: FROM MISTRESS TO WIFEY
BY ERICA HILTON
NOVEMBER 8, 2011

TEA♥
MELODRAMA

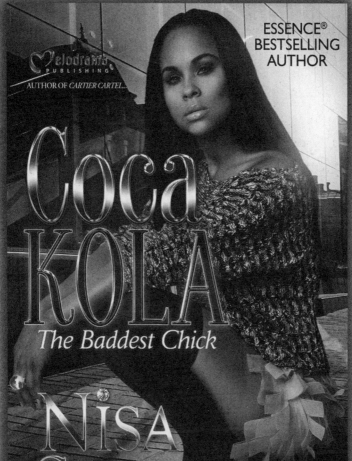

ESSENCE® BESTSELLING AUTHOR

AUTHOR OF *CARTIER CARTEL...*

Coca KOLA
The Baddest Chick

NISA SANTIAGO

COCA KOLA
BY NISA SANTIAGO
MARCH 13, 2012

TEA♥ MELODRAMA

THE ESSENCE® BESTSELLER!

Wifey 4 LIFE

"Kiki captures the heat of the streets."
—Wahida Clark,
New York Times Bestseller

Kiki Swinson

WIFEY 4 LIFE
MASS MARKET EDITION
BY KIKI SWINSON
FEBRUARY 14, 2012

TEA♥
MELODRAMA

Melodrama Publishing Order Form
WWW.MELODRAMAPUBLISHING.COM

Title	ISBN	Qty	Price	Total
10 CRACK COMMANDMENTS by ERICA HILTON	978-1-934157-21-3		$15.00	$
BAD APPLE by NISA SANTIAGO	978-1-934157-45-9		$14.99	$
CARTIER CARTEL by NISA SANTIAGO	978-1-934157-18-3		$15.00	$
CARTIER CARTEL MM by NISA SANTIAGO	978-1-934157-34-3		$ 6.99	$
COCA KOLA by NISA SANTIAGO	978-1-934157-48-0		$14.99	$
DEAL WITH DEATH by ENDY	978-1-934157-12-1		$15.00	$
DIRTY MONEY HONEY by ERICA HILTON, NISA SANTIGO, KIM K	978-1-934157-44-2		$14.99	$
DIRTY LITTLE ANGEL by ERICA HILTON	978-1-934157-19-0		$15.00	$
DRAMA WITH A CAPITAL D by DENISE COLEMAN	978-1-934157-32-9		$14.99	$
EVA II: FIRST LADY OF SIN MM by STORM	978-1-934157-35-0		$ 6.99	$
I'M STILL WIFEY (PART 2) by KIKI SWINSON	978-0-9717021-5-8		$15.00	$
IN MY HOOD by ENDY	978-0-9717021-9-6		$15.00	$
IN MY HOOD MM by ENDY	978-1-93415757-2		$ 6.99	$
IN MY HOOD 3 by ENDY	978-193415762-6		$14.99	$
JEALOUSY: THE COMPLETE SAGA by LINDA BRICKHOUSE	978-1-934157-13-8		$15.00	$
JEALOUSY by LINDA BRICKHOUSE	978-1-934157-07-7		$15.00	$
LIFE AFTER WIFEY (PART 3) by KIKI SWINSON	978-1-934157-04-6		$15.00	$
LIFE, LOVE & LONELINESS by CRYSTAL LACEY WINSLOW	978-0-9717021-0-3		$15.00	$
LIFE, LOVE & LONELINESS MM by CRYSTAL LACEY WINSLOW	978-1-934157-41-1		$ 6.99	$
MENACE by MARK ANTHONY, AL SAADIQ BANKS, J.M. BENJAMIN, ERICK S. GRAY, & CRYSTAL LACEY WINSLOW	978-1-934157-16-9		$15.00	$
MYRA by AMALEKA MCCALL	978-1-934157-20-6		$15.00	$
RETURN OF THE CARTIER CARTEL by NISA SANTIAGO	978-1-934157-30-5		$14.99	$
SHEISTY CHICKS by KIM K.	978-1-934157-47-3		$14.99	$
SHOT GLASS DIVA by JACKI SIMMONS	978-1-934157-14-5		$15.00	$
A STICKY SITUATION by KIKI SWINSON	978-1-934157-09-1		$15.00	$
STILL WIFEY MATERIAL (PART 4) by KIKI SWINSON	978-1-934157-10-7		$15.00	$
STRIPPED MM by JACKI SIMMONS	978-1-934157-40-4		$ 6.99	$
TALE OF A TRAIN WRECK LIFESTYLE by CRYSTAL LACEY WINSLOW	978-1-934157-15-2		$15.00	$

MELODRAMA PUBLISHING ORDER FORM
(CONTINUED)

THE CRISS CROSS MM by CRYSTAL LACEY WINSLOW	978-1-934157-42-8		$ 6.99	$
THE DIAMOND SYNDICATE by ERICA HILTON	978-193415760-2		$14.99	$
WIFEY (PART 1) by KIKI SWINSON	978-0-9717021-3-4		$15.00	$
WIFEY 4 LIFE (PART 5) by KIKI SWINSON	978-1-93415761-9		$14.99	$
WIFEY 4 LIFE (PART 5) MM by KIKI SWINSON	978-1-934157-43-5		$6.99	$
WIFEY: FROM MISTRESS TO WIFEY by ERICA HILTON	978-1-934157-46-6		$14.99	$
YOU SHOWED ME by NAHISHA MCCOY	978-1-934157-33-6		$14.99	$

Instructions:

*NY residents please add $1.79 Tax per book.

**Shipping costs: $3.00 first book, any additional books please add $1.00 per book.

Incarcerated readers receive a 25% discount. Please pay $11.25 per book and apply the same shipping terms as stated above.

Mail to:

MELODRAMA PUBLISHING

P.O. BOX 522

BELLPORT, NY 11713

Please provide your shipping address and phone number:

Name:_____

Address: _____

Apt. No: _____ Inmate No: _____

City: _____ State: _____ Zip: _____

Phone: (   ) _____-_____

Allow 2 - 4 weeks for delivery

Bulk orders call 347-246-6879 FOR DISCOUNTS